RESTORED

STACI JOST

For the women of the world who take care of everyone around them and have trouble putting themselves first. You're strong, you're seen and you're so important. Now take a break.

CHAPTER
ONE

CRACKED WHITE BONE PROTRUDES FROM THE BOY'S skin, his mangled arm bent on the bed at an awkward angle. An acrid smell wafts from the wound. At one time, that smell would have made me gag. Now, it hardly fazes me as I reach forward and place my shaking hands over the injury.

I take a deep, steadying breath, and white light seeps from my sweaty palms. My power purrs as it skates over the teenage boy's mangled arm—pockets of white pus ooze from the injury, and guilt courses through me. Had I gotten here sooner, I could have saved Oliver days of pain and discomfort.

I can't think of such things now. Time is not on my side tonight. I close my eyes, concentrating on drawing out the infection. It burns up my fingers and into my hands.

"How did you get this?" I grit my teeth as I push my healing power further into his arm.

"I, uh, fell off a horse," Oliver stammers nervously.

I know he is lying. I can feel the faint pulse of the power he's trying to conceal. I've healed him before, always a broken bone. I don't dare ask what his power is. The less I know the better, but if I had to guess, I'd wager he could levitate, maybe teleport. "Why don't you report your power to the King?" I ask instead, as much to distract him as anything else.

The burning sensation in my hands fade as the infection dissipates. Oliver's face pales, and he begins to fidget. "You, of all people, should know why, Layla." His voice is a soft, pleading whisper. "I have family here. My mother is growing old. She wouldn't make it long without me," he responds, just as the pounding of fists on wood sounds from a few doors down, so close that we both jump.

It can only be the King's men out collecting the monthly tithe. It's the very reason I was able to sneak away, but now, it means I'm running out of time.

"You know your secret is safe with me," I assure him as sweat drips from my forehead. The cramped room Oliver shares with his mother is hot and stuffy; my clothes cling to my body from perspiration.

I open the stopper to my abilities, releasing as much power as I dare, attempting to close the wound. It's hard to concentrate on anything but my heart thrumming wildly in my chest.

Pounding sounds again, closer this time, and the floor creaks loudly as Thea rushes in. Panic is clear on her face.

Oliver's breath catches, but I tamp down on my own panic, focusing on my breath. I close my eyes, picturing exactly what I want. The skin of my palms heats as bone resets, and the damaged skin starts to mend itself.

I'm nearly finished when the dreaded pounding at the front door reverberates through the worn-down wood.

Oliver and his mother freeze, but I refuse to stop. I need only a few more seconds to complete the healing. Thea touches my shoulder gently. "You must go." I barely hear her over the hammering of my heartbeat.

"OPEN UP." The guards beat at the door again, so hard I worry the dilapidated wood might splinter away leaving a gaping hole.

"Coming!" Thea calls, shooting me a worried look.

I trail my power along Oliver's arm one last time to make sure I've healed everything before cutting it off. His eyes are wild when I look back up.

"Be smart and try to be more careful," I whisper as Oliver helps me shove the window open. Splinters shuck off the frame as I climb out.

"Thank you, Layla," he whispers after me, a moment before the guards burst in.

I sprint down the street as fast as my feet will take me. I gulp down the chill night air, ignoring the foul smells that waft in my direction and instead relish in the way it cools my overly heated skin.

Hurtling down the cobblestone streets, I cloak myself in dark corners and trip on the raised stones. I'd never been particularly adept at being stealthy, but after years of sneaking around and intimate knowledge of what would happen to me if I was caught, I'd learned how to stay hidden.

Screams pierce the air abruptly halting my legs. I scramble over loose gravel fusing my back to the crumbling building behind me. I peer down the empty streets to see an older man writhing on the ground, lit up by the street lanterns.

Not just any older man, Mr. Buford. He was a carpenter. I'd worked on his back, healed the tendonitis in his wrists, repaired the joints in his knee. He was a quiet man but kind.

My stomach flips when King Sandor and Tamish, the king's hand, come into view. Tamish has his palm raised and a sadistic, gleeful look on his face.

"I'm quite certain that you are aware of the law." He drops his hand and the man stills. "Anyone born and blessed with power from the Gods is required to serve the King."

"I have no power." Mr. Buford croaks, pushing himself to his knees.

"I don't have an affinity for liars." Tamish sneers. "You waste the King's time."

King Sandor calmly glances sideways to the guard next to him, I think his name is Adriel. He nods, stepping forward, and raises a palm.

Mr. Buford turns rigid before twisting and turning in on himself. A choking noise is thrust from his throat, echoing down the street. Water begins to pour from his mouth, leak out his ears; it seeps from his palms and puddles around his bent knees.

"Water ability, interesting," drawls the King as Mr. Buford grabs at his neck, fighting for an inhale, but the water keeps flowing. I hold my own breath as I watch, grasping the worn stone under my fingertips hard enough to crack my nails.

Adriel glances at King Sandor, waiting for the order to stop, but he doesn't move, watching the man with a blank face as his lip tips up in the corner.

He is going to kill him.

I tense, ready to push myself into the street. I could create a distraction, and then run. Maybe I'd make it back to the castle unrecognized before they could catch me.

A cold sweat drips down my back and just as I go to push off the building, Sandor gives the command to stop. I sag with relief as Mr. Buford sputters and gasps, wheezing air into his lungs.

"As you well know, I could kill you for such an injustice, but I am a merciful King. Pledge your loyalty to me. Allow me to command your power like it is my own and you live." My head spins and the world tilts.

Mr. Buford straightens, lifting his chin, and dread courses through me. *No.* "The Gods gifted *me* this power, and it is *mine* and mine alon—" His sentence is cut off in a garbled noise as King Sandor drives the tip of sword straight through his throat.

I slap my hand against my mouth, fighting back the scream and the bile that coats my tongue. He yanks his sword back and Mr. Buford falls to the ground with a lifeless thump. His blood swirls in the puddles of water. Power swells inside of me, raging and thrashing against my ribs.

My head spins and my knees go weak as I fight to stay upright. My throat threatens to close as panic overtakes me. I struggle to control my raging heartbeat and hysteric breaths.

I pinch my arm and squeeze my eyes shut. Flashes of my father's lifeless, open eyes replay in my mind, my mother's screams ring in my ears. My toes curl inside my boots.

"Drag his body back to the castle and string him up. The people of Bellehaven need a reminder of what is expected of them. Such blatant insolence will not be tolerated."

I need to *move. Get ahold of yourself.*

I hear the guards shuffling in my direction and beg my body to cooperate. I force myself to slink noiselessly, step by painstaking step, away from them until I come to the open alley. I sprint down it shakily, but as fast as my feet will carry me.

I don't stop until my lungs are burning and my legs are aching. I lean against the cool, rough brick of a closed bakery, trying to catch my breath. My head spins from exerting so much power and energy.

I'm at the edge of the town and the castle is in full view. I *need* get back to my room; I've been out for too long and used all the luck the universe has spared for me today.

I see the open moonlit field. I wait breathlessly to make sure there are no footsteps and then race through the thick grass. The long blades slap against my skin as I weave, navigating in the dark as the light from town fades.

As I near the castle, the crunch of boots and hammering of steps draw my attention. I duck and peer up through the vegetation. My stomach plummets when I see a limp figure dangling from the main entrance, swaying in the cool night breeze.

Nausea threatens to overwhelm me. I fist the dirt at the anger and sadness that fills me. Another innocent life, wasted.

I force my eyes away and crawl, dragging my body through the dirt until I am met with the familiar chilled stone of the castle. I fumble around in the dark until I feel a stone give way beneath my touch and lean against it with my quivering arms. A small passageway appears, and I slip through, shoving the entrance closed behind me.

The King may have started to catch onto my nightly antics, but thankfully, he hasn't found this servant passageway yet. I mean to keep it that way.

I press my hand against the damp walls, the sticky scent of earth strong as I push through the darkness. It is so inky black I see nothing but keep trudging ahead.

After several minutes of stumbling along the corridor, my shoulder hits the entrance to my room. I lose a relieved breath as I stumble through and squint as my eyes adjust to the light.

As soon as the door closes, I replace the picture that hangs in front, concealing it from the rest of the world, and rest my head against the wall to catch my breath and calm my racing heart.

"Naughty, naughty."

I jump at the voice, swallowing the yelp that lodges in my throat. My head snaps up in search of the source, but there's no one to see. It appears I am alone.

"Maddox." His name comes out as more of a plea than I mean it to as I sink to my knees.

He blinks into focus, pushing up from where he is lounging on my bed. His face pinches in concern as he rushes over to me.

"Lay, are you alright? What's wrong?" His hand comes to my shoulder as his eyes search my face.

I wrap a shaky arm around my middle and squeeze my eyes shut against all the horror that keeps replaying in my mind.

"Mr. Buford." I wince as I say his name.

"Who?" Maddox asks confused.

"Your father killed Mr. Buford tonight. He drove a sword right through his throat." My eyes burn as I open them to look into Maddox's round whisky-colored ones. "I just stood there."

"Did my father see you?" His brow furrows and a trace of fear flickers over his face.

"No." He visibly relaxes at my answer.

"Thank the Gods. I don't even want to think of what Tamish and my father would do if they caught you again. I wish you would stop. Why must you *insist* on leaving the castle?"

"You *know* why," I sigh. "The King could cut off all my fingers and toes, and I'd still find a way out of this room. The people of Bellehaven need me."

"One of the boys I worked on tonight had a broken arm with such a bad infection if I had not come, he would have been dead by the week's end." The slums tended to be a place where infection spread fast and viciously.

"You work all day, every day using your power until near burnout, and still, somehow it's not enough for you." He puts his arm around me and helps me to stand.

Maddox sighs, curling and uncurling his fist. "I know I've told you this before, but you can't save everyone." His hand finds my chin and tilts my face, so that I'm looking into his warm eyes again. "I love your heart and support you, but if you get caught, I can't watch Tamish torture you again. I was almost driven mad with how badly I wanted to kill him and my father for that matter."

Fear skates up my spine fast and acute as I remember my latest punishment. "You and I both." I lay my head against his strong shoulder and breathe him in, instantly relaxing.

For the first time my racing mind finally slows. I have to stay focused on all the people that I can save, not the ones that I can't. I tuck the memory of Mr. Buford away and turn it into resolve remembering his last words. *"The Gods gifted* **me** *this power and it is* **mine** *alone."*

"Lay." Maddox pushes again, clearly not wanting to drop it yet.

"I'll be more careful, alright? No one wants your father's attention off them more than me." I tell him what he needs to hear and then attempt to change the subject before the events of the day drag me under. "Now, please tell me you brought food or alcohol?" I am utterly drained and desperately in need of one or both of the latter.

"I wouldn't show up to your room empty-handed." He turns and I right myself as he crosses the room, pulling out a bottle of wine and some chocolate croissants from his bag.

He holds them up and his full lips tip up in a crooked heart-stopping smile. He's always been objectively attractive with a strong jawline and shaggy brown hair that curls when it gets too long. He has carved-out cheeks, and a body that makes many women forgive him after he fails to contact them for weeks at a time.

"Gods above, I love you," I exclaim, as he pops the wine cork and pours us two glasses.

"I know; I'm the perfect man. The Gods gift to women, really," he jokes, and I roll my eyes as I snatch a croissant from his hand.

"There you go, ruining it with your mouth again." I take a bite and swallow a moan when the buttery, chocolate flavor coasts over my tastebuds. "Aren't you going to hand me my wine?"

"You were supposed to meet me for training this morning and never showed. That means you make it up to me tonight, and after, you can have a glass of wine."

I wince remembering how I slept in this morning.

"If you want to sneak out of the castle, especially without Hecktor or me, then you need to know how to defend yourself. Now finish your croissant, you're not getting out of it tonight." He points a gleaming dagger at the pastry in my hand.

"Keep the wine, I don't want it anyway." I collapse back onto my bed.

"Layla," he growls, "you've got to take this seriously. I don't know what I would do if anything ever happened to you."

"Fine." I shove the remaining croissant piece in my mouth and stand. "Please show me your ways."

"That's the attitude," he declares, and I swallow as he fastens his dagger to his hip. "Okay, first lesson. You need to be able to disarm someone. See if you can take my dagger from its sheath."

"Why can't I have my own dagger?"

"Because I am rather attached to all my appendages."

"Very funny." I peer down at where his dagger sits and attempt to grab the handle. Maddox slaps my hand away. "Hey, that hurt!" I cradle the back of my hand.

"You weren't fast enough and your eyes gave you away. Try again."

I keep my eyes on his, only glancing at the handle before trying to swipe it from where it sticks out.

He swats me away. "Stop looking at the dagger, Lay."

I swallow my frustration and focus my eyes back on his warm brown ones. I step closer to him getting a whiff of his freshly showered skin. I whip my hand out, and it brushes the hilt before he smacks it away.

"Better, but you need to use your body, fake like you are going to go one way, then move in the opposite direction. Distract and confuse."

I bend my knees, resetting my focus back on him. I step to the left and try to jerk to the right but end up tripping over my own feet and grabbing for Maddox, hooking my arm around his neck before we both fall to a heap on the floor.

Maddox lands on top of me. "Really?" He smiles into my neck.

"Sorry, I really thought I had that one."

Maddox huffs a laugh as he props himself up. His face hovers above mine and I realize every other part of me is intimately pressed up against him. His muscled thigh rests between mine and every time I inhale my chest brushes his.

He must notice as well because his smile fades, and his eyes drift down, snagging on my mouth. I bite my bottom lip nervously.

"Don't do that, Lay." He groans in a soft whisper.

My body heats with his tortured request. "Do what?" I release my bottom lip, and my breath catches as he leans in further. My mind spins, and I know, without a doubt, he is about to kiss me.

I can't let this happen. I have spent our friendship watching him charm his way from woman to woman and swore to myself I would never fall victim to his seduction.

Just as his full lips brush mine, I grasp the handle of his dagger and give it a firm yank.

"Got it," I squeak. Maddox's brows furrow as he pulls back. I half-heartedly brush the tip against his neck, drawing his attention. "You've been effectively disarmed," I croak out, trying to bring some tension-breaking humor into my voice.

"I knew you had it in you." He pushes up. I can see disappointment and possibly confusion pass over his face. I follow suit, rising on weak knees. He rubs the back of his neck, and I stand awkwardly, gripping the dagger.

I'm dumbfounded, attempting to figure out what the hell just happened. Maddox was my best friend. I'd never allowed myself to go there because he was all I had here and losing him wasn't an option for me.

"Um, okay." He clears his throat. "Now that you have the dagger, what are you going to do with it? I assume stabbing someone goes against the whole healer thing. The most effective move you could make would be to slam the hilt into the attacker's temple. You've got to be quick and precise, but if you do it correctly, you can successfully knock them unconscious."

"Show me." I'm eager to avoid talking about what just almost happened.

He stalks closer and stops a foot from me. I hold my breath as he gingerly grabs my wrist and tilts it back, so the blade now faces me hilt out.

"Grip the hilt harder," he commands, and my knuckles turn white with effort. "Now, you want to aim here. He guides my hand to his temple and presses the hilt there. The hit must be fast, and more importantly, it must be hard. Try the movement a few times." He drops my wrist, and I give the dagger a squeeze before swinging in an up motion and stopping right before his temple.

"Nice, again."

I repeat the motion a few times, getting more confident with each swing. On my fifth attempt, my movements get sloppy. I'm so tired from the day I miscalculate and accidentally strike him.

"Shit, Layla." He grabs his head, and the dagger clatters to the ground as I lower it before him.

"I'm sorry, I'm sorry. Let me see it." I grab for him and am already reaching for my depleted power when he stops me.

"Don't even think about using your powers on me. You have nothing left in your reserve; I can feel it."

"Maddox, I have enough, just let me—"

"I'm fine." He straightens, and I push up off the floor, standing on my tiptoes to get a better look at the hit.

"It's already bruising." I brush the tender skin and feel a whisper of my power pull from deep in my belly.

"Good, I don't mind bruising, it gives me more sympathy and attention from the women around me." His eyes are soft as they sweep over me, watching as I fuss over him.

I have no doubt that is true and he is not lacking in that area. I snort, grabbing a few pieces of ice from the bucket the wine sits in and wrapping them in a cloth. "Lay down." I grab the two filled glasses of ruby liquid. "I'm assuming training is over, and I can drink now?" I hand him the glass from where he now lays on my bed.

"I thought you didn't want any?" He smiles into his wine and downs half the glass in one gulp.

"I lied." I sit on the bed and pat my lap. He moves his head to lay there, and I place the ice over his bruised temple.

He winces. "You're really playing this up." I grin as I brush a few stray brunette strands off his forehead.

"How is the search for your future queen going? Any contenders for your heart yet?" I take a sip of wine and try to sound nonchalant.

"Well, Beth Anne nearly got me to propose this week. She's perfected the art of cock sucking to masterful levels." He wiggles his eyebrows, and I slap him in the arm as he laughs. Maddox has always been a ladies' man who likes to indulge in women often and doesn't discriminate much.

"You are truly a scoundrel." My cheeks reddened at his crass words.

He takes a sip of his wine and then turns to me. "What about you? Are you ever going to get your head out of a book or take any time away from the infirmary to find company with a man? I think an orgasm or two would be exponentially helpful to you." He smirks as my cheeks heat to the color of my wine.

"This isn't about me, stop changing the subject." I'd had only one male encounter before; it was quick and left me deeply unsatisfied.

"Seriously, Lay. I can't remember the last time I've seen you with a male that wasn't me. I certainly can't remember the last time you laid with one. Don't you ever get lonely?"

"Of course I don't get lonely, I have you. Now, mention my sex life one more time and the contents of this glass are going to end up overturned on your head." I hold my glass high and raise my eyebrow.

"Alright, alright. I'm just saying, it wouldn't hurt to indulge occasionally. Let yourself have a little fun."

"I let myself have plenty of fun. I am the definition of fun." I stand, setting the glasses down and Maddox gives me an amused look. "Maybe you're right. There has to be a male out there less insufferable than you." Grabbing my pillow, I throw it, and it hits him square in the face.

"You wound me." He grabs the pillow and throws it back at me.

I laugh, tipping my head back as my body begins to feel light and heady. I sway around the room, humming happily when I hear a tearing noise. Turning, I see Maddox set a book back on my side table, waving the singular piece of paper in the air, grinning.

"You did not just rip that out of my book!" I huff exasperated. He holds out a hand as if to keep me at bay and begins to fold the paper. "What page did you rip out? I wasn't finished! Now how will I know what happens?"

"We have an entire library of books; I'll get you another one." He waves me off and continues to crease the page until he holds up a small paper rose. "For you."

I narrow my eyes at him but take the offering, spinning it between my fingers to admire it. "That's what you always say. I'd rather know what happens in my book...but thank you." I smile despite myself and sniff the faux flower before placing it in the drawer of my bedside table next to the others.

Maddox continues filling our cups until it is so late my eyes grow bleary. I sway around the room, bumping into my cluttered dresser. Some of my many trinkets topple to the ground, a collection of all the offerings people had given me over the years in lieu of coin.

"Okay, I think it's time to sleep." Maddox saunters over to me and his hands grasp my hips to steady me. I drunkenly smile up at him, and he stills as his eyes track the movement. His hand comes up, his thumb brushing over my cheekbone. "You are exquisite. Have I ever told you that?"

"Oh no." I push at his chest and stumble away towards the bed. "No, no, no, no. Save it for Beth Anne; I am immune to your charm."

"Lay." Maddox grabs for me as I begin to topple over. My head is pleasantly buzzing, and my body feels heavy and relaxed. "Don't push me away like you do to every other man." His words sober me for a moment as I peer up at him. He looks down at me with a pleading look that scares me.

"I watched what it did to my mother when he died." I murmur, "I watched how it changed her. It ate away at her mind, body, and soul." The drunken confession tumbles out of me. I vowed to never let the same thing happen to me.

"I know," he whispers, pulling me into his lean body. "I know," he says again, and I wrap my arms around his middle, allowing my sadness to rise to the surface.

He rests his chin on the top of my head. "Come on, let's get you to bed." He walks me backward a few steps before lowering me onto the soft sheets. Pulling up the bedding, he slides in behind me and pulls me against his chest. "You aren't her."

CHAPTER
TWO

I WAKE ABRUPTLY THE NEXT MORNING TO POUNDING on my door. I shoot out of bed, my body moving so fast on its own accord I slam into my door before yanking it open. "Yes, I'm awake," I croak, rubbing at my sleep coated eyes.

Hecktor, my guard stands at the entrance, looking anything but amused. "We leave in ten minutes for the infirmary. The King won't be happy if we are late."

He gives me a disapproving look when he sees Maddox asleep in my bed. "You may want to wake the prince; he has matters to attend to this morning."

"Good morning to you too, Hecktor," I grumble as I shut the door. Every muscle in my body aches and my head pounds furiously as I make my way to the closet.

A few empty bottles of wine litter the floor. I groan, knowing I have a full day of healing ahead fighting through this hangover.

I pull on a white, long-sleeved undershirt, tossing a plain black dress over it. Black is my color of choice lately to hide any of the blood that will unwittingly find its way onto me.

I stumble over to Maddox and give him a good shake. "Maddox, wake up! If your father finds you in here, I'm sure he will be less than thrilled."

He moans, pushing himself further into my bed while securing a pillow over his head.

"You have two minutes to get up before I pour a pitcher of ice-cold water on you."

"What time is it?" he grumbles.

"A quarter to eight."

"Oh, fuck." He jumps out of the bed and begins searching around the room.

"Where did all your clothes go?" He stands before me in a pair of drawers. I'm momentarily stunned, his long sinewy body catching my attention.

I've seen him shirtless many times, but for some reason, I suddenly understand why so many ladies willingly welcome him into their beds. My eyes linger on the planes of his body for longer than appropriate.

He finds his pants, pulling them on quickly, catching my stare. "What? You know I get hot when I sleep."

I nod stupidly, looking away hoping he doesn't notice the red staining my cheeks. I see his shirt lying on the floor and toss it to him.

"Thanks."

"Where are you in such a hurry to?" I run a brush through my long, tangled blonde hair. When I catch a glimpse of myself in the mirror, I cringe. Heavy bags line my bloodshot, light blue eyes. Eyes I've always thought were too big for my face. My cheekbones have a gaunt appearance, a stark reminder of how poorly I'd been taking care of myself lately. My tongue darts out to wet my dry, heart-shaped lips. They are wine-stained, and I rub the back of my hand over them to try and rid them of evidence.

"I am to welcome some visitors from Westray to the castle." He grabs the brush from my hands and runs it through his tousled locks. I lick my fingers and flatten them over a few stray pieces of hair sticking up; he grins down at me.

"Westray? That's quite a distance to travel. What business do they have here?" We both pull on our boots.

"I believe they are just passing through. Calum, the King of Westray used to be close with my father." He finishes tying his laces and stands. His brows pinch together and he rubs at his temples. "Gods, I feel awful; I blame you."

"How is it my fault?! You brought the wine!"

"If you weren't so hell-bent on proving 'just how fun you could be' maybe we wouldn't have gone through three bottles!" He gives me a once over, pulling down the side of my dress and attempting to smooth some wrinkles.

I swat him away. "I don't have time to argue with you; Hecktor will have my head. And for the record, I was the embodiment of fun last night." I open my door, stepping out to meet Hecktor. The three of us walk down the hallways and I rub my arms to wear off the cold that seeps through all the old stones lining the walls. They vary in shapes and sizes, each one a drab grey.

"Oh yeah, was that before or after you passed out drooling and snoring?" His lips tip up in that crooked smile eliciting a grin from me.

I bump him with my shoulder. "I don't snore, and you know it." Our footsteps echo in the empty corridor.

"Dinner tonight after you're done in the infirmary?" Maddox asks as he buttons his shirt. We pass a window, and I get a glimpse of the dead tree that Maddox and I used to climb when we were little.

"I have to visit my mother tonight, but maybe after." I grimace at the sudden onslaught of emotion that assaults me at the mention of her.

"Do you want me to come with you?" Maddox notices my sudden change and his hand comes up to brush the small of my back.

"I think it's better if you don't; she's been getting worse. She barely recognizes me these days." I frown remembering our last interaction.

"You think she would recognize me? It would be very difficult to forget a face as perfect as mine." My lip lifts in a halfhearted smile at his attempt to pull me out of my thoughts. "Really though, Lay, if you need me, I'm there."

"I know, thanks. I'll see you later, okay?"

"See ya, good luck today!" He gives my side a squeeze before going in the opposite direction.

"Are you quite ready?" Hecktor looks impatient as he turns to me, approaching the entrance.

"As I'll ever be." I try to ignore the way my head pounds and my stomach churns unpleasantly.

"Can't you use some of those healing abilities on yourself?" he grumbles, taking in my appearance.

"You know it doesn't work that way, and anyway, I feel great." I feign a big smile hoping to appease him, and he looks away shaking his head.

We arrive at the healing wing of the castle, and he turns to me, handing me a small sticky bun before leaving me with a nod. He may appear grumpy and impatient, but he'd been my guard for many years, and we had a mutual bond.

"Thanks, Hecktor," I call after him before entering.

The healing wing is already full, and I squint against the sun gleaming off the white floors and sterile walls. I rush over to the beds in front; they tend to have the more life-threatening cases and patients who need more urgent care.

One of the new castle guards is on the first cot. Sky, my assistant, is already cleaning the wounds on his back and she gives me a tense look when she sees me.

Looking at the sticky bun, I sigh, my appetite instantly gone, and toss it into the bin. I cleanse my hands as my power awakens, itching my skin.

My stomach flips uneasily as I approach, already knowing what I am going to find. Deep gashes line his back, red and angry. It pains me just to look at them. The guard is dirty, his shoulders slumped and head down.

I kneel in front of him, noting the way his body twitches and spasms and recalling all the times I've suffered similarly. "I'm Layla," I introduce myself, and he tilts his head enough to glance at me.

"I know who you are," he responds gruffly narrowing his eyes.

"Alright," I start lamely, struggling for words. "You look like you're in pain. If it's okay, I'm going to relieve some of it for you."

He grunts in response, and I stand awkwardly, positioning myself behind him. "You may feel some heat as I work; it's helpful if you stay still," I explain, and he nods.

I hover my hands over the lacerations, watching as the muscles and skin carefully knit back together. His body responds, visibly relaxing, and his breathing becomes less labored. "Better?"

He nods again, and I notice his clenched fists as he tries to conceal the tremors. "Tamish?"

His eyes snap to mine when I ask the question. "I just wanted to see my family and make sure they were doing alright. Tell them I am—was, okay." He clenches his jaw before continuing, "The King keeps us locked away to use us as he pleases. Told me my family was nothing but a distraction, to forget them." He huffs a humorless laugh, and Sky glances around nervously.

"May I see your hand?" I ask, at a loss on how to respond to him. He curls his lip at me before shoving his hand in my direction. I take it, pushing some of my powers into him, working to relieve the damage Tamish caused.

"Must be nice being favored by the King. I've heard he keeps your mother here, right in the castle." My body stiffens at his words, and I abruptly stand. "The rare healer gets special privileges. I bet you spread your legs for him, too."

My face burns at his words and I haven't a clue what to say. "You do not get to speak to me like that. Leave." I point to the doors as I say the word.

He shoves off the bed, brushing past a wide-eyed Sky. She pushes her thick rimmed glasses up her nose and nervously tucks a piece of short auburn hair behind her ear. Her mouth opens but I hold my hand up.

"It's fine." I stop her before she can say anything. "Patients are waiting." My shoulders rise with a deep inhale as I close my eyes to collect myself. I exhale my exasperation and slip on a mask of professionalism, knowing what is expected of me.

Once I am back in control, I move to the next bed, and my heart clenches. The next patient is a small girl with a horrific cough. She's with her mother, both in clothes covered in holes and emanating a stench I'd only smelled in the slums. They have protruding collar bones and gaunt cheeks.

The woman looks desperate, and I'm not sure how she's managed to scrape together the amount of money the King demands to see me.

I am sure they didn't have coin to spare and probably had to choose between food and health. I fist my palm as anger licks up my spine. No one should have to make that choice. My cheeks heat as I tamp down on my anger, guilt replacing my rage.

My father would have been so disappointed if he knew how I let the King exploit my sacred power. A power he died for. I swallow the lump in my throat as I approach the little girl and force a smile on my face. "What's your name?"

"Amelia."

"Hello, Amelia. I'm Layla. Would it be okay if I touched you right here?" I point to her chest, where I can already hear her lungs rattling.

She nods hesitantly after looking at her mother, and I gently press my palm to her small chest. I try to ignore the way my fingers brush her protruding collarbones.

She lets out a few barking coughs that leave her breathless. "Okay, I'm going to begin. This won't hurt. You'll feel my palm get hot; my hand will start to glow a bit. She nods just as my power dives inside of her. I can almost see it wrapping around her little lungs.

I picture her running, jumping, playing, laughing. Being a healthy child. I picture myself at that age and how I used to chase my father through the fields behind our worn-down cottage. He would turn with open arms, and I'd jump into them before he'd spin us around and around.

I rein in my power, looking to her mother. "Her lungs are clear; she should be without ailment now." She takes her child's face in her hands and scans her. "There is one more thing. I saw something in your ear." I make a show of looking in her ear before pulling a silver from behind it.

"Wherever did that come from?!" A smile spreads across the girl's face as I feign shock. "I suppose because it was behind your ear it is yours." Her and her mother's eyes widen as I hand it to her. "I'm so happy you came to see me today. I will forever talk about the girl with the silver in her ear."

She clutches the coin, reaching up and touching her ear before smiling over at her mother.

"Thank you," the mother says, the worry behind her eyes easing a touch.

"Glad I could help." I make my way over to Sky, who is cleaning some empty beds.

"I wish you would stop doing that, if the King or Tamish ever found out, I don't even want to think about what they would do," she grumbles, not bothering to look up.

"They aren't going to find out. What was I to do Sky? They were skin and bones. Am I expected to heal their ailments only to have them starve to death?"

She sighs and then tenses as King Sandor enters the room. He is an average-sized man, not very tall, but manages to appear imposing. His very presence demands respect. He wears an affable mask, but I can always feel his cold, calculated demeanor underneath. He is followed by Tamish, Maddox, and a few people I don't recognize.

A man on a stretcher is brought in behind them, moaning in pain.

"Layla, there you are." The King approaches us, and I go rigid. "I have brought some spectators today. This is Ledger, Prince of Westray." He points to a man with severe yet attractive features next to him. His black hair is short, a dusting of rugged facial hair lining his jaw and full mouth. His expression is unreadable as his forest-green eyes study me. "And his travel companions, Mia and Archie." He sneers as he looks at the tall, blonde, boyishly handsome man. Archie clenches his jaw, and Mia brushes his hand with hers discreetly. She is a beautiful, dark-skinned woman with hazel eyes.

I nod, giving them a tight smile.

"Miss Sutton is one of the only healers left on our continent. She is as talented as she is beautiful."

I despise when he does this—using my power as entertainment, showing me off like a prized possession.

"What are you waiting for? Continue—we want to see that power of yours. Work on him next." He nods over at the man who was just brought in. "His moans are starting to grate on my nerves."

"Yes, Your Grace," I grind out before walking over to the man. I fight to control my face as my anger grows.

The man is writhing wildly on the bed. His shirt is tattered, and his shoulder is leaking blood. Cutting the shirt away, I can see familiar black venom running through the veins of his arm.

I give Sky a look, and she pins his arms down so I can begin. The black venom from the bite is already spreading to his fingertips. I wonder what the animal looks like that inflicts such wounds.

Heat scalds my skin, my power already threatening to erupt out of me. I hold my hands steady as they begin to glow. I brace myself as the poison starts to leave his body; it creeps into my veins, sizzling them and stealing my breath.

I clench my teeth together to ease the blinding pain. Sweat beads on my forehead. I desperately want to stop but force myself to continue. The agony is almost crippling. My back bows.

I shift my focus and recede into the recesses of my mind to drown out the pain. I think of Maddox last night. His devious smile and how his perfect teeth were stained red with wine. I think of my father and how proud he used to be when I would conjure a spark of my power.

I sag with relief when the pain subsides, and the man's struggle stops. His moans cease and the shredded skin on his shoulder knits neatly back together.

My power snaps back with such force my knees hit the floor. I must have been holding my breath because I am now greedily gulping down air, unable to satisfy my lungs. My mouth waters, a familiar putrid taste filling it, making my stomach sour.

I reach for the closest bin and vomit the contents of my empty stomach. Maddox is next to me in the next breath, his hand finding mine and his other going to my back. "Are you okay?" he whispers, and when I look up at him, his jaw is set. His whisky eyes are focused on me, and his eyebrows are furrowed in concern.

I nod as I wipe my mouth with the back of my hand.

Clapping echoes off the bare, white walls. "Such a show you put on; I could watch you all day." The King wears a face of delight. "Honestly, Layla, get up, you embarrass me. She has always been one for the dramatics." He addresses the visitors at his side, who all stare with wide eyes and their mouths ajar.

I grit my teeth at his comment and take a deep breath through my nose. I force my wobbly legs to stand with Maddox at my back, steadying me.

My brain feels like it is thrashing around in my skull, and my vision has gone slightly blurry. I curse myself for not eating the sticky bun Hector gave me earlier. My body is desperate for fuel.

"Maddox, get over here, the girl is fine; you're making her look weak. Should I be concerned, Layla? Does this display have anything to do with your nightly escapades?" The King lifts his eyebrows, looking at Tamish who stands on the other side of him. Maddox goes fully still beside me.

I don't even have time to brace before Sandor is in my head. His power slithers over my skull, sinking its teeth into the flesh of my mind.

I gasp as every muscle in my body tenses. My instinct is to rage against his power but the harder I fight, the more intense his grip becomes. Razor sharp claws drag against the sensitive crevices of my memories. Maddox's hand grips my hip bone and I can practically hear his thoughts. *Stop fighting, give him something that will satisfy his intrusion.*

I manage a small gasp, forcing my body to relax. I let The King's power creep into my mind. The feel of it is so repugnant that I nearly vomit again.

I reach for a memory from last night. I think of Maddox and I lounging on the bed drinking wine, me swaying around the room, Maddox catching me and listening as I wail about my mother.

King Sandor's scoff echoes and when I look up, he is rolling his eyes. Everyone's stares bounce between the King and me. The blonde man—Archie, His nostrils are flaring as his gaze vaults from me to Ledger. Mia has a death grip on his hand.

I can feel the King's dissatisfaction as his grip tightens on my skull. I wince, but before he can violate me again a crash makes us all jump. Sandor's concentration breaks and relief is immediate as his power slowly reels back.

Medical supplies chime off the ground and the metal tray they are on rattles as it bounces, reverberating off the stone floor. Maddox releases the breath he must have been holding and it ruffles my hair. The King turns a shade of red as he whips around.

The prince of Westray stands, unbothered, forest green eyes glued on me. Tourniquets, tweezers, needles, and shears are at his feet. He doesn't even spare Sandor a glace as he speaks. "My apologies your Grace, how very clumsy of me." He kneels to retrieve the supplies, and I intervene before Sandor can think too much of it.

"I must also apologize my King," I exclaim, drawing his scrutiny. "I forgot to eat this morning." Sandor's gaze moves back to me, and he makes a noise of displeasure before leveling Maddox with an expectant look.

I don't dare glance over at Maddox as his hand lingers on the small of my back before he drops it, moving to stand by King Sandor's side once again.

I grip the end of the bed, my knuckles white as I fight to form some semblance of control over my body. Sky scrambles over to Ledger to grab the tray from him. He is still staring at me, studying me, like I am the answer to all his problems. Maddox seems to notice as well, his eyes narrowed and his jaw tight as he stares the man down.

"Incredible," King Sandor's attention shifts to the sentry I just healed. "He looks to be the picture of health." He marvels, as his lips spread, gaping. The guard's skin is no longer pale; it is flushed with color. His cheeks are rosy, and the skin of his shoulder a fresh pink.

"What do you think? Isn't she marvelous?" He turns to the green-eyed man and his party. "It is not every day you get to see something like that."

"Indeed," Ledger replies, glancing at the sentry. His deep voice makes goosebumps erupt on my arm. I frown as I look down to see them pebble my skin.

"Wonderful! Layla, back to work, these people aren't going to heal themselves, and for God's sake, eat something," King Sandor says lazily, snapping me out of my daze.

A snarky response sits readily on my tongue, and I fight to keep it inside. My gaze flicks to Maddox, who wears a warning look.

"Tell me, Ledger, has Callum had more luck at keeping Archie in line than I did?" the King asks, and the blonde man tenses.

Ledger's jaw feathers as he follows King Sandor out of the room.

"Of course not, what fun would that be?" I hear Archie respond as the doors swing closed. I frown at the interaction before refocusing.

The sentry I just healed starts to come to, letting out a groan and attempting to sit up.

"Whoa, take it slow." I rush over to his side placing my hands on his upper back to assist him. "You've lost a lot of blood. How do you feel?" I take in his handsome face and hazel eyes for the first time.

"I feel..." He pauses, his eyes straying to his mended shoulder and then back to me. "Alive, thanks to you." He flexes his fingers and rolls out his arm. "You have quite the power."

"It certainly has its uses." I run my fingers over the pink raised skin of his shoulder pressing gently. "Does that hurt?"

"No." His breath brushes the side of my face, and I'm instantly aware of how close we are. He studies me and smiles softly when I finally look up. "You have soft hands, a gentle touch."

I stand, clearing my throat, and busy myself pouring him a glass of water. "Here, you need to stay hydrated."

He accepts the glass, intentionally brushing his fingers against mine. "Your name is Layla, right?"

My response is a small nod.

"I'm Jonah."

"Nice to meet you. I have a few more patients, so if you're alright, I really should tend to them." I motion over my shoulder, where I can sense Sky eavesdropping. "Take all the time you need, but when you feel ready, help yourself out." I begin to turn away hoping to dissuade what I know is coming.

"I'd love to repay you in some way, perhaps dinner?"

I wince before turning back to him and answering, "That is unnecessary." My shoulders stiffen as I take a step back.

"I insist."

"It would look poorly on me to be seen at dinner with a patient, so as much as I appreciate it, I must decline."

He tilts his head, an amused smile tugging at the corner of his mouth. "Alright, well if you change your mind, the offer stands." He hesitates giving me one last look, as if expecting me to take back my words before continuing. "Thank you, ladies."

I let out a breath as he disappears behind the doors.

"What was wrong with that one?" Sky asks, stripping the bloodied sheet off the bed.

"Nothing was *wrong* with him. I simply do not entertain patients, you know that."

"He seemed nice and was rather attractive."

"Sounds like you should track him down and tell him all the ways he can repay you then." I grin as Sky swats my shoulder.

Sky leaves and comes back with some pastries we gobble down. I work for a few more hours, healing patient after patient until my power begins to fizzle. The skin I keep trying to knit together rips back open, leaving behind jagged, horrible scars. My hands start to shake, and my concentration is shot.

After the third try at knitting together a knife wound, Sky places her hand gently on my shoulder. "I can take it from here Layla, you've healed all the serious injuries for the day, all the rest of the wounds can be taken care of with a simple needle and thread; go, rest."

I return her smile the best I can and cautiously stand. I only have enough energy to agree with her, offering a small nod and a thank you before I sluggishly make my way out of the infirmary.

CHAPTER
THREE

I STAND IN FRONT OF MY MOTHER'S ROOM TRYING TO talk myself into knocking. I pace, spinning the ring on my finger. It had already been three days since our last visit, and I couldn't keep putting it off. I was just so tired, utterly drained.

As if making the decision for me, the door swings open. My mother's chestnut eyes scan me. She looks beautiful, her blonde hair pulled back into a thick braid.

I hold my breath, stilling, as she looks at me. My heart trips over itself as I look for any sign of recognition on her aging face.

"May I help you, dear?" she questions, a crease appearing between her eyebrows. I swallow around the lump of disappointment in my throat, letting out a small whoosh of air.

"Sorry, I believe I have the wrong door." My ribs are tight as I say the words, scanning her face again.

"Oh, that's quite alright. Since you are here, have you seen my husband? I was just going out to look for him." She squints as she studies me. "You have his eyes."

My breath hitches as I fight to form a response. "No, I'm sorry, I uh- haven't seen him." I stumble over my words.

"That's too bad; I do hope he comes home soon. I miss him," she says, and my heart clenches.

"I do too," I whisper.

"What was that, dear?"

"Have a good night." I force a smile.

"You too." She steps out the door and shuts it. Brushing past me, her floral scent invades my senses, dragging up old memories. As she walks down the hallway, my shoulders drop. She always ends up in the gardens around sunset. Being outside soothes her in ways I deeply understand.

I stare after her until she disappears around a corner before accepting my defeat and slumping to my room.

Opening the door, I am greeted by Maddox sitting at my table, a glass of wine in hand.

"Welcome home, honey, I hope you're hungry. May I offer you a glass of wine?" He holds out his hands emphasizing the feast in front of him.

"I don't know what I am more desperate for, food or a bath." I groan as I kick off my boots. "And the glass won't be necessary." I grab the bottle off the table and take a few gulps of the fruity liquid.

"You need a bath." He grimaces as he sees the dried blood on my clothing. "Lucky for you, I already have one drawn. I even used your favorite bath salts."

"Thank the Gods." I set the bottle down before walking over to the bathroom and discarding my crusty shirt. "Maybe you really are God's gift to women," I call over my shoulder to him through the cracked door.

"I knew you'd see the light one day." I hear the smile in his voice.

I stumble over to the countertop and uncork a tonic Sky had made for when I'd depleted myself. It relieved the more daunting effects. I throw it back and cringe at the vile liquid. It tastes like shit but helps.

I peel off my pants and undergarments and then lower my body into the wet heat. The water instantly eases my aching body and thundering head.

"I'm assuming my father failed to retrieve any damning memories of yours from last night?"

"I gave him as little as I could. Nothing of me leaving the castle walls. How did it go with the people from Westray?" I touch some of the bubbles floating on the surface of the water.

"Fine. The prince of Westray seemed a little too interested in you for my liking, but luckily, they were just passing through. As usual, my father had to flaunt who he commands with the most treasured and valued abilities. Sorry, I know how much you hate when he does that."

He did this often. He liked to flaunt his power; his every so infinite army of soldiers blessed with abilities. He had the biggest legion on the continent. He knew how to scare loyalty into someone and if that didn't work, he had a way of reading people, seeing their inner most desires and using it to his advantage. He thought of himself as untouchable.

"Maybe if I continue puking every time he brings someone, he will eventually stop," I say and Maddox laughs from the other room.

"You missed my father getting rip-roaring drunk before they left. He started his whole, 'May our kingdoms be ever united and may those blessed with sacred power continue to grow in strength and numbers' speech." He imitates the king, and I huff a laugh.

"Sad that I missed it." I scrub at my skin until it is pink and raw and then stand, wrapping a towel around myself. "After the day I've had, I'd like to also get rip-roaring drunk," I swing the bathroom door open.

Maddox's cocky smile falters as his gaze snags on my bare legs. His eyes linger on the exposed skin of my chest, and his Adam's apple bobs as he swallows.

I fidget with the corner of the towel, suddenly self-conscious. "What?" I question, and he clears his throat.

"Nothing, get dressed so we can get you something to eat." He looks away.

I walk to my closet, pulling on some leggings and one of Maddox's plain shirts. Sometimes, I'd steal one when he left them in my room, finding them comforting and gloriously loose.

"What did your father mean when he asked about that man Archie?"

"He used to reside here when he was a child coming into his powers. From what I remember, he was difficult for my father to manage and was always getting in trouble and punished. I think he ended up working out some kind of trade with Callum so he could be rid of him."

"If only we could all be that lucky." I sigh, sagging into the chair next to Maddox. He seems lost in thought as I pop a grape into my mouth. I grab some fresh meat and cheese and chew thoughtfully. I moan as I eat, throwing my head back. When I crack my eyes open, Maddox is staring at me with a strange look on his face.

"What is going on with you Mads? You're acting strange." I was used to him being cocky, funny, carefree. I'd rarely seen him shaken up or acting the way he was now.

He abruptly stands, his chair dragging against the wood beneath it. He walks to the middle of the room, pacing back and forth, undoing the top button of his shirt and ripping it away from his neck.

I finish chewing my food and swallow. Standing, I walk cautiously over to him. "Maddox, are you okay?" I touch his shoulder gently and he whirls around to face me.

He leans down so his face is mere inches from mine. My brows crease in confusion as his eyes flicker from my mouth back to my eyes.

I don't have a chance to register what he's thinking before he crashes his lips against mine. I'm so stunned my body doesn't react at first.

My lips freeze against his. He doesn't stop, and I can sense his frustration as his lips continue coaxing. His arms band around my waist and he walks me back a few steps until my back hits the wall. His lips are soft, pleasant even, and when his hand cups the side of my neck I melt into it.

The hard ridges of his body press against mine, and I want to feel more of him. His lips move over my mine expertly, his tongue meeting mine in strokes that have me fisting his shirt.

It had been so long since I'd been kissed by a man. I can hardly breathe, hardly think, as the desire I'd buried so deeply becomes a prominent ache in my belly.

One hand stays fisted in his shirt while the other tangles in his hair, pulling him closer. His teeth tug lightly at my bottom lip.

He shifts closer, and his hard length brushes my stomach. His lips break from mine, kissing down my neck. I heave a breath as my eyes flutter open.

My lust-addled brain clears for the briefest moment, and I freeze. My hands find Maddox's chest and push. He steps back a fraction, his gaze fixated on the ground as his own shoulders heave. "What in the hell was that?" I try to calm my breathing as my mind reels. Why did he kiss me? Why did I kiss him back? And why, for the love of the Gods, did I like it?

"Maddox, look at me." I take his face in my hands and force his caramel eyes to meet mine.

He sighs and his warm breath fans over my face. "I've been under a lot of pressure to wed lately, you know that."

I nod.

"I've been trying, I really have, but you keep popping into my head. It got worse after we almost kissed the other night. I can't stop thinking about you. I even called Beth Anne your name while we were having sex."

I drop my hands from his face, my eyes wide.

"She will probably never speak to me again, and I don't even care!"

I take a step back, trying to form a response. "What every girl wants to hear." I roll my eyes. "You know this can't work between us. You're my best friend, and your father would most definitely not approve!"

"You always say that, but what if it could work, Lay? I take everything I said back, I don't want you spending time with other men. Spend time with me; give us a shot." His eyes are hopeful as he closes the distance between us.

"It wouldn't work." I smile sadly at him. "You would get your fill of me just like you do every other woman, and then I'd be completely lost. You are one of the only things that make this life bearable, Maddox, and I can't lose you."

"You could never lose me, Lay. You felt it, I know you felt it." He pushes me back gently until my back hits the wall again. He leans down so our mouths are almost torturously touching.

I close my eyes against the desire that stirs in my veins. His hand cups the side of my face and his fingers curl in my hair as he brushes his lips against mine in a devastating kiss.

I push up on my toes, chasing more as his tongue traces the line between my lips. His other hand grips my hip firmly, yanking me against him so I can feel just how much he wants me.

Gods, he is good at this.

My heart pounds as blood surges through me. I want to wrap my legs around him, to tear off all the clothing that separates our skin.

My brain screams at me to stop, but my body demands I continue. He is the one person in this world who means the most to me, and I am playing a dangerous game. A game that, if lost, would cost me dearly.

I manage to pull myself away and drag in a ragged breath. "Stop, we need to stop." I barely get the words out and have to fist my hands at my sides to keep from reaching for him as he steps back.

He notices my reaction and smothers the grin from his face. "If you need time, I can give you time, but I know I want this."

I touch his stomach and let my head fall onto his chest. I breathe him in. He smells clean and familiar. "Time would be good," I murmur, and he nods, rubbing his hands down my back before putting much-needed space between us.

"I'll be in my room if you want to finish what we started." I can hear his smirk as he walks to the door.

"I fear you severely overestimate the effect you have on women."

He chuckles as he leaves.

I don't know what to think about what just happened. I'd always been attracted to Maddox, but we'd been strictly off-limits to each other.

He is my best friend, and I'm terrified to mess up what we've built over all these years. Kissing him is easy, natural, and I can't deny the pining I'd felt for him during it.

I take a few deep breaths to quell the desire still stirring in my belly before making my way back to the table. Tearing at an uneaten baguette, I pull my knees to my chest.

The balcony door swings open, drawing my attention. The wind whips around the room, sending a chill over my skin. I drop the bread and swallow.

My brows furrow as I stand, taking a few slow steps towards the creaking door. "Hello?" I call softly, craning my neck and peering out into the dark.

A soft breeze blows loose tendrils of hair around my face and a shiver skitters up my spine. It's faint, but I swear I sense a pulse of power. The hair of my arms stands on end, and my heartbeat ratchets up a few paces.

My eyes bulge as gray smoke drifts into the room. I spring back as it trails through the air towards me. It reaches my ankle, and I suck in a startled breath as it caresses up my calf, around my middle, and over my neck. A shudder rolls through my body. It feels cool and euphoric, and my own magic awakens in response as if curious.

I nearly yelp as the emerald-eyed man from earlier steps through the doors. My eyes dart around the room looking for a weapon as I jolt back.

"Don't scream. I'm not here to hurt you." He holds up his hands in surrender, and his power recedes into him.

"What do you want?" I take a step back, my eyes flicking to the door. I know Hecktor is standing at attention on the other side.

"I want you."

I raise an eyebrow at him.

"Your power to be more specific." When I don't speak, he continues, "Someone I care for is very ill and doesn't have much time left. I have tried everything to no avail and am out of options. I saw what you did today, what you are capable of."

"Is the person you speak of in Bellehaven?" He shakes his head no, and I let out a disbelieving huff of air. "So you are proposing I leave and travel to Westray? King Sandor would never allow it."

"I am well aware of the fact your King does not like to share. That is why I do not ask him, but you. I can pay you handsomely."

"I am sorry about your circumstances, but I can't leave. The punishment would be too great, and the risk is one I can't take." My mother's face flashes in my mind.

"You could have a better life in Westray. Serve a King that isn't a selfish tyrant." He spits the last part, a scowl on his lips. I've dreamed of a life away from Bellehaven since the moment I was brought into this God's forsaken castle.

I distract myself with books and ease my guilt by sneaking out to heal the powerless. I am not foolish enough to believe I can exist away from here as long as my mother is alive. Besides Maddox, she is the one thing I have left, and my father would have wanted me to keep her safe.

"You need to leave before I alert the guards outside my door of your presence," I threaten.

"Name your price."

"I cannot be bought. I can't help you."

"Ple—"

"LEAVE," I cut him off, my mind already made up.

His eyes harden and the muscle in his jaw ticks. His magic pulses harshly around him and my stomach flips. I hold my breath, bracing for his next move.

"You deny me so easily. Without thought of what will happen as a result."

"I do not have a choice." I plead with him to understand.

"One always has a choice." His eyes are hard, his presence even more intimidating as I take another nervous step back. He clocks the movement and after several seconds of silence, when he realizes I will not be swayed, he finally speaks in a clipped tone behind gritted teeth, "As you wish." He backs out of the room, the balcony doors slamming shut, causing me to flinch.

"Everything okay?" Hecktor cracks the door.

"Yes, the wind just caught the doors. I think I'm going to call it a night." He does a sweep of the room, and I hide my hands behind my back so he doesn't see them shaking.

"Okay, I will be here at eight tomorrow to escort you to the infirmary. Be ready." He shuts the door.

I wipe sweaty palms against my thighs and pace around the room attempting to calm my thrashing heart. Unease eats at me, filling the pockets of my mind and unsettling my stomach.

I stagger to the bathroom, lathering my hands in soap. I scrub rigorously, watching numbly as the bubbles swirl down the drain. The water might as well be tinged red. All I can think is I've just condemned someone to their death.

CHAPTER
FOUR

"Is everything okay?" Sky finally asks me after it takes four tries to heal the ailment of our last patient. I've been painfully struggling to heal every patient today, warring against my straying thoughts. "Why don't you take a break? I can handle it for a while," she offers with an encouraging smile.

"Okay," I agree, my shoulders sagging. "I think I'll get some fresh air." I wash my hands, leave the infirmary, and make my way to one of the side terraces.

The sun immediately warms my skin as I sink down the heated stone wall dropping my head onto my knees and pinching the bridge of my nose.

I startle as Hecktor's knuckles rap against the glass window, alerting me of his presence. A second later the terrace doors swing open. Hecktor waves a sweet roll in the air before tossing it to me. It's still warm when I catch it.

"Thank you," I call after him, hearing his responding grunt as the doors swing closed. I *need* to eat—to replenish my power reserves but have no appetite. My stomach is tight, churning with unease and I can't shake the bad feeling that has rooted itself inside me.

The look in the prince of Westray's eyes keeps flashing in my mind. It had been desperate at first but was replaced rapidly with something like determination and before he left, malice. The interaction is on repeat in my mind and makes me wish for King Sandor's memory-altering powers.

I want to find Maddox, seek comfort in him, and tell him of the interaction but am too much of a coward to face him. If our kiss had revealed anything, it's that I am weak, and if he tried to kiss me again, I'm not confident I wouldn't fold entirely.

We are good together, him and I. We complement each other and know one another intimately, but until I have time to think clearly, I can't give him the answer he deserves.

I force a few bites of the sweet roll down, the sweet, buttery flavor tasting like ash on my tongue. Brushing myself off, I inhale deeply and begin walking back to the infirmary.

The rest of the day doesn't get better. My healing is sloppy, but I manage to fumble my way through it. It's a grueling few hours that leaves me feeling completely inept.

Sky is gracious enough not to ask me about it again, but I don't miss her surprised and concerned stares as she pays witness to me laboring with my abilities.

I wash the day away once back in my rooms, dress in one of my white under dresses and then attempt to distract myself with a book. Upon further inspection, I realize Maddox has ripped out multiple pages of my current novel.

Sighing, I make my way to the door. Hecktor is standing at attention, and he doesn't move, only lifts an eyebrow. "Do you have the report from your shift in town today?" Hecktor always has a report of the townsfolk's needs after his shifts. It is how I know who needs my powers most.

He pulls a small piece of paper out of his front pocket. "Did you eat dinner yet?" he questions, holding the paper out of reach.

"Yes," I answer, and he nods once before handing it to me.

"Good." He looks around to make sure we are alone. "If you decide to leave the castle grounds tonight, I'd like to escort you. You should not be without protection." His voice is low, and he stands at attention as he speaks.

"Thanks, Hecktor." I smile at him as I shut the door.

I pace the room as I scan the paper and my stomach sinks. This must have been the reason I've had a bad feeling all day. Oliver's name is written boldly in the middle. "Seriously? Again, Oliver?" I whisper to myself.

Thea used to be friends with my mother; she had a meager garden she would share with us from time to time, which relieved the constant ache of our hunger. It was why I always looked for her, and her son's, name and visited their cottage when they needed me.

What power I have left from the day lashes around inside of me, demanding I go. I know I don't have much time to waste, especially if I want to avoid being caught. I debate accepting Hecktor's offer to escort me to town, but I don't want to put him at risk.

Throwing on my cloak and a pair of leggings to go under my dress, I move the picture off the wall. The door to the tunnels creaks open. I uncurl my hands and look back at the report with Oliver's name on it. Grinding my teeth, I grab my boots knowing I won't be able to rest tonight until I make sure he is okay.

Stumbling out of the exit, I squint up at the full moon. My head swivels around, making sure no one spotted me and once I am satisfied, I start the journey to town.

The walk feels longer tonight. My mind is racing, burning with paranoia. When I see the town lights, I breathe a sigh of relief.

"Just this one stop and I'll go back. Quick in, quick out," I mumble to myself, pulling my hood up and closer to my face.

I amble through the quiet, empty streets. My head swivels and my heart pounds. My palms are slick as I brush them over my pants.

Thea's dilapidated cottage comes into focus at the end of the road, and I briskly make my way over to it. I glance towards the spot where our humble cottage used to sit, now just a heap of withered remains and forgotten memories.

Sighing, I knock softly on the decaying wood of her front door. There is scuffling inside, and I only release the breath I'm holding when Thea herself cracks the door.

"Oh, Layla, thank Gods you came, love." She swings open the door, sweeping me into an embrace. She smells of cinnamon and apples. "Quick, please come inside." She ushers me in. I'm met with the cozy haze of fire in the hearth.

"Oliver was caught stealing a loaf of bread yesterday. Times have been tough lately, and he just wanted to help." Her already bloodshot eyes rim with unshed tears. "I begged them to leave his hand. Pleaded they take my own instead. They didn't care, barely heard me as they—" Her sentence is cut off by a heart-wrenching sob.

My stomach churns. Anger burns inside of me at the senseless act of violence for such a minuscule offense.

"Listen." I take her hand in mine. "I'll heal him the best I can. He's a strong boy, he will make do. Everything is going to be alright." I wish my father was here; he always knew the right thing to say in moments like this.

She squeezes my hand before dropping it and wiping at her eyes with a handkerchief. "He developed a fever today. I've been using cold compresses and trying to get broth into his system. He is in a lot of pain." Her voice is distraught as she leads me back to a stuffy small room. She touches his forehead and then rubs her thumb over his pale cheek.

Oliver's skin is sheet white, and beads of sweat gather on his forehead. His eyes are closed, but his face is pinched with pain. He grabs at his arm and moans. He seems in and out of consciousness.

I wash my hands in the water basin next to the bed and begin to build my power. My palms itch as I pull on the dwindling energy I have to offer.

I gently pick up his wrist, unwrapping the ruddy bandage encasing it. I wince as his bloodied nub is revealed. It is a gruesome scene of blood, bones, and veins. It's a nasty, jagged cut, as if the guards had to hack at it twice.

I clench my jaw to chase away the burning anger I feel for him. He is just a boy, and it was just a loaf of bread. The crime hardly matches the brutal punishment.

I know without my healing ability, an injury like this could be fatal. The powerless relied on their ability to work, and if he chose to stay among them, I feared he would now be fighting an uphill battle. He is spunky and strong, and I have to believe he will be okay.

I brush his curly, damp hair from his forehead, feeling the heat there. Taking a deep breath, I call on my power and channel it to my palms. The room fills with a dim glow that seeps from my hands.

I'm prepared for the sharp stings of pain that shoot up my arms as I draw out any infection. Thea watches me with bated breath in the corner until a knock rasps at her door.

"I can't imagine who that would be at this hour. Keep working, dear, I'll be right back." She excuses herself and leaves the room.

I'm too focused to pay much mind to what Thea says or even the knock at the door. My hands move confidently over Oliver's injury, taking great care. I imagine his howling laugh, his face full of color, his adorably shy smile. I picture him healthy and happy. I wish I could regrow limbs, but I know my limits. I instead regrow the flayed skin, pad it with muscle and fix the damaged nerves.

His furrowed brow soothes, and his moaning ceases. His skin, while still pale, takes on a healthier sheen.

Satisfied, I attempt to reel my power back. It continues flowing, straying from Oliver. I stagger as a violent tug comes from deep in my belly.

The light from my hands is no longer seeping into Oliver's hand but now trailing away. Curiously, I follow the light to where it is being channeled, and my very bones go cold.

There, standing in the doorway, a pair of familiar green eyes stare back at me. I'm momentarily stunned. Ledger gives me a menacing look. His hands are raised as if channeling my abilities.

His power trails along mine latching onto my wrists. I fight against it, yanking on my own power with all the strength I can muster. He grunts but otherwise shows no sign of stopping.

My energy wanes at a rapid rate, and I'm helpless to stop it. I look around for any other weapons but unsurprisingly, find none.

A trail of warmth trickles from my nose, the droplet of blood splashing onto my boot.

It hits me all at once. My already weakened power drains too swiftly and not of my own accord. My knees hit the ground so hard it makes my teeth clang together. My head swims and my vision becomes spotty.

I grab at my head, melding into a fetal position. My brain pounds painfully against my skull and a dry sob leaves my lips. To have my power so violently stolen from me evokes a bone-deep fear.

I think I am begging the man to stop, but I can't focus on anything else besides the agony of having my power reserves drained. I can't even scream. My veins feel like they are on fire, a sign I am near burnout.

All at once, the pain stops. My body sags into the dingy floor as I gasp for air. I don't even have the energy to raise my pinky finger.

The floor creaks as Ledger makes his way to me. "Sorry about that, nothing personal." His voice is smooth, calm even, and it makes me furiously angry.

He pulls me into his arms, and I can't seem to contract even a singular muscle to fight him. A garbled moan leaves my mouth as my head lulls. My vision blurs, darkening around the edges.

Thea sobs as we walk through the house towards the front door. "Please don't hurt her," she pleads with my captor.

"You speak a word of this, and we will take your son's other hand." A gruff voice threatens, which just makes Thea sob louder until she's promptly cut off by the front door slamming.

"I can't believe that worked. I wish I could stay to see the look on Sandor's face when he wakes up and realizes she's gone." The words drift in and then out of my ears.

My breathing is shallow and labored as my head swings limply. Panic creeps into my consciousness, and I can't seem to get enough oxygen into my lungs. I think of my mother, Maddox, and the townspeople. They need me. This couldn't happen. How could I have let this happen?!

I am placed on solid ground, feeling the coolness of the cobblestones against my skin.

"Breathe, blondie. Don't go dying on me now." I can feel his lips brush the shell of my ear before the world goes black.

CHAPTER
FIVE

Pain slaps me back to consciousness. There isn't a place on my body that isn't aching. My wrists are tightly bound behind me, and the rough bark of a tree scratches against my back.

It is still dark out; I'm not sure of the hour but I figure I couldn't have been out for too long.

With the light from the moon, I can make out a camp about thirty feet away with a few tents next to each other. I can't see horses but can hear them nickering. The camp appears quiet, and I wonder where everyone is.

I pull uselessly at the bonds and let out a frustrated noise, cursing myself.

There is shuffling beside me, and I turn to see a boy who can't be older than sixteen, sitting on a stump. He fidgets, staring at me, looking unsure. "Oh! Uh, um hello," he starts nervously. "I'm Cam."

I stare.

"Are you thirsty?" He gestures to the canteen in his hand awkwardly.

My mind reels and my tongue sticks to the roof of my mouth. My throat is scratchy and dry. I nod over to the boy, accepting his offer.

"Okay." He makes his way over to me, uncorking the canteen. His hands tremble as he brings it to my lips. The water is warm as it slides over my tongue and down my throat, but I'm grateful, nonetheless.

I study the boy as I drink. He's skinny and tall. The dim light of the lantern glows off his short blonde hair.

I roam the length of him, my eyes snagging on a tear in his shirt. The fabric is stained a dark red. When he pulls the canteen away, I watch him walk back over to the log. He winces as he sits, and that's when I know I have my opportunity.

"I'm Layla," I start. "Are you hurt?" I ask innocently, my face feigning concern. "I saw you wince."

His eyes drift down to where I am referring, and he waves me off. "It's nothing, just a flesh wound."

"Those are some of the most dangerous ones. I've seen many men with flesh wounds. Wounds too shallow to kill immediately but deep enough to sting, to bleed, to become infected. Wounds that are difficult to keep clean that end up festering."

I see the moment he second-guesses himself. His hand drifts down to his wound.

"I could look at it for you," I offer.

He hesitates, looking wary.

"You can just lift your shirt. Let me check for infection."

He is quiet for so long I think I have lost him. "Just a quick look, okay?" He looks around nervously as he stands and then bounds over to me. He rips up his shirt, exposing the cut on his rib.

The skin is red and angry, but the cut is shallow. It could use a good clean and a bandage but nothing too serious—however, I need him to get these bonds off.

I let out a gasp and contort my face into a mask of concern.

"What, what is it? Is it bad?!" Cam looks at his cut and back at me, his eyes wide and worried. Right where I want him.

"Don't panic, Cam, but it's worse than I thought. It looks like it could be infected."

"I knew I should have been cleaning it more. It's only a few days old, but it's starting to hurt more and more." I let him ramble on, waiting patiently. "Could you heal this?" He stops abruptly and looks expectantly at me.

I nod up at him. "I could."

"How long would it take to heal something like this?" He points to the still-exposed cut.

"I suppose I could do it in less than a minute, but I'd need at least one hand free." *Come on, Cam, untie me.*

"I'm not sure." He backs away and lowers his shirt. "Ledger wouldn't want me to untie you." *I'm losing him.*

"It is up to you, but the infection could spread to your heart if not treated. I'm sure you'll be fine though," I say as nonchalantly as I can. "You don't have to untie both hands, I could do it with just one."

He considers my words before relenting, "Okay." He looks around again before continuing, "I can give you twenty seconds." He begins removing one of my bonds.

As soon as my hand is free, he is retying the rope to the tree branch next to my head. I caught a glimpse of a dagger strapped to his side when he lifted his shirt. I know how to make this work, I have to be fast and calculated.

When he is sure the rope is secured, he turns to me and exposes the wound again. "Hurry, please."

I nod, raising my hand to hover above the cut; I reach for any trickle of power but can't seem to find even a whisper of it beneath my skin.

"Just a moment," I assure him.

He shifts restlessly as his head swivels around. Once I'm sure he is fully distracted, I strike.

My hand grips the hilt of the dagger and in one fluid motion, I swipe it from the sheath and bring the end of it down on his temple just like Maddox taught me.

I'm so shocked it works when Cam hits the ground, he conveniently takes me down with him. He lands with a thud on the ground. I struggle to sit up. My arm strains as the rope digs into my wrist, still connected to the tree.

"I'm so sorry, Cam," I murmur as if he can hear me, a pang of guilt eating at me.

I squeeze the handle of the dagger and slice the rope shakily, freeing my other hand. Then I'm running like hell.

I trip and stumble through trees and the uneven forest floor wanting to get as far away from their camp as I can. The adrenaline pumping through my veins is the only thing that keeps me moving.

My body has such little energy to pull on I have no choice but to grasp at my sheer will to live. The thought of stealing a horse crosses my mind, but I've never ridden one by myself and haven't a clue if I'd even be able to get one to move without being caught.

I continue like this for what feels like forever, every noise or snap of a branch making my heart race. My breathing is ragged, and my shoulders heave from exertion. My body rebels with every move, forcing me to stop and rest against a tree. My legs all but give out the second I stop and my back scratches roughly against the bark, leaving scrapes in its wake.

I'm gasping for air as I squeeze my eyes shut, trying to conjure anything that will help calm me down. I place my palms into the cold, damp earth, and my nails claw around it, hoping to ground myself.

A twig snaps, alerting me of another's presence a second before a body hits forcefully into mine. A warm hand snaps roughly around my mouth, muffling the scream that tears from my lips.

I struggle, grappling with the form, my dirty nails scraping against the firm hand at my mouth and waist, my feet kicking blindly.

"Lay! Stop! It's me; it's just me." I immediately stop struggling, and his hand leaves my mouth.

"Maddox, what the hell are you doing out here; you scared the shit out of me!" My whisper is shrill as I roll out of his embrace to face him.

"Oh, just having a nightly stroll," he retorts. "What the fuck do you think I'm doing out here?! I go to check on you, and when I search your room, to no one's surprise, you're not there. I found your report with Oliver's name on it and knew you couldn't help yourself." He continued, "When I get to their house, Thea is hysterical and tells me you were carried out of her house unconscious by two men! She pointed me in the direction they took you, and you're about as quiet as a wild boar, so it didn't take long to find you. I knew this would happen!"

I grimace listening to my foolish decisions as he finishes and then blurt out, "The prince snuck into my room last night asking me to go with him to Westray. He needs my power. I told him no and thought that would suffice, but clearly, he didn't like that answer." Maddox's eyes bulge at my omission.

"You didn't think to tell me that?" he questions, and I open my mouth to respond before he cuts me off. "Never mind, we have to keep mov—"

Before he can finish, a branch snaps in the distance. I freeze.

"I nearly drained all her power; she couldn't have gotten far. Mia, you go left. Arch, you go right. I'll look around here. If you find her, you are under orders not to harm her, just restrain her and call for me." I recognize Ledger's voice.

Maddox gives me a panicked look and gestures to the tree next to him. "Climb it" he mouths. I shake my head furiously back and forth.

"I will not leave you, just turn us both invisible," I mouth back.

"We will have a better chance if we split up. Listen to me for once, Lay." The plea is barely a whisper in my ear. "I'll distract them and be back for you." He squeezes my arm before activating his power and blinking out of sight, invisible to all around him.

I gulp and start to climb the tree. Every muscle in my body contracts. I grab limb after limb, climbing as quietly as I can, praying I won't fall. My injured ankle rebels against the action but still responds to my requests.

My body freezes when I spot Ledger walking right beneath the tree. "Come out wherever you are. We can do this the easy way or the hard way."

My skin pebbles much like it did the first time I heard him speak. Sweat trickles down my spine. *Do not look up,* I chant repeatedly in my head.

My tired legs tremble so violently as they hold my weight, I fear I'm shaking the tree. I attempt to readjust, moving as carefully as I can.

Without warning, my ankle gives out, my boot scraping a small piece of bark that falls in slow motion to the floor of the woods. I can't make out where it lands but I can make out the moment Ledger freezes.

Oh fuck. I shrink into the tree hoping to blend in through the dark.

"You can come down, or I can bring you down; your choice," he calls from below. I squeeze my eyes shut against the onslaught of panic.

After a few silent moments, he sighs, and I can hear the scraping of tree bark. I look down and see vines snaking up the tree. My eyes bulge, and my body begins to move.

He has two powers... that is almost unheard of.

I frantically grip the branches in front of me hauling myself higher. My feet scramble for purchase as the vines beneath me continue their ascent.

I'm a little more than halfway up the tree when the vines wrap around my ankles. A strangled noise escapes my mouth as they yank me back with surprising force.

The rough wood of the tree grates against my palms as my grip slips. With one more furious pull, I'm ripped from the branch. My body bounces and cracks off the tree as I fall to the earth.

The wind whips through my tangled hair and a scream tears from my throat. I brace my body for impact, ready to hit the hard ground.

Instead, I land with a huff caught by two strong arms. Instinctually, I throw my elbow out, catching Ledger in the face.

My ass hits the damp earth as he drops me, and I scurry back trying to get some distance in between us. Maddox screams my name in the distance, followed by sounds of struggling.

Vines tighten around my ankles, and I kick out trying to dislodge them. New vines rise from the ground, lashing out and wrapping up one of my wrists and forearm.

"Maddox!" I scream his name like a prayer, if I could just get to him, we could be each other's salvation.

The vines grow too fast; they slither up my body like vicious snakes, and it isn't long before they tighten painfully around both my ankles and wrists, binding me to the earth.

I struggle against the binds, but they seem to tighten with each movement until I'm completely entangled, kneeling in the dirt.

Ledger saunters over to me and crouches down so he is at eye level. I taste iron as warm blood drips over my split lip and down my chin.

"I underestimated you." He studies me as I struggle. "I don't want to hurt you further, but you need to stop fighting me."

In the same moment, a struggling Maddox is dragged out between Archie and Mia. He's bleeding and still fighting furiously.

Our eyes meet and my stomach sinks.

"Great of you to join us. Awfully far from the castle, Prince, don't you think?" Ledger stands to his very generous height.

"You have no right to her. Leave her now, and my father will learn none of this," Maddox replies.

"I don't believe I will leave her. Westray is in need of her services. Your father would never graciously accept our request. So now, we have no other option but to take her." He pauses, glancing at me. "Tell your father what you will. Maybe he will learn to be more reasonable."

I grit my teeth, my body too beaten and weak for me to do anything. The feeling of helplessness overwhelms me.

"He won't just let you have her; you have no idea what you are starting if you take her, Ledger."

Maddox gives me one last determined look before he somehow frees himself from Mia and Archie's hold. His hand flies to his belt retrieving his dagger. He swings it wildly, connecting it with Mia's arm.

He disappears in the next breath, and they are left grappling with nothing. Maddox gets in a few slices, the two of them hissing in pain and lunging, failing to make contact with his invisible form.

Ledger takes a few steps forward, holding up his hand until I *feel* the rumble of his power. The rumble grows louder and stronger as he latches on to Maddox's abilities.

A strangled noise surges from the darkness before Maddox flashes into view. His form flickers as he fights against Ledger's siphoning powers.

Ledger looks at Archie, and in the next breath, Maddox is thrown through the air, his back slamming roughly into a tree. A scream erupts from my raw throat.

Maddox's dagger is torn from his grasp and floats into Archie's hand. The same vines imprisoning me emerge from the ground and wrap around his body binding him to the tree. One wraps around his neck and tightens.

Maddox chokes; he struggles against the binds, gasping for air.

"STOP!" My voice is high and shrill and panic rises in me as he loses consciousness.

"We've wasted too much time, we need to leave now." Ledger comments and turns back to me.

"You can't just leave him out here; there are deadly creatures!" I shriek fighting the vines.

"You can only begin to imagine the things that exist in these woods. Now, I suggest you stop fighting me or I'll have Archie here send this dagger straight into his heart."

He tosses a dagger into the air, and it spins, suspended. Archie twists his fingers and the dagger points at Maddox. He flicks his first two fingers and the blade sails right for his chest.

"So, what's it going to be? Are you going to come willingly with me, or are we going to leave Bellehaven without an heir?"

"OKAY!" My body goes limp and the dagger stops a mere inch from Maddox's chest.

"What was that?" Ledger looks at me expectantly.

"I'll go with you," I manage to croak out.

"Good choice." He gives Archie a nod; the dagger drops with a dull thud. The vines disappear into the earth freeing my limbs. Ledger lifts me, tossing me with ease over his shoulder. I crane my head to give Maddox one last regretful look. He's still unconscious. I wish I could tell him I was sorry or even just see his brown eyes one last time.

"Let's get Cam. Camp should be packed up, and he'll be ready to go."

There are horses tied close by, and Ledger tosses me into a saddle before climbing up behind me.

The horses canter through the moonlit, peaceful woods so conflicting with the war that wages inside of me. Defeat is a bitter taste on my tongue. I want to scream, to fight, to wage war on this man who thinks himself entitled to rip me away from my life but can't find the strength.

My thoughts are sluggish, any movement I make is difficult and languid.

The full weight of the day closes in on me, my body throbs and aches all the way down to my toes. My power is but a dull spark in the depths of my belly.

With the adrenaline fading from my system, I fight for consciousness. Exhaustion falls over me like a heavy blanket and I sway to the side.

"Whoa." Ledger's arm catches me and slides me back into the saddle. His other arm cages me in, stopping me from going over the other side.

I weakly elbow him away, the feel of his body, the way it warms my chilled skin, an unwelcome sensation. "Rest, blondie, don't worry, you'll have plenty of time in the future to fight me." His arms remain strong.

And fight him, I fucking would.

CHAPTER
SIX

I FEEL THE SLOW CANTERING OF THE HORSE, A WARM hand wrapped around my middle, and the dull throb in my head and ankle. Birds chirp all around me. I blink my heavy eyelids, squinting as the brightness of the day engulfs my vision. My tongue sticks to the roof of my mouth.

My eyes flicker around the surroundings. There are trees as far as the eye can see, moss and ferns cover the ground. The scent of damp earth and wet tree trunks fills my nostrils. A blanket of haze coats the air. My hands are tied in front of me, numb and leached of color.

I stiffen as the memories of the prior night come flooding back to me. Clawing at the hand encircling my waist I manage to shout, "Stop the horse." The words scrape my throat, unfamiliar and raw.

My gaze darts frantically, searching for anything recognizable in the dense, shadowy forest. We're far from Bellehaven now, farther than I've ever been.

"Stop the horse!" I lunge for the reins, my voice rising with desperation.

"Whoa." Ledger's arm snakes around my chest yanking me back against him. His breath is warm on my ear as he growls, "We are not stopping. We need to make up time."

I lean to the side, and his arms tighten around me.

"What makes you think I will help you?" I spit the words at him as I try to shrug him off. My anger sparks anew.

"You are under no obligation to help me, but you will."

"And if I refuse?"

"You won't." His short presumptuous answers stoke my growing outrage.

All I see are trees and I wonder just how far I'd get if I could get off the horse and run.

"You wouldn't get ten feet. And if, by the off chance, you did escape me, you would not live to see the sunrise. The creatures that roam these woods are the fuel of many nightmares."

My body feels heavy, discomfort gnawing at me from all angles. It takes substantial effort to sit up without swaying, so my odds of outrunning him or escaping are low.

"If I help you, what are your plans for me after?" I glare back at him through my eyelashes, holding my chin high.

"Haven't gotten that far, blondie." He hardly pays me a glance and that sends a bolt of fury down my spine.

"Layla," I grit. "My name is Layla."

"Noted." His face is bored, void of any discernable emotion.

I elbow him in the ribs needing to draw some kind of reaction from him, and he grunts.

"Do that again and I will tie a rope to your ankles and drag you behind Apollo the rest of the way." I catch a glimpse of his neck as it turns a tinge of red. It brings a triumphant smile to my face knowing I was able to anger him.

"Please do; that sounds much more pleasant than being stuck pressed up against your brick of a body," I snap back, accepting the fact I would have to come up with a different plan of escape.

The hours tick on, and I nearly weep with joy when we come to a halt. My mouth pops open as our backdrop comes into clear focus. We've stopped at the most idyllic body of water I have ever seen. The water is a crystal-clear teal, and a soft roaring is coming from a freely flowing waterfall in the middle of the spring. There are trees and moss-covered rocks surrounding it. My breath catches at the beauty; it is beyond anything I could have imagined.

I continue to stare, mesmerized as Ledger hops down from behind me. "Don't get out much, do you?"

"I didn't know such things existed; it's incredible." I'm breathless as Ledger's hands come around my waist and set me on the ground. My legs are stiff, and parts of my body still throb angrily.

I can't stop from greedily drinking in my surroundings. The sun shines bright and hot, indicating it must be late afternoon.

When Ledger turns to tend to his horse, the dagger strapped at his hip gleams against the light, catching my eye. I barely have time to contemplate my next move before I am foolishly snatching it from his belt. I dig the tip into his back, where I know his heart beats a few inches away.

"I must go back. I cannot leave my mother." My heart pounds in my chest. I grip the dagger in my tied hands. "She is all I have, and I cannot leave her to the antics of the King." Ledger remains still as I hold the dagger firm.

"Is she healthy?" he asks, and by now the other party members are staring at us.

"Of body but not of mind. You need to return me." I glance over at them nervously.

"I can't do that," he responds. I push the dagger further into his skin until red droplets soak through his shirt. "Do it, stab it right into my heart." He leans back and the knife slips further into his skin.

I gasp and my grip falters.

Ledger moves swiftly. He turns, and his foot knocks into my ankles, sending me careening to the ground.

He's on top of me in a breath, the dagger still in my hand between us. His palm closes over mine, forcing my wrists towards myself.

The cool metal of the dagger brushes the delicate skin of my neck.

"I'm sorry about your mother but that is none of my concern. Just like my loved one was not of your concern." His nostrils flare. Vines wrap around my already bound wrists replacing his hand and squeezing so tightly my fingers spasms, releasing the dagger.

Ledger grabs the blade and stands, leaving me struggling on the ground. Mia appears in front of me, shaking her head. Her dark skin gleams in the sunlight, her hair shiny and neat, tied in a long braid that hangs to her lower back. "I'm Mia," she says, and I kneel awkwardly in front of her.

"Is this really necessary, Ledger?" She takes out a knife and slashes at the vines and binds until I'm free. I sigh with relief as I rub my wrists, moving my fingers to get blood flow. Ledger steps up to us, and she places a hand on his chest. "I've got her."

She raises her eyebrow until he relaxes and turns back to the horse. "If she attempts to escape, it will be you that goes after her." He scowls down at me.

"Gladly." She grins. Her demeanor is light and playful, and despite the circumstances, I instantly like her. "It is a pleasure to meet you. I'm so relieved to have a female join us; men are such headaches to travel with." She glances obviously at Ledger and my lip twitches.

"Do you know how to swim?" she asks; her teeth are a dazzling white as she smiles at me.

"No, I can't swim. There aren't many bodies of water in Bellehaven." Embarrassment floods me, and I fight to keep it off my face.

"No worries—the water doesn't get very deep here." She begins to remove her clothes until she is left in her undergarments. I blush at her nudity, looking away. "Come on, Layla, the water feels amazing." She calls, fully submerged in the enticing water.

I look around, seeing Ledger and Cam tending to the horses.

Archie approaches me when I catch his eye. "Hey, we didn't get off to the best start yesterday. I'm Archie." He holds out his hand, and I stare at it, remembering the way he sent that knife towards Maddox's chest.

He drops his hand after a few moments and rubs at the back of his neck. He looks to be in his mid-twenties with smooth unblemished skin. I wonder idly if he is capable of growing facial hair. He's very handsome with thick blonde hair that is tousled and down-turned bedroom eyes.

"Sorry about last night. We had to get you away from Sandor. I thought you'd come willingly, but clearly, I was mistaken." He looks at me sheepishly. "How about we start over? I promise you're going to like me; I've yet to meet a female that doesn't."

I have no doubt that much is true. He winks at me, and it reminds me so much of Maddox it melts some of my initial reserve.

"Let's all go for a swim, maybe if I smelled better, it would help my case." He sniffs his armpit and makes a face, tugging off his shirt.

I catch a glimpse of gruesome scars littering his back before he jumps into the water.

Cam shoots me a nervous look before moving a few feet away and shucking off his clothes. The guilt I felt the previous night returns when I make out purple bruising at his temple.

Everyone swims through the crystal waters. They all look so happy and carefree. I can't remember the last time I truly let go and enjoyed something like that. I wasn't sure if I was capable of those emotions.

My eyes snag on Ledger, who is removing his shirt. He folds it neatly next to him, leaving him in only a pair of briefs.

My blood heats at the sight of him and my power surges to the surface. He is all muscle, scars, and tanned skin—a harsh kind of beautiful. I can't decide what is more breathtaking, the spring or him.

I force myself to look away, annoyed by my thoughts. My own pale skin is dirty and stained, and my bones ache for reprieve. I itch with the desire to feel the enchanting waters against my skin. I'd only ever read and heard about places as magnificent as this, and it would pain me to miss the opportunity.

It doesn't take me long before I remove my boots. Once I have them off, I test the water with my bare toes. It feels glorious.

Spotting a bush, I walk over and remove my leggings. I opt to keep on my dress, cursing myself for not putting anything under it before leaving the castle.

I walk hesitantly into the water until I am shoulder-deep, and sigh when the water laps against my heated skin. My head tips back, and my hair splays around me.

"Doesn't get much better than this, does it?" Mia is next to me, now floating on her back. The water pebbles on her skin, reflecting off the sun. Archie pushes Cam's head under the water, and he pops up laughing and splashing. They both swim toward the waterfall.

Once they make it, they stand and let the water cascade over their heads. "Come try, Layla," Archie shouts.

The normalcy of the moment perplexes me. I thought I'd be chained in a dungeon somewhere by now, not swimming leisurely in a beautiful spring with my captors.

I contemplate for a moment before my feet are coasting over the stones beneath me as I make my way over. I'd never seen a waterfall before, much less stood underneath one, so I decide to allow myself this.

Once I'm next to Archie I extend my fingers, letting them skim over the cool flowing water before moving my head under the stream.

I smile as the crisp water cascades over my head, down my face and shoulders. I have never felt anything so refreshing, so wondrous.

"What do you think?" Archie asks as I open my eyes, stepping away from the flow.

"It's magical," I answer with a small, hesitant smile. I look over at Cam, seeing him under the waterfall one second and then disappear the next.

At first, I think he has a similar ability to Maddox, but then movement catches my eye on shore, and Cam appears shaking his shaggy hair out.

"He can transmit?" I ask incredulously.

"Short distances; he's still mastering it."

I turn back to Archie curious. "Can you show me your power again?"

He turns to shore, raises his hands, and sends an array of flowers floating in the air towards us. He wears a satisfied smile as the flowers breeze magically around me. I reach out, running my fingers through the air above and below the flowers before I delicately grab one.

"Brilliant." I'll never not be stunned seeing other people's powers come to life.

"Well, I can't mend bones and save people's lives, but it comes in handy." He shrugs.

"It fits you," I say as the flowers drop, filling the water around me.

Mia takes that moment to come up and splash Archie, darting back under the water to swim away. "Real mature," he calls before he dives in after her.

I'm still marveling at the beautiful flowers when Ledger approaches the waterfall a few feet down from me.

The water stops just below his belly button. My mouth goes dry as he steps under the surging water. I watch as it flows over his broad shoulders, down his impressive chest.

The briefs he wears sit low on his hips revealing deep Vs that draw my attention and a dusting of hair that disappears beneath his waistband. I'd seen plenty of shirtless men, I'd worked on hundreds, but I can't ever remember one looking quite like that.

He catches me staring, his face hardening and jaw feathering. My cheeks heat, and I go to look away when his gaze shifts and becomes alarmed.

"Layla. Do. Not. Move." His voice is dangerously low and serious when he steps out of the flow of water.

I freeze at his command and the hair on the back of my neck stands on end. My breath halts as I sense another presence in the water.

Out of the corner of my eye, I see a creature stalk towards me. It sails eloquently through the water. Its green, scaly skin shimmers in mesmerizing blues and purples as it moves. Its face is ethereal, almost human, except for round, alluring eyes that appear too large for its face. Two slits appear where its nose is and a row of razor-sharp teeth gleam from behind full lips.

Its head moves from side to side as it studies me, its unearthly eyes boring into mine. My breath lodges in my lungs as the creature circles me, holding its head at an unnatural angle as its eyes vibrate over me. I'm frozen in place, unable to move as it gets closer.

It dives under the water only to pop up right in front of me. I swallow a scream as it fingers a strand of my hair and then drops its forehead to mine.

It inhales deeply and every muscle in my body locks. I want to squeeze my eyes shut but find myself equal parts terrified and captivated, rooted where I stand.

The whisper of a sword being drawn from shore shifts the creature's attention, and it reacts immediately. It pulls away, eyes growing angry, and releases a hissing sound that makes my knees quake.

"Everyone stand down; Maladra are unpredictable. We are one sudden movement away from it drowning her." Ledger's voice is a low warning.

I assume the sword is put away when the creature's eyes fall back on me.

"What do you mean *drown*? What do you mean, Ledger?" I'm whispering hysterically as a webbed hand shoots out of the water. It skims my cheek, leaving behind a sticky sheen. I don't dare move, but I'm trembling so hard the water ripples around me.

"Stay calm, it's just curious. Maladras tend to be drawn to women."

I bite back a scream as the creature dips its head, nose grazing my neck. It inhales deeply again. This time, its tongue appears, licking me from collarbone to ear. The scent of algae and fish floods my senses, and a strangled, terrified noise escapes my lips. "Ledger!" I beg for him to do something, anything, as he comes into view behind the creature's shoulder.

"Eyes on me," he commands, and my eyes snap to his deep emerald ones. He takes a slow step forward, making the Maladra careen around so fast water slaps me in the face. An ear-splitting screech fills the air. Ledger's hands go up as if to calm it.

In the next second, I see Archie, out of the corner of my eye, lift his hand. He closes his palm and a large boulder sails through the air.

The creature's eyes narrow, and that is the only warning I get before the Maladra grabs me in its clammy grip and pulls me under the surface. I silently scream as it drags me down, bubbles leaving my mouth in a flurry.

The creature swims with incredible speed, so fast I can't tell what direction we are moving in. My ears pop and my lungs burn. I thrash around, considering this may be how I die.

My mouth instinctively opens for air and cold water floods my lungs. Blood pounds behind my eyes. The more I struggle the more disoriented I become.

My vision grows spotty as I catch a glimmer of sunlight rippling on the waters above.

Air screams back into my lungs, searing my throat and nose, and we surface. The air chills my skin as I gasp in choppy breaths, coughing up copious amounts of water.

My mouth tastes of bile and seaweed. I cling to the murky mud of the shore as if that could stop the creature from pulling me under again. When I look up, I see Ledger in the middle of the spring with a look of horror on his face. The Maladra and I are on the opposite side now, too far for anyone to attempt to use their powers.

Gathering my courage, my gaze snaps back to the Maladra. I realize I am now surrounded by three of them and shrink back. They are equally beautiful and horrifying as they tower over me.

One of them grabs onto my wrist and pulls me further into the water until I am waist deep.

"Oh fuck, oh fuck," I whisper hysterically to myself, unable to form a single helpful thought.

It moves its grip to my arm and motions to one of the smaller Maladra with the other webbed hand.

In a frantic attempt, I crane my arm back to pull away, but it grips me tighter, motioning to the smaller Maladra again, more aggressively.

"You need to calm down and take a deep breath, they want something from you. Focus on what they are trying to tell you," Ledger's voice calls as he treads closer.

"Do not fucking tell me to calm down right now!" I hiss at him through my clenched teeth, knowing he is right.

I shake my head, attempting to clear it and take a steadying breath. It is then I realize the smaller Maladra looks sickly; its eyes are sunken in, and its skin is dull, illustrious, and dry. The other Maladra nods at me as if to confirm my thoughts.

"I- I understand, they are sick, you- you need my help?" My voice quivers.

It nods its head once, the side of its mouth tipping up encouragingly, revealing more serrated teeth. I swallow thickly, my tongue sticking to the roof of my mouth.

The Maladra releases my arm, and I move closer to the smaller one. I look at it and try to form a smile. I cautiously raise my trembling hands.

"Is this okay?" I ask, and when it nods back, I realize it must understand. I hover my hands calling my power and letting it ripple over its upper body. My power trickles out, cascading over its scaled skin before delving inside.

The Maladra's eyes close after a few moments and it heaves a breath.

My own eyes fall shut to focus. I picture how the first Maladra looked. I think of the deep green, purple, and blue scales that shimmered off the sunlight. I push my healing light through every pore in its body.

A gasp comes from shore, and I open my eyes to see the water around the Maladra glowing.

I call back my power revealing the smaller Maladra. Its scales now beam radiantly, the colors shimmering. Its skin is now glistening with a dewy glow.

The two bigger Maladras assess it, sniffing and nudging. They all rest their foreheads together in an intimate display before turning to me and bowing deeply. They then dive into the water, disappearing. I stare blankly at rippling waves until I feel Ledger beside me.

"We should get out of the water." He puts his hand on my lower back and leads me to the water's edge. I step onto dry land just as the Maladras reemerge.

Ledger's arm moves from my lower back to around my waist firmly as they approach. I lean back into his grasp, gripping his forearm hard enough to leave fingerprints.

The two larger Maladras lower four large, flopping fish at my feet with a bow. The smaller one then kneels, holding up a small, beautiful shell.

"The legends say if a Maladra presents you with a shell, it is a symbol they are eternally indebted to you," Mia says, coming to stand beside me. "Take the shell."

Ledger's arm flexes around my middle as I hesitantly reach out. I take the shell. The Maladra stays on its knees with its head bowed. "I think it's waiting for your permission," Archie says from behind me.

"Uh, thank you. You may go?" As soon as the words are spoken the Maladra dives into the clear water and disappears.

I sag against Ledger, my palm closed tightly over the shell, eyes transfixed on the now smooth water.

"That was totally awesome," Cam proclaims.

"Not to be insensitive, but they do have great timing because I, for one, am starving." Archie steps up to the fish. "Do you mind?"

"Archie," Ledger growls.

"I'll make you guys a plate." He grabs the fish by their tails and walks away.

I'm still staring unblinkingly at the water as Ledger pulls me away from the edge to set me down against a tree. He studies me for a long moment before his hand moves to graze a strand of soaked hair off my cheek. "You okay?" The question is soft and genuine as if he truly cares to know the answer.

I blink and then smack his hand away. "No, I am not okay. I was almost drowned and eaten alive by the most terrifying creature I have ever seen in my godsdamn life. A creature I didn't even know existed!" My throat is raw and painful as I speak.

"Shake it off. I wouldn't have let them harm you. Your power is too valuable. Maladras—while unpredictable, are curious creatures, peaceful even, usually only harming those with corrupted souls."

"Shake. It. Off? You've got to be kidding me." I push myself up off the ground, and when he stands, I shove him roughly in the chest. "There is no way in hell I am getting back on that horse and riding further into the woods to whatever other nightmarish creatures await us. Take. Me. Back," I demand, my finger prodding his chest with each word.

He glares at me, his gaze snagging lower before he looks away and clenches his jaw. "You know I can't do that. Maybe if you hadn't been so busy staring at me like I was the first man you had ever seen shirtless, you could have avoided the interaction." He mashes his teeth together. "I am your captor, and it would do you good to remember that."

My mouth drops open, and I let out an exasperated breath. "You're really making this about you? I was not looking at you, I was looking at the...waterfall," I trip over my words and will the redness from my cheeks.

"Of course you were," He glances down again. "Go put your clothes back on and get rid of that god's forsaken dress." He leans down, grabbing his black tunic off the ground and tossing it at my face.

I don't have time to be offended as I look down realizing I am in a very see-through, very wet, white dress. I gasp, covering my breasts with Ledger's tunic, and when I look up, the rest of my clothes are floating in front of me.

"Thought you might want these." Archie is grilling up the fish by the fire he must have started. "However, you will hear no complaints from me if you stay in the dress." He looks up from the fire, his eyes doing a quick sweep of me. "Zero complaints."

My face heats further as I snatch my clothes from the air and dart behind a tree. I've never dressed so fast in my life.

As I slide Ledger's shirt on, I'm hit with the woodsy, manly scent of him. I curiously pick up the collar and inhale. It smells like cedar and leather, and I immediately want to take it off. It would make me feel immensely better if this man could have the decency to smell bad.

I place the small shell in my pocket and wad my wet shirt up, stepping out from behind the tree. Everyone is gathered around the fire eating the fish I almost perished for.

With no eyes on me, I decide to take my chances as I crouch down, making my way as quietly as I can over to the horses.

I creep over to Ledger's horse, untying the reins from the tree. He begins nickering, and I shush him. "Listen, while I may not know how to ride you, I can assure you I am much more pleasant than that belligerent man that's been riding you." I pull the reins, attempting to turn him around back the way we came, but he won't budge. "Come on, if you move, I will feed you as many apples, leaves, grass—whatever the hell horses eat—as you want. Work with me here."

I continue to whisper to the animal, pulling his reins as he resists me.

"Belligerent, am I? I'm offended." Ledger's voice startles me as he saunters up behind me. I close my eyes and sigh.

"Having trouble? Apollo and I have been bonded for many years. He won't listen to anyone but me, but it was a nice try." He grips the reins and yanks them out of my hand.

My eyes narrow, and my arms fold stubbornly over my chest. "I do not wish to go any further." I bite out, knowing I have no choice in the matter.

"I do not need to tell you this, but I do not care what you wish or what you want. You *will* get on this horse and make it to our destination, where you *will* complete the task needed from you." He's now in my face, and my fists are itching to punch him right in his stupid, full mouth.

"In case I haven't mentioned it, you are unbelievably unlikeable, and I hope to make this trip as unpleasant as possible for you."

"Mission already accomplished, blondie, and it hasn't even been twenty-four hours."

CHAPTER
SEVEN

Seething with anger, I sit next to Archie, and he hands me a plate of food.

Ledger douses the fire with a bucket of water, sending a plume of smoke into the air. "No more fire, I don't want anyone being able to track us."

I tug at the vine around my ankle uselessly.

Everyone gets up to set up camp as I pick at the fish. They nestle the tents in a group of trees that is somewhat hidden and far enough away from the body of water I hope the Maladras will be deterred from paying us another visit.

The sun begins to set, and I chew thoughtfully as everything around me blazes. It all feels so serene as a hush falls upon the woods, upon my thoughts themselves.

The pastels dance upon my milky skin, and I soak them in, enjoying the lasts of the sun's warmth. I surrender to the moment, giving myself permission to accept the events of the past day. I watch the calm surface of the water and close my eyes letting the roar of the falls quiet my mind.

It feels nice to be away from the confines of the castle. I remember a time when I longed for the freedom to see what lies beyond the borders of Bellehaven. I wonder if the longing had ever really stopped or if I had suffocated any thoughts beyond healing and mastering my powers.

When I open my eyes again, Ledger is standing a few feet away, studying me. He's holding some flowers in his hands that he is absently braiding together. "What are you thinking about?" His eyes skim my face, looking for a hint.

I debate ignoring him but decide against it. "When I was little, I would sit on my windowsill and imagine myself in places like this. Swimming in waters like that." I nod over to the spring. "Lounging under an open sky without a care in the world." I pick a pink lily growing out of the ground next to me and twirl the stem between my fingers.

"I used to resent the power that simmers in my veins, resist it, pray for the Gods to take it back. I knew that with it, I would never truly be free. Whether that meant answering to a King or the Gods, or to someone like you." I give him a withering look.

"What about now? Would you rather be powerless?" He tilts his head as he asks the question.

"Some days. Though now it's such a part of me I'm not sure who I'd be without it. Maybe I'd be a baker, or a seamstress or possibly a blacksmith." Ledger huffs a laugh.

"Is something funny?"

"A blacksmith, huh?" He eyes my scrawny arms with a raised brow. "Do you think you'd be able to pick up a hammer?"

"Yes, a blacksmith." My palm skims my bicep self-consciously. "I can always get stronger; you however, are stuck with your big muscles and small brain. What would *you* be if you weren't an entitled little prince?" I hurtle the question back at him.

"First, blondie, there is nothing *little* about me." His eyes meet mine with an unwavering confidence that forces me to drop my eyes. "And secondly, I've never had the time or privilege of daydreaming." His face gives away nothing, just a mask of cold indifference.

"Right, of course, how silly of me." I roll my eyes, looking away from him. "Well, since you won't take me *home,* I'd like to rest." Darkness spreads, smothering all the warm hues until only black remains.

"*Home?* You mean where the King exploits you and his people for your powers and then locks you safely back away each night?" He spits the words as if they disgust him.

Anger radiates somewhere inside of me but I push it away. "Home isn't always a place. Bellehaven isn't my home. Maddox is my *home,* my mother is my *home,* the people of

Bellehaven are my *home*." His face shifts at my words and he looks almost shocked by my response. "I wouldn't expect *you* to understand."

The lily drops from my fingers as I stand to brush myself off. I'd still not fully recovered from the events of yesterday. My power pulses weakly inside of me, and my injuries nag. I long for blissful, deep, reviving sleep.

Ledger stills as he looks at me; I can't make out his face in the dark. I go to walk away when I'm yanked back by my bound ankle. A frustrated noise claws up my throat.

Ledger turns, hanging the braided circle of flowers from a tree branch before recalling his vines. They recede back into the ground, freeing me. He turns, walking away without acknowledging me.

I stumble and trip after him, my eyes straining in the blackness. He slows as we near the camp. "After you." He motions inside one of the dimly lit tents.

"What do you mean?" The side of his face glows in the lantern light.

"I mean you may go in first."

"First? Meaning you are following me in?" I look at him, bewildered.

"That is exactly what I mean, you can't truly believe I would leave you alone after you tried to steal my horse earlier? Not to mention your little run-in with the Maladra. Seems to me like you need supervising." I eye the dagger sheathed at his hip, and his large hand wraps around it. "Don't even think about it."

"Give me the dagger, and I'll have all the protection I need."

"Not a chance. Something tells me you can't be trusted with a dagger. Now get inside the tent, you've tested my patience enough today."

"I haven't even begun testing your patience." I grumble ducking into the tent.

It's small, with a cot and some furs on the ground, a wash basin, and a dim lantern. It smells earthy and musty. Looking around, I stand awkwardly as Ledger enters. He pays no mind to me as he discards his shirt and starts washing his hands in the basin.

I sit on one of the furs and glance over at him, trying not to get caught this time. His skin is bronzed, his back broad and littered with scars. As he moves, the muscles in his abdomen flex. He has a body earned from training ruthlessly and being disciplined.

My eyes roam over his lean abs and the long scar marring his ribs. They amble over his strong arms and down his veined forearms.

He is intimidating, his presence imposing.

"What did I say about looking at me like that?"

I snap my eyes away. "You think very highly of yourself," I huff. I brace myself as he brushes past me and lays down, covering himself with the furs.

I sit with my back to him, scooting a few inches away, pulling the other fur up over my shoulders.

I can practically feel the warmth of Ledger's body heat as my skin prickles with the awareness of him. I could do this, I could sleep in a tent with this harsh male. It's only temporary.

Despite my exhaustion, it takes me a long time to fall asleep. Every snap of a branch, every whisper of wind, has me flinching and my heart racing.

I am not used to the sounds or the fact that only a thin piece of fabric separates me from the creatures that stalk in the night.

Ledger slumbers peacefully next to me, and I inch closer to him, taking whatever refuge I can.

Eventually, hours later, I must finally drift off, because I'm awoken by Ledger's palm pressed against my lips.

His large body is crammed tightly against mine, and I instinctively begin to struggle beneath him. My brain is heavy with sleep, but the second I hear commotion from outside the tent, I freeze.

There is rustling and footsteps, and my heart hammers wildly in my chest. Ledger hauls me up from the ground, plastering my back to his front tightly and releasing his hold on my mouth.

"Do not make a noise," he warns in my ear and my mouth snaps shut.

I'm too scared to struggle, thinking the worst. Is it the Maladra or another creature I know nothing of?

The cool night air nips at my skin as Ledger pulls me out of the tent. He navigates impressively through the woods with no sound until we run into Cam and Mia, who are crouched together. Their eyes are laser-focused on where the noise is coming from.

I nearly jump out of my skin when Archie stumbles over to us, making such a racket I *feel* the death look Ledger shoots him.

"What was that?" Maddox's voice filters through the night and everyone freezes.

My body reacts almost immediately, kicking out and wriggling in Ledger's tightening grasp. I go to call out to him, but Ledger is ready. He claps his hand tightly over my mouth, and his arm flexes firmly against my small frame.

A group of men about forty feet away appear in the clearing. The moonlight is dim, but I can make out about six of them. Hecktor is in front with Maddox, a flame in his hand lighting the way.

My muffled screams are drowned out by the quiet roar of the waterfall. This is my chance to escape. We are out-numbered, and I recognize some of the King's most power-ful men among the group.

Maddox makes some hand movements, and the men spread out. He and Hecktor begin quietly searching, moving towards us.

I elbow and kick Ledger, my body silently thrashing against him, but he doesn't even flinch. His hold does not waver, his arms iron bands around me.

If Maddox finds us, I could be safe and sound back at the castle by nightfall tomorrow. Back to exploiting the people of Bellehaven for money they don't have in exchange for a taste of my power. The thought gives me pause.

"I think it came from over here." Maddox heads in our direction; he stops just fifteen feet from us. We are hidden in the trees, away from the light of the moon, cloaked in the night.

I track his gaze as he searches the woods. Ledger's hold is so tight around my body and mouth that it's difficult to breathe. His eyes skim over where we lay crouched, cloaked in shadows.

The side of Maddox's handsome face lights up for a moment as Hecktor signals him with his flame. My heart pinches. I can tell by the distance that Hecktor had found our camp.

Maddox gives us one last unseeing look and turns to go to Hecktor. I half-heartedly fight Ledger as he pulls me in the opposite direction through the woods. Despair and confusion flood my emotions.

Did I truly want to return to my life at Bellehaven?

Smoke plumes into the air from where I crane my neck. Hecktor must have scorched the campsite.

Shouting fills the air. "Layla!" I barely recognize Maddox's voice; it is desperate and scared as he screams my name.

We reach the horses, and Ledger throws me in the saddle. "Maddox!" I scream his name as Ledger envelops me with his body. I elbow and scratch at him until he ties the reins around my wrists to subdue me.

"We must make it to Grimwood. They aren't as familiar with the terrain and we can lose them. It's our best bet." Mia jumps onto her horse and nudges it into action.

Apollo doesn't hesitate; his hooves pound on the ground as we race through the dim woods. I'm unprepared for the speed at which he moves, and my bound hands clutch at the saddle.

I can hardly drag air into my lungs around Ledger's grip on me but fear if he lets go, I'll be sucked into the oblivion of this night. The wallop of hooves comes from behind us as Maddox and the soldiers catch up.

A ball of fire whizzes past us, singeing the skin of my legs. I turn my head to get a view of what is going on and can make out the silhouette of the pursuing men. The night flashes brightly as another fireball flies at us.

I'm sure it is going to knock us from the horse when Apollo veers to the left. Ledger pulls me further into him, but fire makes brief contact with my shoulder and Ledger's arm.

I hiss at the pain. Ledger doesn't falter; instead, he urges Apollo faster. His power pulses around me so intense it nearly steals my breath. He commands it, and I can feel the moment it projects behind us.

The air vibrates and a loud creaking sound pierces the night. Ledger's hand is raised, and as we pass a towering tree, it falls crashing with a loud boom.

A gust of air blows my hair and shock courses through me. I crane my neck, praying Maddox is okay, and am briefly relieved to see him still in close pursuit behind us. He has a bow drawn. I remember the times I'd seen him use one expertly and with precision.

"Focus your efforts on him; if we get him, we get her," Maddox's voice commands. There are still four men pursuing us. The tree must have taken out the other two.

Maddox releases the arrow, and I gasp as it makes contact with Ledger's shoulder. He releases a pained grunt but otherwise doesn't react.

A large object comes whizzing past us, a boulder, I surmise. It crashes into one of the soldiers, knocking him swiftly off his horse. Archie lets out a victorious noise.

Another boulder comes careening past us, the wind from it brushing my cheek. This time, instead of making contact, it rebounds, flying straight back at Archie.

"Arch, watch out!" Cam yells and he barely has time to plaster himself to his horse before the boulder sails over his head. They must have a deflector among them, able to redirect someone's power back at them.

Another grunt comes from Ledger, and even though I can't see where the arrow went, I know it met its mark somewhere in his body. My power somersaults in my stomach.

They are gaining on us, and for a heart-stopping moment, I think they might actually catch us. Ledger's grip on the reins and my body is loosening, an iron tinge stinging my nose.

What would King Sandor do to them if they caught us? A strange sense of dread fills me when I think of returning to my life at Bellehaven.

"Almost there," Mia calls from somewhere in front of us, snapping me out of my thoughts.

Ledger's body shudders as another arrow burrows into him. He lets out a rattled wet noise. Maddox gains on us, his horse running so fast they nearly pass us.

My breath stalls as we make eye contact. I wish it was light enough to make out the warm browns of his irises. I slam my head back, my body lurches sideways towards him. I pull at the reins trying to slow Apollo. Maddox reaches out his hand towards me and I extend my tied hands out. Our fingertips brush.

My eyes widen in horror as I catch the movement of vines. They bound out of the dirt, securing over his horse's legs. The animal falters before it comes to an abrupt halt, sending Maddox careening off.

I shriek as his body soars through the air before slamming into the ground. We sail past his unmoving body. I rage against Ledger, and the binds digging into my wrists. I scream for Maddox until my voice is raw.

CHAPTER
EIGHT

By the time we pass the border into Grimwood, the sound of chasing hooves becomes distant.

Our horses keep galloping until all my hope of returning to Bellehaven is snuffed out. Ledger's body sags into me, causing me to pitch forward.

I yank at the reins binding my hands, loosening them.

Ledger's grip falters, and I turn in time to see his eyes roll back into his head. As he loses consciousness, we start pitching to the side, and I'm helpless to stop us from falling.

Apollo slows to a canter as we slide out of the saddle. My hands fall free of the reins, and I squeal right before our bodies hit the ground.

The air is knocked from my lungs as Ledger's limp body lands on top of mine. Warm droplets of his blood drip over my skin as I struggle beneath him.

His bare skin blazes into mine the more I squirm. My hands push against his thick slabs of muscle uselessly.

"Oh shit." Archie must see us in a heap because he dismounts his horse and is over us in the next second. He lifts Ledger's body so I can slide out from beneath him.

Mia comes up, helping Archie get him in a sitting position. "Ledger," Mia calls his name, her hands going to his face, slapping across the cheek.

I gulp in air, trying to quell my swelling emotions. My arm and leg quiver with the pain of my freshly blistered skin.

With Mia and Archie distracted, I jump up and limp in the opposite direction in hopes of seeing Maddox and the guards in pursuit of us. My lungs burn with exertion as I pump my arms and legs.

Maddox. I've got to get to Maddox.

"Godsdammit!" Archie charges after me.

My legs ache as I push them faster. My back spikes with awareness as Archie chases after me. He's fast, running in long strides, and it isn't long before he barrels into me.

We collide onto the wet earth, grunting at the impact. He wrestles me to the ground as I throw unsuccessful punches, eventually pinning my arms to my sides. I let out a defeated sob as warm tears flow down my cheeks.

"I'm sorry, Layla, I'm fucking sorry." His chest heaves as he tries to catch his breath. "I'm begging you, please help him. I know it's the last thing you want to do but if you don't, he will die." He looks over to where Mia is frantically trying to wake Ledger.

"Maybe death is what he deserves." I spit the words, fighting to see past my anger.

"Please, we can't lose him." The anguish in his words matches how I feel, and as much as I want to leave him to bleed out, I know I can't. My father always spoke of the sacred power bestowed upon us and the deep responsibility that comes with it. It didn't matter that he'd ripped me away from my life or that leaving him to die could be my chance at freedom. I would not allow his blood to be on my hands.

I struggle against Archie's grip before the fight leaves my body. "I will help him, and I will heal whoever it is that he requests of me under the condition that you return me to Bellehaven after it is done." I rip my wrists from Archie's grip the second I feel it loosen.

"I will take you back myself if that is what you want." Archie winces at the promise.

Mia is still pleading with Ledger to wake up as I approach running a sleeve over my tear-streaked face.

Fury explodes in my gut, fast and acute, as Ledger's eyes blink open. I think of Maddox sailing through the air and am unable to tame my rage as I stumble over to them.

Ledger sits slumped on the forest floor, the soil damp with his blood. Three arrows protrude from his back, and I waste no time grabbing ahold of one of them and yanking.

A choking gasp leaves him as he pitches forward onto his hands. I reach for the next one before he can recover and yank it out with a sickening squelch. Blood pours from the wounds.

He wheezes, falling to the side and holding up his hand, trying to keep me at bay, but I don't stop. My power thrashes against my skin, and I contest it.

His sticky hand weakly pushes at me as I fist the last arrow. I yank it out roughly. My power laces through my veins and I struggle to ignore it.

"Fuck," he groans as his hands fist in the dirt, and he gasps for air.

"Remind me never to get on her bad side," Archie exclaims. He and Mia are looking at each other with their mouths ajar like they can't decide if they should intervene or not.

I swallow thickly before kneeling next to Ledger. I reluctantly let my power lose, and it whips out of my palms, wrapping around his bleeding body.

Guilt rocks into me as I gain control of myself. Ledger calms almost instantly, his body relaxing into the mist.

His skin knits together, and the burns on his arm smooth out. He fights to control his breathing as he pushes himself up to kneeling. His eyes drift shut as my power caresses his body, checking for any other injuries. His breath shudders out.

I frown when my power clings to him briefly before retreating into me.

I take a moment to brush my fingers over his closed wounds. Gods, what is it with this man? Everything about him is opposing. His features are severe but captivating. His very presence is alluring yet callous. It's a maddening, lethal mix.

I wonder for the first time who this person is he loves enough to capture me. Was it a lover?

Mia and Archie give each other a look before their eyes fall on Ledger. "Are you okay?" Archie asks, and Ledger nods his head, his body taut.

"Give us a minute," he croaks. They consider me with a weary look. I avert my eyes and try to ignore the way my cheeks heat in shame.

"We will be right over here," Mia calls as they walk away.

I sit frozen for a second before moving to my feet. I rip off a piece of Ledger's tunic, grabbing his canteen off Apollo and wetting it before returning to him.

Ledger is sitting, his breathing almost back to normal, and he studies me as I kneel next to him. He flinches almost imperceptibly as I bring the wet cloth to his bloodied back.

"You feel better now?" he asks me pointedly as I wipe away the drying blood with rapt attention.

"You could have killed him, Ledger."

"Trust me, if he can't survive a fall off a horse, I did you a favor."

"You're unbelievable." I wipe roughly at the skin where the arrow wound was moments before, causing him to wince.

"Jesus, I've never been more afraid of a woman in my life."

"It's not too late to return me."

At that, he scoffs. "So, what is the prince to you anyway?" I let my hand drop and peer out into the darkness towards the border of Bellehaven as if I could see Maddox.

"He's my best friend."

"I saw him kiss you that night. Do you kiss all your friends?"

If it were light enough, I'm sure he would see my blushing. "That is none of your business."

"Mmmm." Ledger stands, rolling out his shoulder and peering at his now-closed wounds. "Incredible," he whispers, more to himself. "Can you heal yourself?"

"No, it doesn't work like that," I respond, and he considers my words.

"Then let me see your burns." He walks to Apollo, pulling out a tunic from his saddle bag and throwing it on. Another pouch in the saddle holds some ointment and wrapping.

"I'm fine," I lie through my teeth. The burns throb painfully; the skin affected seems to radiate heat.

Ledger pins me with an unconvinced look that has me rolling my eyes. "Fine, give me the ointment; I can do it myself." I reach for it, and he moves his hand back out of my grasp.

"Does anyone ever take care of you? Or is it just you taking care of everyone else?"

I bristle at his words as they struck, stripping away yet another truth. "I don't need anyone to take care of me, but I suppose Maddox takes care of me. We take care of each other." I square my jaw.

He nods slowly and then motions to a log. "Sit. Humor me, Ms. Sutton." I narrow my eyes briefly before glancing at the log and reluctantly sitting down.

He takes my ankle into his large hand, holding my leg up to the moonlight to get a better look. His fingers dip into the ointment.

I cringe against the sting as he applies it, his fingers surprisingly gentle. "It won't heal you completely, but it should ease the pain."

His fingers brush over my calf as he skillfully wraps the burn. "You've done this before." It's more of an observation than anything.

"A time or two."

He moves to my arm; the skin is raised and blistered worse than my leg. I hiss when the rough skin of his fingers glide over it. However, his touch is light, opposite of what I imagined it would be.

"Payback." He grins, the dimple in his cheek popping ever so slightly as he continues.

"Vengeful," I quip.

"You're not anything like I thought you'd be, you know?" He pauses, studying my face as if he's perplexed.

"How'd you think I'd be?"

"Different. You don't strike me as the kind of girl that would stay for so long in that carefully crafted prison your king and prince keep you in."

"You're saying it like I have a choice. You think of me as some weak, sheltered girl, easily manipulated and compliant. You know nothing," I spit the words at him yanking my ankle from his grasp.

"Believe me, I am well aware. I have never had less of a grip on who someone is in my entire life. Enlighten me, please." His hands gesture towards me expectantly.

I narrow my eyes at him before speaking. "As you know, healers are one of the rarest abilities, and Sandor loves to have what others do not possess. I was able to leverage my... compliance in exchange for my mother to live in the castle. I do as he demands, and she stays safe."

"You said she was not of healthy mind?"

"The death of my father took a toll on her. For months I begged Sandor to let me see her and once he finally agreed and brought her to the castle–she wasn't the same woman I remembered. In that time her brain had become addled, forgetful, confused, and she could hardly recognize me most days." Ledger listens intently, his expression blank, and body still.

"When I came fully into my power, I attempted to heal her but, it turns out, my powers only work for physical wounds, not mental." I huff a bitter laugh. "She was never the same. And now without me there to protect her, who knows what Sandor will do."

"I was not aware." His expression is almost remorseful. "It sounds like you would do anything for your family. We aren't all that different."

We sit in silence for a long while unsure of how to continue. Archie ambles over to us, a hesitant expression on his face. "We are going to try and get some sleep before the sun rises."

"Good idea," Ledger responds, and we both stand, following Archie to the group.

"It looks like the soldiers burned our camp, so I guess we are going to be one with nature for a few nights." I can smell the smoke in the air and see the plumes of it in the distance. Cam lay back in a pile of moss, crossing his arms behind his head and gazing up at the stars.

"I'll take the first watch," he offers.

A shiver courses through me as the chill of the night sets over my skin.

"It isn't particularly warm tonight, so if you want to huddle together to preserve body heat, I'd be happy to." Archie appears next to me, and I halfway consider his offer.

"Like hell, Archie; go keep Cam warm. I'm sure he'd appreciate the heat," Ledger comments, making Mia chuckle before she curls up on the ground.

Archie sighs and saunters over, collapsing on the ground next to her.

"Don't get any ideas," she mumbles.

Ledger's eyes track me as I sink to the ground and curl my legs into my chest. I begin to tremble, the adrenaline from the day wearing off and the cold seeping into my bones.

Ledger lays next to me, and a second later a root seals around my ankle. I yank at it and huff, too tired to argue. The heat from his body taunts me, close enough to sense but too far to warm me.

As the time drags on, my shivering becomes a violent tremor. I inch myself towards Ledger, my pride fading until my back is inches from the side of his body.

"She is going to wake the gods with the chattering of her teeth, Ledger. Just let me—" Archie starts.

"She is fine." Ledger cuts him off, pushing up and disappearing into the night. A few seconds later, a saddle blanket is thrown over me. It smells of sweat and leather. I grasp the rough fabric and pull it over my shoulders sighing with the relief it brings.

I stare into the void of the night and think of Maddox. I pray that he is alright and hope he can forgive me for what I've agreed to do.

CHAPTER
NINE

Soft sunlight rouses me, and I groan stretching my stiff muscles. I rub the sleep from my eyes flicking off a rouge leaf sticking on my cheek. It's an effort to push my aching body off the ground.

Everyone else is awake and Ledger makes eye contact with me before grabbing the discarded saddle blanket and walking to Apollo.

I shiver against the chill morning air, still exhausted and bleary-eyed.

Archie cuts the vine from my ankle and helps me up, offering me his canteen full of cool stream water.

"Thanks." I take a drink and hand him back the water, rubbing away the goosebumps that pepper my arms.

Ledger comes from behind me and drapes his cloak around my shoulders. "Take it; you'll be of no use to me if you fall ill."

"Gee, thanks." I pull it around me. "You don't happen to have a cup of coffee in that saddle bag? I like it with a touch of honey," I joke lamely as Ledger rifles through it.

"We leave in five minutes, and we will ride for most of the day." He ignores me completely, and I nod.

I find some water and splash it over my face. I sit in silence listening to the small creek and breathing in the morning air.

It is serene and calm and more picturesque than I could have imagined. Even though I am a prisoner, this is the freest I have ever felt. The desire to see more and experience more grows inside of me by the minute.

I pull some wild weeds I remember Maddox feeding to his horse. He said it was their favorite treat.

I bring the weeds back to Apollo and offer them to him. He looks at me suspiciously before turning his head in rejection.

"Alright then," I grumble, dropping them to the ground. He turns his head, eating my offering where it lies as I walk away. Being disliked by an animal is a strange feeling, sparking determination within me. I will get this hardheaded horse to like me.

Ledger holds out his hand when I'm ready, and I take it, bracing. I am not looking forward to another day on Apollo. My body aches in places I wasn't even aware possible.

He pulls me up, and I settle in front of him. My back presses up against his front and his arms encircle me again as he grabs the reins.

I squirm at his closeness all too aware of all the places he touches. "Are you alright?" he asks.

"I'm fine," I reply, scooting forward and effectively silencing him.

We ride for hours until my body is achy, sore, and begging for a break, and then we ride for even longer. Cam struggles to stay awake, nodding off. And Archie keeps shifting in his saddle, proving I'm not alone in my misery.

I don't dare complain or ask to stop. At some point, I give in and rest back into Ledger, and he takes some of my weight, making the ride more bearable.

When he finally announces we must find camp before the sun sets, I blow out a breath of relief.

We choose to set up camp next to a small stream, luckily not deep enough for anything to be lurking in it.

When we stop, Ledger dismounts, and when I go to follow, I nearly fall flat on my face, one of my legs having gone numb.

Ledger catches me midair and places me down with surprising gentleness.

"Uh, thanks," I stammer. He walks away without a response.

"You're welcome, Layla, anytime Layla," I grumble. I can't be sure, but I swear I see the ghost of a grin on his face as I pass him.

I limp towards the stream, shaking out my numb legs. Cam fills up his canteen, and I seize the opportunity to finally catch him alone. "Hey," I say softly, sitting down next to him, unlacing my boots, and wiggling my toes.

"Hey," he responds, glancing back at me.

"Listen, I, uh, I wanted to apologize for my actions when we first met. It was nothing personal, and I feel horrible about it." My eyes flicker to his bruised, swollen temple.

"I have to give it to you, you have fast reflexes and hit way harder than I'd expect from a girl your size."

"Thanks, I suppose." I grin at him. "That bump looks pretty nasty. Would you let me heal it for you? This time, I won't knock you unconscious, you have my word."

"You promise?" he asks hesitantly.

"I promise."

"Okay, what do I need to do?"

"Just be still, it won't hurt," I encourage.

We both turn our bodies to face each other. I lift my hand to his head and the other to where the cut still marks his ribs.

My power flows out of me in a glowing mist. It warms my skin and fills my palms. It coasts over the injuries in a matter of seconds and snaps back inside of me.

Cam touches his temple gingerly as if he is expecting it to hurt. His eyes widen when I assume he doesn't feel the bump or any pain. He then rips up his shirt revealing his pale skin that is now free of any cuts or scratches.

"You're so awesome," Cam says, and I smile softly.

"Rein it in, Cam. You're too young for her." Archie comes up and ruffles Cam's hair.

"I feel like her type is blonde, incredibly handsome, strong, brave, can move things with his mind?" He smirks down at me as Cam pushes his hand away.

"Okay, I'm out, it's nauseating watching you try to flirt." Cam stands but before he walks away, he turns to me. "Thanks for healing me." His cheeks turn a light shade of pink.

"It was the least I could do." I grin at him. My toes delve into the water as he walks away.

"So, was I right about your type?" Archie plops down next to me and I huff a laugh.

"I'll have to get back to you on that one."

"I can be whatever it is you like, you tell me what you like, and I can be that." My lip tugs up at his flirty banter, a distraction I welcome.

"What if I told you I liked murderers and dirty cheats?"

"Hmmm," he considers. "For you, I'd send this dagger through Ledger's heart right now."

I snort, knocking his shoulder with my own. "Tempting."

Archie chuckles, removing his shirt and splashing some water on his chest and neck. I glance over at the mangled skin of his back and swallow thickly as I assess the severity.

He catches my stare before I can look away and stiffens before rigidly putting his shirt back on.

"Did King Sandor do that?" I ask softly, my stomach flipping as I await his answer.

"Did you know I grew up in Bellehaven?" he asks, and I shake my head no. "My mother died giving birth to me, and my father didn't want to be involved. My aunt raised me, and when my abilities began to surface around age six, she brought me to King Sandor."

I listen as he speaks.

"I was a difficult child. I didn't like authority, or being told what to do. I was unserious, unruly, and stubborn—all traits King Sandor detested and attempted to rid me of. He would get especially angry when I would make a quip after his discipline attempts, and that would lead to more beating, whipping, or sessions with Tamish."

The color drains from my face and my throat squeezes. I reach for his leg and give his thigh a gentle squeeze.

"One day, Callum and his son came to visit. Ledger and I met, and we connected almost instantly. When we were playing, he must have seen some of my scars or healing skin because the next thing I knew, we were all on our way back to Westray." He looks at me as he finishes.

"King Sandor never releases anyone willingly from his grasp. He hoards and collects the powerful like they are something to be possessed," I say surprised.

"Callum won't admit it, but I'm almost positive he traded one of his own for my release." His nostrils flare as he blows out an angry breath. It's the first time I've seen him affronted. It's an emotion I'm very familiar with, one I've shoved down for years. "Either way, he gifted me a second chance, and I'm thankful for that."

"Sandor did that to you when you were just a boy?" I ask the question, looking at his now-covered back. I already know the answer, and it makes me sick. Ledger glances up from a few feet away where he is moving brush around. Archie stays silent so I speak again, "Callum—is he a better man than Sandor?"

"I wouldn't have stepped foot back in Bellehaven and assisted in your kidnapping if he wasn't." He tosses a rock into the water. "Did Sandor ever hurt you?"

I pause, contemplating my answer. "He killed my father." From the corner of my vision Ledger goes predatorily still, clearly listening. "And then he plucked me from my home. He could sense that I had power and is not a patient man. He spent weeks experimenting on me, attempting to bring it fourth. His methods were–cruel." I frown at the dreadful memories. "That was the worst of it." With my mother safe in the castle any treatment after felt bearable. "I'm glad Callum got you out." When I look up at Archie he wears a look of understanding.

"Me too." He stands, brushing his pants off. "I don't know about you, but I could use a comfy, luxurious bed right about now. And a beautiful woman warming it."

"Sounds like you have been sleeping on the cold ground alone for one too many nights," I tease.

"You'd be correct. If you get tired sleeping next to a brooding Ledger, know I'm a few feet away, waiting with open arms."

"Archie, get over here and leave that poor girl alone. The last thing she needs right now is your advances." Mia's voice carries over to us as she shouts at Archie from where she is taking supplies out of her saddle.

"Well, that's my cue. It's been a pleasure, Layla." He gets up, bowing to me before grabbing his boots and heading over to help Mia.

I force a smile as he walks away and begin putting my boots back on, still shaken by what he had revealed. He seemed to be a few years older than me, leading me to believe this all must have happened before my arrival at the castle.

I wasn't surprised at all by the actions of King Sandor. He spared no mercy even for a child.

I take a few deep breaths trying to quell the burning anger that flares in my chest.

"Was your father a healer like you?" Ledger walks over to me as I tug my boots back on.

I pause looking up at him. Once again, he's weaving flowers together with his fingers. "He was, he'd heal the powerful and powerless alike. He'd never deny anyone. He evaded the king for a long time until he was caught. Sandor implored him to join his ranks but my father spit at his feet. He believed that if one was gifted a power it belonged to them alone and should not be wielded by another." I stand brushing myself off.

"Sounds like he was a wise man." Ledger's eyes linger on me thoughtfully before he crouches placing the loop of flowers into the stream and watching as they float away.

"He was."

It starts to rain as the sun is snuffed out. Ledger uses his powers to thicken the tree branches above us to create somewhat of a barrier. We huddle beneath the tree as it continues to pour.

I lay on my side on the spongy moss-coated ground. I allow my mind to wander, conjuring Maddox's familiar face, his crooked, self-assured smile. I rub at the center of my chest, missing him fiercely.

I can't help but feel like I am betraying him the closer we get to Westray. I know he is worrying about me, thinking the worst.

I think of how he fought for me twice now.

My mind snags on how he'd kissed me and the confession of his feelings that followed. What would have happened if I had given in and ignored the report? Would I be wrapped safely in his arms tonight instead of shivering in the cold?

I worry about what had become of my mother in my absence. Would the King allow her to stay in the castle until my return? Would he dump her in the slums to fend for herself? Or worse. Would he allow Tamish to inflict his power upon her? Would he inflict his own pain as he did to Archie? The thoughts make me sick.

I could not go back to Bellehaven now; I made a deal, and I would follow through.

I toss and turn, finally landing on my side, peering over at Ledger, who is lying on his back a foot from me.

The moonlight highlights his sharp jawline, straight nose, and long black lashes as he blinks. My stomach flips as he turns to his side, letting his eyes roam my face.

They burn a path over my skin, and it is an effort to not squirm as they continue their perusal. His deep green eyes find mine, and we stare at each other as raindrops cascade off our skin from the leaves above.

I shiver, and Ledger moves closer to me. My skin pebbles in the cool night air. I can tell he wants to reach for me but stays perfectly still.

As the night drags on, I long for my cozy bed. Would sell my soul for warm fur. My clothes cling to my skin as the rain persists, making my teeth chatter.

I beg for sleep to take me but even Ledger's tepid body so close provides little reprieve.

I jolt as a sharp howl cuts through the thick air of the night. Tensing, my ears strain as another piercing howl follows. I plaster myself against Ledger, my hands fumbling for the dagger in his belt.

His large hand finds mine, stopping my exploration. "I don't think now is the place or time, blondie."

I elbow him roughly in the ribs, freeing my hands. "Something is howling out there!" My whisper is somewhat hysterical. "Give me a weapon," I demand.

"Not a chance." Another howl penetrates the night, and Ledger's hand moves steadily over my stomach until it lands on my hip. He pulls me closer to him while he sits up, searching the woods.

"What in the hell is that?" I whisper again, clawing at Ledger's hand. Archie wakes, looking to Ledger for direction.

"We are in the woods; there are creatures everywhere. That's a dire wolf; they are looking for something larger than a human to eat. Typically, if you leave them alone, they will leave you alone."

"Larger than a human? How big are these things?!" My heart is a wild chorus in my chest.

"Layla." He forces my face away from the woods. "I will not allow anything to happen to you. You are far too valuable. You will make it to my kingdom unharmed, I swear it." He nods over to Archie and they both lay back down.

I sit up, my ears straining to hear any further howls or footfalls. "As reassuring as that is, I'd still like a weapon."

"Not going to happen," Ledger grunts as his hand shoots up and pushes me back down to the springy moss. "Sleep," he demands.

"Fine, but I am staying as close to that dagger as possible," I mumble as I roll onto my side, my back to Ledger, and scoot myself closer to him.

I stare into the shadowed misty forest fisting the moss beneath me in an attempt to quell my pounding heart. I picture a horrific beast bounding from the trees and tearing my flesh apart as I flail around in its mouth, unarmed.

Ledger sighs from beside me. I flinch when his fingers skate along the back of my neck. "What are you doing?"

"Easy." He moves my hair to the side and the sleeve of the tunic down to expose my shoulder. "Relax."

My breath shudders out as he strokes soothing circles into the skin there. His fingers breeze down the curve of my neck and sail over the freckles of my shoulder.

I loosen into his touch, the tension in my body easing. My power slithers through my veins to meet his fingers, warming my bones.

I'd never let a man touch me like this and I couldn't for the life of me figure out why I was allowing him to continue.

A surprising wave of desire washes over me at the stroke of his fingertips. I squeeze my thighs together as his rough calluses drag over my damp skin.

I should pull away, but I'm so lost in the foreign feeling that I hardly notice when I press myself closer to him. Before I make contact, he pushes himself back. He blows out a rough breath that skates across my skin making me squirm.

His fingers tighten on my neck briefly before he yanks them away. I mourn the sudden loss of them. When he scoots away from me my mind sobers and shame floods me.

What would Maddox think of me right now and what I'm doing? I need to get a grip.

"Sleep, Layla." Ledger's voice is gravelly and grates against my pebbled skin. My cheeks flame at my unexpected reaction to his simple touch. Fear creeps back into my consciousness, but it's directed now at myself, and the feelings Ledger was able to elicit from me.

Chasing after the touch of a man was something that I did not do.

He turns roughly to the side so his back is to me. I yank up my sleeve, staying as still as possible, no longer trusting myself.

I sleep in fitful bursts begging for the sun to rise each time I wake. I am not sure what terrifies me more, the dire wolf or the way my body reacted to the Prince of Westray.

Ledger and I don't even brush each other the rest of the night. The miserable cold sets deep into my bones, making me question if I will ever be warm again.

My fingers and toes are stiff and numb when the golden rays of the sun finally settle over the land.

I rise, taking care of my needs before finding the small stream and gulping down a few long handfuls of water.

"Ah, good morning, sunshine." Archie approaches, squatting down before doing the same.

"Morning."

"You look..." He pauses, taking in my haggard appearance. "Uh, well rested." I roll my eyes at him, practically feeling the dark bags underneath my eyes.

"If we cover enough ground today, we could end up at The Lazy Archer, the only inn in Grimwood. A hot meal and a warm bed sound pretty good right now, am I right?" He wiggles his eyebrows.

"Heavenly," I grunt as we make our way over to the horses.

Mia hands me a few pieces of what looks like dried meat and a stale piece of bread. "Sorry, it's all we have; our rations are running low."

"This is fine, thank you." My stomach grumbles as I take a bite of the salty meat, grateful for any sustenance.

Ledger is quiet, avoiding me as he saddles the horses.

Cam smiles over at me from where he is tending to his own horse. "Morning, Layla," he says, smiling shyly.

"Morning, Cam." I smile back at him.

"What do you think about riding with me today?" Archie questions, throwing his arm around my shoulder.

I open my mouth to gladly accept his offer when Ledger cuts me off, "Not happening." He pointedly looks at Archie's arm until he removes it.

"I get lonely, Ledger. I can't keep her warm at night, can't ride with her on my horse. What can I do?" Archie grins and winks at me and I smother a smile.

"You can focus on yourself. I'm in no mood for you two today. Blondie, get your ass up here."

"What did I do?" I accept his hand as he yanks me up into the saddle.

"You exist."

CHAPTER
TEN

The sun begins to rise as we leave, and I am reluctant to blink as the oranges, reds, and purples fill the sky.

My mouth hangs open in awe. "Did the King have you so locked up in that castle you never saw a sunrise?" Ledger asks, glancing at me.

"I had a lot of late nights, and I'm not much of an early riser, though I have seen a sunrise before. Never one quite as beautiful as this one."

"Where I am from, they are like this fairly often."

"Do you always wake early?" I ask genuinely curious.

"Since I was a boy," he answers before pausing. When I peer up at him, he looks like he is debating if he should continue. "I used to get up early to watch the sunrise with my mother. She believed there was no problem that could defeat a sunrise. She'd always tell me that they represented a new beginning, a new opportunity to live life, breathe freely, to love. She would then bask in the sun for hours claiming there was no other way she would appreciate the break that night brought." A genuine smile breaks out on his face as he speaks, revealing the dimple on his cheek that halts my breath.

His face glows with the reflection of the sky. The only thing I can think is no sunrise could ever rival him with that rare smile. A flutter erupts in the pit of my stomach at the sight of him, and I struggle to look away.

Fearing he will catch me, I take a mental picture of him and force my stare back at the now brilliant, crimson hues. "When I arrive in the kingdom, I may have to wake early to lay my eyes upon them. I can't think of anything more important in a day that would justify the loss of something so breathtaking." I had no idea if I was still talking about the sunrise.

"I can guarantee you will not be disappointed," he remarks, staring ahead.

The day passes mercifully uneventfully; we stop a few brief times to tend to the horses and eat some small rations of food. My thighs ache from the long hours and hard saddle.

It's an effort to convince myself back on Apollo each time we stop. I bite back moans of pain as my joints and muscles bark angrily at me.

"Just a few more hours, blondie." Ledger's voice comes from behind me, and I nearly whimper at the word 'hours.'

"Oh, that's all? I can't imagine why we'd stop at all; this is so enjoyable." The sarcasm in my voice is thick.

"Glad you're enjoying yourself," Ledger responds, and I have to stop myself from turning around to see the pop of his dimple.

We ride for another hour when a sense of unease comes over me. The woods turn eerily quiet as we pass through them.

"Is there another way we can go?" I scan the trees wearily. "I have a bad feeling."

Ledger's body goes stiff behind me as he surveys for danger. The horses slow; they bristle as we stop, and everyone's hands start to move to their weapons as they scan the trees.

A tree branch snaps, and my eyes flicker to the sound. The blood drains all the way to my legs, leaving a trail of ice in its wake as I take them in.

Creatures stand on massive, sharp, clawed paws. Their short black hair shines red in the sunlight. The arms are long and sinewy, their body packed with slabs of muscle. They crouch, flexing and tensing their muscled thighs. Huge horns protrude from each side of their heads and drool drips menacingly from the overbite of bottom fangs jutting from their lower jaw.

"Kerolu," Archie exclaims, drawing his sword as others start to appear around us. "We need to try to distract them from the horses. If they manage to kill them, we are going to be fucked."

The clang of weapons being drawn has me reaching for the dagger I no longer possess. Mia dismounts her horse and notches an arrow into her bow in one fluid movement.

Ledger cautiously lowers himself off the horse and reaches for me as the creatures' red, piercing eyes study us. They creep closer, sniffing the air.

I sit frozen, staring, terror working its way through my limbs. I hardly notice when Ledger gently brings me down and puts a dagger into my hand.

"Get to Cam, he will get you out of here, and if the Kerolu get anywhere near you, ram this straight into their skull." His lips brush my ear as his hand closes my palm over the glittering dagger.

"Ledger," I squeak as I count at least eight of the sinister creatures. These things make swimming with Maladra look appealing.

"Layla, there is no time to panic." He draws his sword and shields me with his body. "Get. To. Cam."

A siren-like noise pierces the air before the clearing in the woods becomes chaos. The already-spooked horses make a run for it. One Kerolu tracks their movement, bounding after them.

Mia begins to loose arrows at an impressive speed as the Kerolu bound towards us. Arrow after arrow hits the Kerolu she has her sights on, but it doesn't slow until an arrow flies right into its eye.

Seconds after the arrow buries deep into its skull, the Kerolu drops, its lifeless body twitching.

Archie sends another careening into the air so fast it snaps the first tree it meets and slams into the one behind it. The Kerolu is stunned for a second before it recovers, charging in his direction.

Archie raises his hands, sending the sharp end of the broken tree into a Kerolu's stomach. The tree branch cuts clean through its torso, the pointy end sticking out of its thick, furry back, dripping blue blood.

My palms sweat as I grip the dagger so hard my knuckles turn white. The scene in front of me ensues in slow motion, and I watch in horror. I only remember Ledger's words when a Kerolu comes bounding towards me, its red eyes angry and locked in.

I swivel around, frantically searching for Cam. He is dodging a Kerolu, disappearing and reappearing behind it, swiping his sword into its side.

There is a clash behind me as Ledger intercepts the Kerolu coming for me.

Rocks careen around, knocking the Kerolu off balance. This distraction is enough for Ledger to brandish his sword right at the creature's neck skillfully. His movements are sure and strong and hit their mark, decapitating it. Dark, navy blood spurts into the air.

My stomach sours, my mouth watering, a gag working its way up my throat at the sight. I force myself to turn away and take a deep breath, trying to quell the nausea. I do not have time to be sick; I must get to Cam.

Archie is now at Cam's side; his movements are incredibly fast. He slashes at a huge Kerolu, making contact a few times, splattering his face in navy droplets.

Cam takes one strong swipe at the Kerolu, but its head swipes up, the sharp horn tip plunging right through his arm.

He grimaces in pain, yanking his arm from where it is impaled by the Kerolu's horn. Archie yells something to Cam, and his head snaps up, meeting my panicked gaze.

We run for each other almost instantly. He reaches his hand out to me when we are close enough and mine meets his. The second our skin touches, the world goes black, and a moment later, comes rushing back.

My head is spinning as I orient myself. We are only about fifteen feet away from the mayhem. "Sorry." Cam's breathless voice comes from next to me. "I can't teleport far when I have someone with me and am under pressure."

Before I can answer, Cam grabs my hand again, blackness taking over before we reappear. He does this two more times before he is satisfied with how far away we are from the Kerolu.

We are both trying to catch our breath as he turns to me. "Stay here, Layla; I must go back to help. We need you and your powers so please stay quiet and hidden. I'll come get you as soon as it's safe."

I nod, not able to form words yet and he disappears.

Almost as soon as Cam vanishes, a rustling comes from a few feet away. I freeze, straining to hear, and shakily lift my dagger, desperately trying to coerce myself into turning towards the noise.

Heart racing, I ever so slightly turn my head, my body poised to strike. I nearly sob with relief when I see Apollo.

"You scared the shit out of me." I take a few steps towards him, realizing his reins are stuck on a tree branch. His eyes are wild, and he is trying to pull himself free.

I follow his stare to see the Kerolu from earlier that had run after the horses.

"Just great," I mumble to myself. "I suppose you don't want to be friends?" I call to the creature. "I could heal you, and you could give me a cute little seashell and send me on my way?"

That gods-awful siren screech is all I get in response, the drool from its mouth peppering the air. It moves first, its strong thighs sending it hurtling through the air towards Apollo. I yank his reins free, and he blots.

I careen around, racing as fast as I can through the trees. I *feel* the rush of air on my neck as the creature lands behind me. The pounding of my heart thrums through my ears. The greens and browns of the woods blur my vision as I run.

A scream rips from my throat as the Kerolu barrels into me. I hit the ground with such force the breath is knocked from my lungs. My head pings off the ground, making my ears sing.

I don't even get a second of reprieve before the creature locks its horrible jaws around my thigh. It's gnarled serrated teeth dig deep into the muscle of my leg drawing fresh rivulets of crimson. Its eyes are wild, unseeing, lost in bloodlust. My body jostles as it shakes its neck in an animalistic predatory way.

White spots fill my vision as the pain laces through me. The dagger in my hand gleams in the sunlight as red, beady eyes lock with mine. My thoughts are empty as I slam the dagger as hard as I can into its fleshy neck.

Its head snaps to the side, its bloodied teeth scraping across my thigh. It wails in pain, and I can barely feel my own as I scramble to my feet.

The dagger slides around in my palm, slick with blue, sticky blood. I limp away from the Kerolu, putting precious distance between us. Hot blood drips down my thigh, the crimson color telling me it's mine. *I am so royally fucked.*

The scrape of the creature's nails on the dirt signals its pursuit. The Kerolu's anger billows off it.

I foolishly chance a look back, my injured leg snagging on a root, sending me crashing to the ground.

It pauses briefly, eyes narrowing on my precarious position. It's then that I realize how truly terrifying this creature is. Its massive body is almost like a mans but with black skin and thick hair. It is stacked with brawny muscle. It poises itself to attack, a heart-rending moment before jumping. Its sharp claws gleam ominously in the light of the day.

I grit my teeth and push myself up, dagger raised and ready to fight. If I am going to die, it will be fighting, not cowering on the ground.

I brace myself for contact a second before a figure jumps in front of me, taking the blow.

There is skin and fur, growls and grunts. Ledger's muscled body grapples with the Kerolu. It snaps its fangs viciously in his face, coating him with frothy spit. Scarlet blood leaks through Ledger's shirt soaking the ground.

My power awakens at the sight, thrashing under my skin, attempting to reach him. Ledger's sword catches my attention a few feet away, and I waste no time scrambling over to it.

"Ledger!" I call his name, grabbing his attention for a split second before sliding his sword across the forest floor.

I pray it reaches him because I unwittingly draw the Kerolu's undivided attention. It jumps off Ledger and runs at me full speed.

I don't have time to react as its curved horns ram into me sending me flying into a tree. The rough bark scratches my skin as I sink to the ground, struggling for breath.

I run my hand over my stomach, relieved when it doesn't come away bloody.

My eyes snap closed as the Kerolu approaches. My hand trembles when I clutch my dagger. My body stays perfectly still as it sniffs the air around me that's drenched in fear. The moment its putrid breath fans across my face, I strike.

My eyes fly open, and my daggered hand soars straight up, right into its fleshy chin, and deep into its brain. The Kerolu releases a grunt before it falls over with a thud.

I yank the dagger from its flesh, blue blood coating it and running down my arm. As soon as the dagger is free, I puke. Stomach acid burns the back of my throat as I retch and retch until my body relents.

I'm trembling from adrenaline and fear trying to compose myself. "You're okay, you're alive," I whisper attempting to calm my racing heart while rubbing my bloodied, blue hands against my clothes, trying to rid them of sticky blood.

"I keep underestimating you." Ledger approaches where I'm crouched. The front of his shirt is ripped, and crimson is pouring rapidly out of four perfect claw marks. He sways on his feet before collapsing onto his knees before me.

I hurtle over to him, everything else forgotten. "Jesus, Ledger, that was so stupid. Why would you jump in front of me like that?! I had the situation under control!" I grab his shoulders, attempting to steady him.

Ledger snorts. "I think what you mean to say is, 'Thank you, I'm forever in your debt.'" His normally bronzed face is ghostly pale.

"I need you to lie back, okay?" My power is roaring under my skin, already misting out of my palms, and I can do little to stop it. Once I get him propped on my thighs, I rip his shirt open, assessing the deep wounds.

"This is not quite how I pictured you taking my clothes off for the first time."

"Oh yeah?" My shaky hands hover over his skin, heating. "You have pictured me taking off your clothes before?"

I had healed plenty of wounds like this, especially as of late, but I'd never been this scared. Ledger's face contorts with pain as the poison works its way further under his skin. My power is as chaotic as my racing thoughts, and I have to fight to control it.

"Oh, I've pictured many things since meeting you, Layla." The way he says my name makes me flush.

I grit my teeth as I draw out the first trickle of poison. I wince as the poison burns its way up my veins. "Does it hurt?" I can feel his eyes on my face.

I don't answer, concentrating as sweat beads on my forehead and down my back. I take a deep breath, attempting to calm my raging abilities and focus.

"I don't deserve your power; you should save your energy. I do not like being the cause of your discomfort."

"You're right, Ledger, I'll just let you die." My hands tremble more violently now. The puddle of blood beneath Ledger is growing, and fear threatens to cripple me.

"You should. Then you would be free. Yet you expend your power on me twice now. Why?" he grunts.

The last of the poison leaves his body, and I shudder a breath of relief. I glance at Ledger's face briefly just as his eyes shut and his head falls limply to the side. Panic swarms me with surprising force. "Ledger, open your godsdamn eyes." I swing my leg over his body so I'm straddling him and slap his face.

I know I need to close the wounds that are still bleeding but my heart is beating so fast, and my mind is so scattered I can barely keep a grasp on my power.

"Please, don't do this, wake up, wake up." My bloody fingers smear gore onto his beautiful face as I attempt to rouse him. "Don't you dare die." My heart squeezes before his eyes crack open. Relief floods my veins.

"Not dead yet," he croaks.

"Do that again and I'll kill you myself." I refocus on the claw marks, realizing how deep they are. "Oh, gods," I breathe, sucking in a shaky breath. I grip onto my powers, sending a white mist over them.

Ledger's hand closes around my hip, his body taut and eyes closed.

"Are you in pain?" My power should have muted his pain by now.

"No, quite the opposite." His voice is strangled. "Your power feels rather nice."

I try to focus on everything good I have experienced these last few days. I think of the sun, of the waterfall skating over my skin, of the bright stars and the blue lagoon.

His thumb is resting against the bare skin of my hip and when he swipes it over the sensitive spot, my power flickers. My control slips.

His skin isn't knitting together nearly as fast as it needs to. I let out a frustrated huff. "If you don't want to bleed out on the forest floor, I would remove your hand from my hip."

When he doesn't immediately release me, my eyes snap to his to see him staring at his hand. His thumb swipes over my hip bone one last time before he slides it slowly down my hip and over my thigh. My power surges at that small act.

I clench my teeth desperately, trying to focus. My thoughts flood with images of Ledger's smile, that damn dimple, his fingers swirling over my neck, the heat of his body shielding me from the elements.

When I recall my power, all that's left of the wounds is dried blood and four long, pink scars running down his chest and abdomen. I run my fingers down them, feeling their slightly raised texture against his smooth, tanned skin.

Ledger releases a shuddered breath as I continue my perusal. "You never answered my question." His voice is strained.

"What?" I suck in air trying to catch my breath.

"Why didn't you let me die, with the arrows—now. I've given you more than enough reason to justify it. You could have had your freedom by now."

Ledger sits up, his fingers lifting to brush the hair from my face behind my ear, resting them on my neck.

"I'm a healer, it's what I do, it's who I am." I breathe.

"You are so much more than a healer. You are kind, and brave and entirely too good for this world." My breath snags and my heart stumbles in my chest. His thumb brushes up my neck.

My hand is pressed against his abdomen, and I am suddenly all too aware of how close we are, too close. Panic slices through me, and in the next second I am hurtling myself off of him. Distance, I need distance.

"Ledger!" Mia's voice cuts through the air as I scurry away from him. She jumps from behind a set of trees, arrow drawn and lethal.

"Thank the gods." She drops the bow. "Are you two okay?" Ledger has yet to move; his eyes are still trained on me. The second Mia sees all the blood, she is on her knees in front of him, inspecting his body.

"I'm okay, Mia," he assures her, stilling her hands. She turns to me, her eyes searching my body. My face is hot as I nervously brush my hands down the front of my tunic.

"I'm also alright." I can imagine what I look like. Both sticky and dried blood coat my hands and body. Her eyes bulge when she sees the dead Kerolu lying just feet away. The sight makes my knees go weak, and I force my eyes away.

"I heard your screams and the Kerolu's screeching. What the hell happened?!" Neither of us answer her right away, tension still hanging thick in the air.

Mia's eyebrows furrow. My mouth flounders open and closed, struggling to find words. "Never mind." She cuts me off. "You can tell me later. We need you; can you heal?"

"Yes, I can heal." I'm relieved at the change in subject. Healing Ledger had taken a significant amount of power, and I was feeling weak as well as battered, but I would never deny someone in need.

Mia grabs my hand, pulling me up, and I nearly double over in pain. The bite wound in my thigh pulses with white-hot agony as blood drips down my leg. My stomach aches from where the horn slammed into me. I had been so distracted with Ledger I'd hardly noticed.

"You're hurt." Ledger pushes to his knees in front of me, examining the injury. "You're bleeding too much; I need to wrap it to stop blood flow." He rips off a piece of his already tattered shirt. "It will need to be cleaned later. This isn't going to feel great," he warns, bringing the pieces of his shirt to the back of my leg.

"Ready?" His fingers graze the inside of my thigh, and I brace myself before nodding.

He pulls the cloth hard, and my vision goes black, a guttural scream getting caught in my throat. I can hardly breathe around the agony, fisting Ledger's shoulders and fighting not to pass out.

He waits patiently on his knees in front of me, his jaw locked and his hands resting on the backs of my thighs, supporting me. "Breathe, blondie."

"Trust me, I'm trying," I wheeze. He allows me to grip him until the pain dissipates enough that I push to stand.

My head spins as he wraps a few more pieces of fabric around my thigh, gentler this time.

His attention moves to my stomach. "May I?" He fingers the hem of my shirt.

"Do I have a choice?"

"I'm not letting you bleed out here, not when we are this close."

I yank my shirt from his fingers and pull it up enough for him to assess. The skin is already purple and blue, but somehow the horn didn't pierce the skin.

"You got lucky." Mia peers at my stomach.

"The bite isn't venomous?" It's a question, but I feel as if I would have felt the venom by now if it was.

"No, the venom is in their claws."

"We need to find the horses so we can get out of here." Mia scans the trees as Ledger drops my shirt.

"Apollo can't be far; he was caught in some branches back that way before I freed him." I point in the direction of his horse.

"Mia, I'll go with Layla to get Apollo. You look for the rest. I'll drop her with the group and ride back to find you." Ledger finally stands.

She agrees. "I'll stay around this area. If Apollo is here, the other horses can't be far."

I flail in Ledger's arms as he picks me up. "Put me down right now! Even though your gashes appear healed, you should certainly not be lifting me. Not to mention I can—"

"Layla, I'm carrying you, it's not up for debate." He shuts me down.

I fight him a little more for good measure and his arms tighten around me. I huff, crossing my arms, but my body never fully relaxes into his hold. We find Apollo in a clearing not too far away. His eyes look wild as we approach.

"You okay, buddy?" Ledger puts me down, and I place my hand on the white patch of fur on his forehead, resting my own on his nose.

He nuzzles against me, and I scratch his neck. Ledger watches us curiously.

"What?" I question.

"Nothing. I've never seen him let anyone touch him like that."

I shrug, and Ledger picks me up. I wince as he places me in the saddle. The wound on my thigh is starting to throb intensely.

Ledger mounts but doesn't immediately spur Apollo into action. He sits perfectly still, his chest pressed up against my back.

"Thank you for what you did back there," he says softly as his arms brush my sides, grabbing the reins. I know he means for healing him.

"It was the least I could do. You did jump in front of a rabid creature, saving me from being mortally wounded. You must need my power pretty badly to go through all of this," I say, but he doesn't respond and when I turn my head to glance at him, he looks troubled.

"Are you sure you can heal? You expended a lot of power back there, and you're hurt," he questions glaring down at my thigh.

"I'm fine, I'll be fine," I assure him as we approach the others. I slide out of the saddle as delicately as I can.

"Don't push yourself too hard, I'll be back soon." He presses the hilt of his shiny dagger into my hand. "You keep that, just promise not to use it on me."

"I don't make promises I can't keep." I swear I see Ledger's lip twitch as he rides away.

CHAPTER
ELEVEN

I GO TO CAM FIRST, REMEMBERING HOW THE KEROLU'S horn had pierced through his arm. He's drinking from his canteen, his other arm hanging limply at his side, blood dripping from his fingertips. My power purrs weakly under my skin at the sight.

"Let me see your arm." I reach for it, thankful when I see the horn didn't pierce all the way through.

I channel enough power to stop the bleeding and repair the skin, but he still has a hole in his arm. "Once my power returns, I can heal it more, at least now it won't get infected." He nods.

"It feels better. Thank you, Layla." I nod turning to find Archie.

He's sitting against a tree. I assess him, seeing a few cuts and scrapes, but when my eyes drift to his leg, I see his pant leg tattered and wet with blood. "You look like hell." I force a smile, kneeling. I use my dagger to cut his pant leg to get a better look.

"Hey, I liked those pants, and we both know I've never looked like hell a day in my life."

I chuckle softly. "Looks like the Kerolu got you pretty good." A decent-sized chunk is missing from his calf, and my hands are already glowing as I bring them up to hover over the wound. "Don't worry, I'll get you all fixed up. I don't have enough power to make it perfect; you're going to have a nasty scar. The ladies will go crazy for it."

"I'm no stranger to scars as long as I can keep my leg." He braces expecting pain.

"It's not going to hurt, Arch. If anything, you'll feel some warming, maybe itching." I take a deep breath, letting the stopper off my power, pushing what I can spare into him.

White glowing mist cocoons around his leg, swirling around the skin until I'm fully satisfied. The newly healed skin almost completely matches his healthy skin, except for a rugged scar.

"Astonishing," Archie remarks as he moves his leg around, testing it.

"It might be a little sore for a few days, try to take it easy on that leg. Mind if I take care of that head wound?"

"You really are the best, Layla," he says, and I smile, lifting one hand to his temple, the other on his chin to keep him still.

When I feel like I am done, I lick my thumb to smear it against Archie's temple, removing the dried blood. "Thanks, Mom." He grins. "I could really get used to having you around." He stands up and offers me his hand.

I sway as I stand up. "Whoa, you okay?" He steadies me.

"I'm fine, just a little weak." I want nothing more than a hot bath and a comfy bed. My thigh and stomach are throbbing in time with my heart. I fight to stay conscious as blood loss and use of power catch up to me. My body lurches sideways, and Archie catches me before I can hit the ground.

"Layla!" His voice is laced with concern, and I can't seem to find the words to answer him. "Hey, stay with me." He is shaking me gently. I struggle to keep my eyes open but the darkness creeping in becomes impossible to resist.

I COME TO AS THE HORSES SLOW. THE NOISE OF HOOVES clomping on pebbles echoes off the empty streets. The smell of the forest and leather is at the forefront of my senses.

When I am conscious enough to open my eyes, I realize my face is nuzzled into Ledger's neck. The only thing keeping me up on the horse is his arm banded around me. My body goes a little rigid as I pull my face from his neck.

"Thank the fucking gods," Ledger breathes as he looks down at me. "You scared the hell out of all of us back there. You shouldn't have pushed yourself so hard. There is a limit

STACI JOST

to everyone's abilities, and you seem to have no regard for yourself."

"He's right, you know? I thought we almost lost you back there," Archie chimes in.

"You guys aren't going to get rid of me that easily," I respond, trying to lighten the mood. If I'm being honest, I'd scared myself. Expending so much power mixed with my wounds had been a dangerous combination, and I am feeling the punishing effects of both.

"Where in the world are we?" We canter down a cobblestone street. The houses we pass are built with spruce wood walls covered in green moss, the roofs a rich copper.

It looks charming and smells earthy and floral. I hear a babbling creek somewhere in the distance that must run through the town.

"This is Grimwood. Westray is about a day's ride from here." As we turn the corner, a few heavily armored men on horses ride by, barking hounds trailing after them. "They are known for animal tracking, herbalism, and leather working here. That is how they make a living."

"Are they tracking Kerolu?"

"Amongst other things." Ledger pulls Apollo's reins as we come to a halt in front of an enchanting inn. The sign above the red wooden door reads, "The Lazy Archer."

Everyone dismounts their horses, Ledger getting off himself and then reaching up to gently place me and my numb legs on the ground.

My head swims, and I reach out to Apollo to steady myself.

Ledger lifts an eyebrow at me, and I force a pleasant look onto my face, giving myself another steadying second before dropping my hand.

Ledger lifts me into his arms, and I'm too weak to fight him as he walks us into the inn.

The inn is warm, the smell of something savory and delicious in the air makes my stomach rumble. There is a fire in the hearth giving the dining room a glowy appearance. Mounted animal heads litter the walls, some seemingly innocent while others still appear as viscous as the day they perished.

I spot a monstrously large Kerolu head on the wall behind the front desk, I can practically see the drool dripping off its fangs. I shiver at the sight, unconsciously rearing back.

"What, blondie, you don't like the furnishings?"

"No, they are very inviting. Why wouldn't I want to see a creature that almost violently killed me right when I walk in?"

A faint smile spreads across Ledger's face, and his right dimple pops just a tad. My eyes dart away, willing myself to be unaffected.

"Stiny!" I hear Archie exclaim as a stout older man walks out from behind a curtain to the front desk. He has a rounded belly, a white mustache, and rosy cheeks. His long, white hair is pulled back into a straight ponytail at the nape of his neck.

"Archie, it is so good to see you. I expected you earlier and was about to send Forde to look for you all."

"Well, that was the plan, but we got ambushed by a rogue set of Kerolu. Let's just say they were not overly friendly."

"Those are some nasty creatures; I had a run-in with this guy a few years back. Ended up losing my hand to him but in the end, I got his head." He lifts his left arm revealing a small, rounded nub. I avert my gaze, not wanting to stare for too long.

"Get cleaned up, and I will get some plates of nutriment for you when you're ready. You know I am going to want to know all the details from your little run-in today. Keeps my life exciting." He holds up some rings of jingling keys.

"Oh, trust me, we know, Stiny. We will be back down here soon with all the gory details." Mia steps up to him, grabbing her key and giving him a pat on the shoulder. Everyone else takes their keys greedily, wanting to bathe off the days of travel and gore or maybe just get a moment alone.

"Do you need another room for the lady, Ledger?" He eyes me, and I open my mouth to respond in the affirmative.

"No," Ledger says before I can. I glare at him, and he ignores me, taking the key from Stiny, who wears a wry grin on his face.

"Don't you think if I was going to escape, I would have let you bleed out, taken a horse, and been long gone by now?"

"We are almost back to my kingdom, and I am not taking any chances."

"Does my privacy mean nothing to you?!" I snap in a low whisper at him, my anger spiking.

"Your privacy is none of my concern. When we get to Westray, I'll make sure you have your own quarters; for now, you're with me." His nonchalant tone boils my blood.

He puts the key into the lock as we approach the door and swings it open. It is a simple room with a dresser, and one singular mattress on a sturdy wooden bed frame. The air is stale but smells of rich mahogany.

"Great. One bed. I suppose you're going to vine bound me to the headboard and watch me sleep?"

"If anything, I would 'vine' you to the bathtub and give myself the comfortable bed." I see a flash of a dimple as he walks into the room and straight to the washroom. He sets me gently onto the creaky vanity.

The smell of eucalyptus and lavender permeates the steamy bathroom.

"Someone already brought up some hot water. Get cleaned up and keep that tourniquet on. I don't want you bleeding out in the bath. I'll get some clean clothes for you and medical supplies."

"Anything else, master?"

He looks down at my thigh thoughtfully and then pulls out his dagger. Before I can object, he slices my leggings from ankle to wound. Then drags the tip carefully from my upper thigh to my hip. The flimsy fabric frays and falls limply away from my skin. I snatch the fabric covering myself.

He doesn't look again or wait for my response, just brushes past me. "Do not open the door for anyone." He shuts the door, and I hear the faint click of the lock sliding into place.

"You should have let him bleed out, Layla. This is your fault," I grumble to myself, pushing off the vanity. A whimper escapes me as white-hot pain laces up my leg. I shrug my other leg out of the leggings carefully, eager to scrub the gore and dirt from my body.

The bath looks like heaven. I dip my toe in the water, testing, before lowering my body in with a sigh. I'm careful to leave my injured leg out, but I deeply wish I could submerge it. The wrap dangles, and when I move my leg, it dips into the water, wetting the fabric.

I grit my teeth against the pain emanating from my ribs. My middle is already blue and purple as the bruises set in.

I've never felt such bliss and agony at the same time. Ignoring the discomfort, my eyes drift shut as I enjoy the warming of my skin and the rejoicing of my aching muscles. I submerge my head for several seconds, willing nothingness into my brain, blocking out all the unpleasantries of the last few days.

I grab a cloth sitting on the lid of the tub, dumping lush lilac-smelling liquid onto it. I scrub my skin until it's pink and raw and the water has cooled.

I hear what I assume is Ledger coming back into the room. My toe pops the stopper out, and I watch the dirty-tinged water swirl down the drain.

Sighing, I lift myself out of the bath, squeezing out my hair. Then, I realize my leggings are shredded and my tunic is covered in gore.

Scanning the area, I'm relieved to find a dark green robe hanging on the back of the washroom door.

It appears to be a worn silk material and only comes to my upper thigh, but I'm thankful for it no less. When I put it on, it drapes nicely against my skin.

Opening the door, I see Ledger laying out some clothes on the bed.

"Stiny was able to find me some women's clothing. Not sure how they will fit you, but I figured they would be better than your torn and tarnished...ones." He stops dead in his tracks as he sees me. His eyes drag down my body. He swallows thickly, and his eyes linger before he clears his throat, looking away. He scratches the back of his head before speaking. "Sit down; we need to get those wounds re-wrapped." He juts his chin to the bed a few feet from me while turning to grab whatever supplies he snagged.

I glance down at myself, knowing it's too late to change now and head over to the bed.

Before I can sit, Ledger lowers himself down the front of my body. My eyes nearly bulge out of my head as he passes along all my most sensitive parts until he is kneeling before me.

I brace myself, holding my breath. My hands fist the front of my robe, closing it further, and my eyes drift to the ceiling.

I let out a squeak of surprise when cool metal brushes my thigh. My eyes dart down as he cuts the wrap in two with his sharp dagger. "Would you stop doing that." I say through gritted teeth as the wet fabric slaps onto the ground.

My eyes stay laser focused on Ledger on his hands and knees before me. I nearly quake at the sight of him.

The cool side of the dagger and his fingertips linger on the warmed skin of my thigh.

He studies the wound with a tight jaw. My toes dig into the floor as he blows out a breath.

"So, doc, am I going to live?"

"Sit, Layla," he demands, and I do as I'm told almost immediately. "This is not funny; you could lose your leg if this gets infected." My mouth is suddenly dry, and my palms slick. Wait, was I *nervous?*

Gods, I hope that my sudden feelings for this man are just from near-death experiences and blood loss. There is no other explanation—mere days ago, this man ripped me away from the only place I have ever called home.

The excruciating sting of the alcohol snaps me out of my thoughts. I choke as the cool liquid drips down my leg. Flying back, the bed thuds loudly against the withered wood walls causing particles to dust the air.

"Jesus, Ledger, you could warn me first." I cradle my knee in my hand, carefully keeping the wound facing away from him.

"Give me back your leg; this must be done if you are fond of it."

"Can't someone a little more in tune with emotions do this—like Mia? I'm not one hundred percent convinced you feel pain— or really anything at all."

"Alright, go ahead and stay like that. I'm rather enjoying the view."

Remembering I am in a very small robe, I fling my leg back down, my hands scrambling to the ends of it again and pulling it as far down as I can. "You're a pervert." I glare as I slide back over to him. He wets the rag again, his lip ticking up for a moment.

"Brace yourself." My hands move to the edge of the bed, squeezing, and when the alcohol-drenched rag touches my skin, a pained noise I didn't know I was capable of is thrust from my throat.

Ledger's hand drops as he fists the rag. "How does your healing ability work?" He stands.

"What?" I grit my teeth against the pain in my thigh.

"What do you think about when you heal? What activates your powers?"

"I don't know, Ledger. What does this have to do with anything?"

"Please humor me, Layla. What were you thinking about when you healed me from the Kerolu?"

"I was thinking of things that provoke good feelings: the sunrise, the lagoon we stopped at." I look away from him. "Stuff like that."

"You're not telling me something."

"Well, I can't remember *everything*..."

"Layla." He snarls my name.

"The alcohol wasn't that bad. I'm ready, dump it on the wound."

"Say. It." His demand has me spewing the truth faster than I would spoiled milk.

"Your fingers. I was thinking of how your fingers felt that night when you were distracting me from the dire wolf."

He stiffens at my confession as he stares at me, my cheeks aflame. The silence in the room is deafening as seconds tick by. Ledger slowly lowers to his knees again in front of me. "I'd like to try something with your permission."

"What? Try what?! No, I'm fine, really, I'm not that attached to my leg anyways—" I start to push myself back across the bed, away from him.

His strong hands snake around my calves, pulling me to him. My mouth snaps shut. "Just give me two minutes.

I need you to trust me for two minutes. Can you give me that?" My body is taut, my back rigid, my hands fisting tighter on my robe.

Ledger exhales, his breath skating over the top of my thighs.

His words ricochet around my brain, making my heart thunder. Trust. The only man I've ever trusted is Maddox. Now, my captor of all men, wants me to let down my walls for him. To allow him access to me, and for what? I'm not sure I am even capable of a verbal response.

The second his warm, callused hands ascend on my calves, my resolve begins to melt away. Two minutes. I could allow him two minutes.

"Layla, I need a yes or no."

"Time's ticking." I rasp. His hand pauses before his fingertips slide down one calf. His eyes don't leave mine as his touch caresses my foot, dragging his fingers up the sensitive arch and skimming over each toe. His touch is feather light as he begins his perusal back up.

I shiver, and I'm sure Ledger notices because it seems to spur him on. His green eyes heat as his fingertips deliciously skate along my skin. My brain narrows in on his touch, the sight of him, and all thoughts of anything else vanish. His fingertips glide around my ankle, and the back of my knee. When his powerful hand works its way up my uninjured thigh and squeezes, I nearly groan.

I watch as his tongue darts out to lick his lips. He lowers his mouth to my inner knee and places a kiss there. *Oh hell.* He moves leisurely up my thigh, his warm breath scorching my sensitive skin. He places one more tantalizing kiss on my inner thigh, and it is an effort to stop them from spreading for him.

I let out a shaky breath. Heat pools in my belly, and somewhere in all of that, I can feel the slight tingle of my power awakening as if curious.

"I'm going to lay you back now." His voice is rough, and his scruff grazes my ear as he speaks. He pauses, listening for my answer, and a humiliating squeak of agreement is all I can muster before his corded arm guides me down to the bed.

Ledger knocks my thighs open enough for his knee to slide in between them. I pray he can't feel the radiating heat coming from me. He leans down, his nose skimming where my robe meets in a V between my breasts. He drags it up my chest, following the fabric to my shoulder, his sultry breath fanning across my skin. He tugs the robe down and places a torturous kiss on my bare shoulder.

On instinct, my eyes fall shut, and my head digs into the mattress. My chin tips up ever so slightly, giving him better access.

One of his hands moves to my waist, his incinerating touch soaking through the thin fabric. His nose drags up my clavicle and coasts agonizingly slow up my neck, making my flesh and nipples pebble. My back arches, chasing more.

He shifts above me, and when he does, his hard length caresses my upper thigh. My hands fist in the blanket on either side of me. The urge to touch him, feel his manhood, is almost enough to drive me insane.

His hand moves languidly up my rib cage, and I nearly whimper in frustration when his fingers tighten around my side, his thumb stopping just below my breast.

His mouth, however, continues. His damp lips dust over my hammering pulse point, and I grind my hips into the mattress to keep them from lifting. Unhurriedly, they skim my jaw, making my breath hitch.

His labored breaths match my own as he stops at my mouth. His lips barely brush mine, and I am so lost in the moment, and the feeling of him, the desire for him to keep going, his words barely register when he chokes out, "You're glowing."

I blink, meeting his lush forest-green eyes. I catch a glimpse of his unfiltered desire, a look I'm sure my own face mirrors. We stare at each other for a long moment, catching our breath, the tension almost suffocating.

My eyes drift down our bodies, a faint glow emanating from my pale, buzzing skin. Ledger stays stock still, hovering inches above me. I notice he hasn't showered or changed yet. That small detail, the fact he is taking care of my needs before his own, gives me a surge of satisfaction.

The skin on my thigh is now unmarred, slightly pink, and smooth. I touch the milky skin of my belly and am met with no pain.

The bed shifts as Ledger's hand comes up to rest on my thigh, his thumb trailing over the freshly healed skin. "You're remarkable." He looks incredulously at me.

All I can do is stare dumbly at him, processing that he just seduced me into healing myself. *I actually healed myself.*

His fingers tighten on my thigh and his eyes trail up my body. When they land on my face, they linger on my lips. I run my hand over his forearm and up his bicep. When I get to his neck, I pull gently, lifting my head a fraction of an inch, itching to taste him.

Ledger makes a faint throaty groan, abruptly dropping my thigh as he unravels from me and pushes back.

His sudden absence feels like a bucket of ice water being thrown upon me. I jolt up and grab the robe, hugging it to me tightly. Disappointment fills my veins, and it's a struggle to keep it off my face.

There is a thick silence in the room as we both collect ourselves. I keep my eyes firmly on the ground. I can feel Ledger's presence everywhere, the scent of cedar and leather clogging my senses.

"Layla." My name on his lips sounds tortured. "You must understand. I refuse to take any more from you than what I have already demanded."

"I'd like to get dressed." I feel too exposed, too vulnerable, and if he didn't give me space, I knew I would bolt, tiny silk robe and all.

He pauses for a pregnant moment before nodding and walking into the bathroom. The door shuts with a click.

A man has never made me feel even half of what I'd felt in those minutes. The worst part was he'd barely touched me, hadn't even kissed me. I was grateful he'd stopped it. I *should* have stopped it myself.

My face falls into my hands, and I groan. "Get a grip, Layla."

I look at my stomach again, no bruising to be seen. I did that; I used my powers on myself. I get a glimpse of my thigh and marvel at the freshly healed skin. Just moments ago, it was an open, jagged wound. I stand up, testing it and moving my leg around, not a twinge of pain. This is something so foreign, something I was sure was not possible. I wonder if I can do it again.

I hear Ledger shuffling in the bathroom, and yank on the clothes he brought up. They are simple: some undergarments, a pair of britches, and a black top, both big, but I am grateful, nonetheless.

I'm pulling on my boots when Mia walks through the wall into our room. She looks gorgeous, her brown skin and black hair now clean and luminous.

"Hey, I thought I'd check on you two. Make sure you haven't put that dagger Ledger gave you to use on him yet."

"You can walk through walls?!" It hadn't occurred to me; I had not seen Mia's powers in action yet.

"Walls, doors, trees, an array of objects, really." She shrugs, walking in further. "Where's Ledger?"

"He's in the bathroom."

She raises her eyebrow, and a sly grin comes over her full lips. "Shall we go get some wine?"

"Please." I nearly jump off the bed at the offer.

"First, let me fix your hair, what in the Gods' name were you doing after your bath?"

A blush breaks out on my face, and I try to hide it from her as she fixes strands of my hair.

"Oh, girl, I totally get it. Where do you think I've been for the past hour? Travel gets long; I'd be a crazy person if I didn't take care of my needs occasionally." She gives me a wink, and I smile awkwardly back.

CHAPTER
TWELVE

Mia and I shimmy up the mahogany bar. The floor is sticky, and the air smells faintly of stale beer. Stiny is behind it serving other patrons, his bold laugh filling the air as he produces frothy pints. "Ladies," he greets as he saddles up to us. "What can I get you?"

"Two glasses of wine, please, kind sir," Mia answers.

"Coming right up." Stiny fishes out two thick-rimmed glasses and fills them with a deep red liquid. "Why don't you take these to a table, and I'll bring you out our special, roasted boar and leeks." He winks at us.

"Sure thing, Stin." Mia grabs our glasses, and we move to a table. I barely swallow a sip of the rich liquid before Ledger comes storming down the stairs. His eyes are wild as he scans the inn.

When they fall on us, I see something akin to relief flicker across his features, before being replaced by anger. He thunders towards us, his hair still wet and dripping. I dare a side glance at Mia and see her rolling her eyes.

"Why did you leave the room? It isn't safe for you to be down here without me. You have no idea of the kind of people that frequent these places." He braces his hands on the table.

"I wasn't aware you wanted to be in control of my every move. Unfortunately for you, I am not a dog and cannot simply be told what to do and when to do it. If you didn't want me to leave the room, you should have used those vines you like so much." I can feel anger licking at my skin as I grate out the words.

"Oh, don't tempt me, blondie. The night is still young." His eyebrow raises in challenge and my palm itches to smack him.

"Ledger, get your hands off the table and calm down. I came into the room and got her. Now, go back upstairs and dry yourself, you're dripping on me." Mia flicks a water droplet off her arm. "I'll have Stiny get you a whisky and some boar."

His eyes leave mine for a second to briefly look at Mia. "Do not let her out of your sight." With that, he pushes off the table and marches back upstairs.

"Don't let him get to you. He's rough around the edges, but underneath all of that, he's an honorable, good man."

I snort as we both take long pulls of our wine. It is rich, heady, fruity, and just what I need after this nightmare of a day.

"He's been through a lot; he's lost his mother, then his sister. He'd do anything for the ones he loves."

I pause at her words, wondering what it would feel like to be loved like that.

My head swims happily as Archie comes to sit with us. "Ladies," he greets and drops down in his seat. He's freshly shaven, and his skin is clear of the gore from the day. Looking at us now, it would be hard to determine we'd been through anything at all.

"You both clean up nice." His hand finds mine and he places a gentle kiss there. This clean, he looks almost younger, and I grin at his charm.

"I could say the same to you," Stiny places the most delectable-smelling food in front of Mia and me seconds later.

Archie drops my hand and immediately takes a bite of Mia's food, earning a slug from her. He closes his eyes and moans. "Stiny, I need at least three bowls of this and a pint, please. And send my utmost compliments to the chef. You're a lucky man getting to eat like this every day."

"Don't I know it," Stiny chuckles and walks back towards the kitchen.

A moment later, a beautiful dark-haired girl passes our table and sidles up to the bar. Archie spots her immediately, and his eyes follow her. "Ladies, while I value your company,

I have been stuck in the woods for weeks. I saw my life flash before my eyes today, and tomorrow is not promised. So, excuse me while I share both my harrowing story and matching scar with the stunning lady at the bar. Thanks again for that, Lay. Oh, and have Stiny send my food over." He winks.

I feel a pang in my chest at the familiar nickname, thinking of Maddox. "Good luck." I smile a little sadly after him.

"We will be here when she turns you down," Mia calls after him. Archie makes an obscene gesture at her with his finger from behind his back as he approaches the brown-eyed beauty, and Mia chuckles next to me.

"You two are like brother and sister."

"Yeah. Ledger, Archie, and I grew up together. Cam is Archie's little cousin. He begged his aunt to let him take Cam when he started to come into his powers. He didn't want him to go through what he went through. She was reluctant but eventually gave in and let Archie sneak him out of Bellehaven. We've all been inseparable since we were little. I take it as my job to check Archie's ego and bring him back down. Women, unfortunately for them, usually eat up every word he says, and the Gods gave him that face to back it up. Could be a dangerous combination."

"Thank heavens he has you." We laugh and cheers to that. "Where is Cam anyways?"

"If I had to guess, probably in his room. He's a little introverted and likes his alone time when he gets it."

"I completely understand."

"How are your wounds? I noticed you weren't limping."

"Yeah, they are good, I'm fine." I take a bite of food, looking away from Mia.

"What do you mean you're fine? Your thigh was shredded?! Did you heal yourself?" She looks at me expectantly.

I pause, chewing thoughtfully. "Yes, I healed myself." I keep my answer short and hope she will move on.

"Oh, well, that's great, so you figured out how to make your power work on yourself? What would happen right now if I stabbed you?"

"Maybe don't do that. I'm still working on it. It was either suffer under Ledger's horrible nursing care or heal, so I chose the latter."

"Speak of the devil himself," Mia exclaims as Ledger drops into the chair Archie was in earlier.

His beard is trimmed, his black hair damp, his shirt rolled up, tanned forearms resting on the table. My face grows warm as I remember what those forearms looked like as he held himself above me.

He doesn't seem angry anymore.

Averting my eyes, I take a long drink of wine. "Layla was just telling me you were the reason she was able to heal her leg," Mia says, and I promptly choke on the wine, sending me into a coughing fit. "Are you okay?" Mia pats me on the back.

"Water," I choke out. "Could you get me some water?"

"I'll be right back; I hate when it goes down the wrong way."

When I manage a look at Ledger, he is sitting across from me with a grin, one of his beautiful dimples on display.

"Wipe that look off your face. That is absolutely not what I said. If you tell anyone about what happened in that room, I swear I will feed myself willingly to a Kerolu."

"Your secret is safe with me." His grin remains as he watches me squirm under his gaze.

Mia comes back with a whisky and water in her hands. I continue eating while looking around the room, keeping my eyes off Ledger. I grimace, seeing a grotesque-looking boar head mounted across the room. "Must they have the head of the boar, that was probably viciously killed for this meal, staring at me as I eat?"

Mia snickers next to me. "They could use a little help decorating, but I love it here—it has a certain charm about it."

"I suppose if you can look past all the stuffed creatures. What is that one?" I point to a particularly horrifying creature on the wall. Its head resembles a horse, but the nose is all bones, and the mouth has serrated pointed teeth. Why did everything have such sharp teeth?

"That's a Suttug. You don't see many of them these days. They used to serve humans. It's legend that once we could draw from them. They had the ability to make you extremely powerful once bonded but humans got greedy, took too much, exploited them. They either died off or went into hiding." I consider Mia's words while staring at the Suttug, feeling a jolt of sadness for the creature.

A woman about my age brings out a plate of food to Ledger. They seem familiar with each other as she drops effortlessly into the chair beside him. Her hands work their way to his shoulders as she whispers something in his ear. His response makes her giggle, and the food in my stomach instantly sours.

My teeth clench as I swipe my glass of wine off the table and finish the contents in one gulp. Her fingers stroke the hair at the nape of his neck, and I'm shocked at the visceral jealousy that assaults me.

The feeling is so intense, so confusing I can't bear to sit any longer. I excuse myself by mumbling something about the washroom to Mia.

I avoid Ledger completely as I beeline through the dining area in the opposite direction of them. I only get a few steps before I promptly run into a hard chest. A pair of large hands reach out to steady me.

"Sorry," I exclaim, craning my neck up to meet a very tall red-headed man.

"My apologies, I was not looking where I was going," the man starts, and once I'm steady, he releases me. "You don't look familiar, I'm Forde," he sticks out that sizable hand of his.

"Are you Stiny's son?" I shake his hand remembering his name from earlier.

"The one and only. Now I feel at a disadvantage. Who might you be? I'm positive I would remember someone so striking."

"I'm Layla Sutton from Bellehaven."

"You're a long way from Bellehaven. What brings you this way?" he questions, and before I can answer, he chuckles, looking past me. "You must be with Ledger's crew."

Looking over my shoulder I see Ledger glaring intensely over at us. The busty blonde from earlier is now playing with the back of his hair while she drapes over the side of his body.

I roll my eyes and look away, my stomach twisting. "I suppose you could say that."

"Well, it would be grossly wrong of me to run into someone so exquisite and not have the opportunity to buy her a drink. Would you do me the honor?"

With one more quick glance over my shoulder, I agree following Forde to the bar.

Moments later, Stiny places a pint and another glass of wine in front of us. "You watch yourself now, Forde. She's with Ledger, and we don't need you creating any problems."

"*Me* create problems? I wouldn't dream of it, Stine." He grabs his pint and takes a sip, a grin playing out on his face. Stiny grunts and takes the order of a customer at the bar.

I bristle, feeling a bit uneasy, but try to keep the conversation going. "So, are you a tracker?" I ask, taking a generous pull of my wine.

"One of the best trackers in all of Grimwood."

"Modest," I respond, smiling.

"There is no point in lying, and if I'm being honest, I'd like to impress you."

"Consider me impressed, we ran into a pack of Kerolu today. I can't imagine tracking and encountering those creatures intentionally."

"Someone must keep them from spreading too far across the lands. We offer population control, and their furs sell for a high price in the markets."

"I bet, but why you'd ever want to snuggle up in Kerolu fur is beyond me." I grimace.

Forde laughs. "I like you, Layla. Tell me, how'd you get mixed up in Ledger's crew?"

I pause, thinking of how much I should divulge. This is someone who knows the lands and the creatures and could be my opportunity to get back to Bellehaven. I frown at the thought, wondering when my desire to return had faded.

Returning to the castle walls and the wretched King holds little appeal to me now. Thinking of returning to the drab castle makes me claustrophobic. Beyond seeing Maddox and my mother again, I can't think of anything I want less.

The thoughts scare and confuse me. What is my life without Bellehaven, without Maddox, and would the King ever really let me live peacefully outside of his kingdom?

I pause my thoughts, seeing Forde's expectant look. "It's a long, unfortunate story, and I wouldn't want to bore you." I wave him off and glance over at Ledger. His eyes are still trained on Forde and me, a quiet simmering rage behind them.

"Ledger seems like a big fan of yours," I pan, looking away.

"He's never really liked me since I was involved with his sister. Even less when she wandered over to Grimwood a year back. Ledger came to us frantic one night, asking for our help tracking her. We agreed but ran into a pack of wild boar not long after we set out. We found her tracks after a few hours, but by the time we came across her, she had already met her unfortunate demise. All that was left was one of the silly little flower crowns she always insisted on wearing."

My stomach twists.

"Ledger went insane; he killed every last one of the Kerolu responsible. I'm sure a part of him still blames me for not doing more, for us not getting there sooner."

My mouth hangs open; whatever I expected him to say, it certainly wasn't that. I set my drink down, suddenly sick. "That's horrible," I respond as Forde's hand finds my arm. He grips it softly as if to offer some kind of comfort. It doesn't feel warm and reassuring; it feels cold, wrong.

I jump as a dagger is slammed into the bar top, the tip securing Forde's sleeve. My arm is torn out of his grip. I see

Archie out of the corner of my eye start to creep towards us with his hand on his own dagger.

"If I hear my name or my family's name come from your mouth again, I will cut out your tongue." Ledger's voice is laced with fury. His face is threateningly close to Forde's.

Forde doesn't even flinch as he takes a sip of his pint. "My sincerest apologies, Ledger. The last thing I would want to do is upset you." His words don't come out as sincere; the look on his face almost taunting.

I frown, looking back and forth between them. Ledger looks like he is contemplating killing him.

"Ledge, what do you say we call it a night? It's been a long day." Archie appears, his hand going to Ledger's shoulder and putting light pressure there.

Ledger's eyes don't leave Forde, his gaze intense and furious. "Ledger," Archie tries again.

I reach my hands out, lightly touching his forearm. At that, his eyes leave Forde's to glance down.

He yanks the dagger out of the wood, the sharp side of the knife nicking Forde's arm. Blood instantly stains the fabric. I notice that, for once, my power doesn't react.

"You stay away from her," he threatens as he abruptly turns, grabbing my hand and leading me out of the bar.

When we make it back to the room, he slams the door, making me wince. I stand awkwardly as he takes a few deep, steadying breaths. "Stay away from him, Layla."

"Okay, maybe we should go to bed. Archie was right, it's been a long day." I can't bring myself argue with him.

"I'll sleep on the floor." Ledger grabs a folded blanket from the foot of the bed and a pillow.

I sit, watching him. Forde's earlier words swirl in my head, an ache forming for him in my heart.

"Do not look at me like that." His movements tense as he unfolds a blanket with too much force, snapping it against the floorboards.

"I'm not looking at you like anything," I reply flatly.

Ledger removes his shirt with one hand, balling it up and throwing it in the corner. He steps out of his trousers and blows out the lanterns.

I lay on my side, staring at the outline of his body as the moon emits a soft glow through the window. Ledger lays down, tossing and turning for a few moments, punching his pillow and huffing back down.

His back is to me, and I can see it moving up and down as he breathes. The bed seems too big and too suffocating all at the same time. I sigh and then make up my mind. Grabbing my pillow, I shuffle over to Ledger. I toss it down next to him and lower myself to the ground.

"Layla," he growls. "What are you doing?"

"I'd rather be down here with you."

"Get back up on the bed."

"No."

"Layla," he grits.

"Ledger," I snap back. "There is no reason for me to be on a comfortable bed while you sleep on the hard floor. If you sleep down here, so do I."

"You're infuriating," he snaps.

I don't respond, instead turn on my side and watch him. He is on his back now staring up at the ceiling.

"Thank you for helping me heal myself today." My voice is soft, and I swear I see Ledger stop breathing at my words.

"Do not thank me for that." His lip curls.

I shift onto my back, mirroring Ledger. "I'm sorry about your sister."

We stay silent for a long moment, staring at the ceiling. Just when I think he's fallen asleep, he speaks. "Legend says that a Kerolu's venom, when extracted and mixed with the right herbs, can have healing properties." I don't move, don't dare breathe too loud in fear that he will stop speaking. "My father had been sick for a long time, and the healing solutions we had been giving him were getting less and less effective. My sister got the idea one day she was going to get the Kerolu venom. She snuck out one night and rode to Grimwood, hoping to find a pack of Kerolu. I'm not sure what she was thinking or what her plan was, only that she was desperate.

"When I realized she was gone, I rode to Grimwood— and...you've heard the rest." His voice cracks. "If she would have just waited, knew we had other options." He pauses. "Knew you existed. She would still be here." The raw emotion in Ledger's voice makes my heart squeeze. My power thrashes inside of me, wanting to help, wanting to fix, but there is no physical wound to be mended.

"The worst part is that Forde could have brought her a Kerolu claw and given her the venom so she could have put that thought to rest. I'm sure it wouldn't have worked, but it could have at least purged the thought from her mind. She told me she'd asked him for it, and he'd laughed at her, told her it was the ramblings of a crazy woman."

I reach my hand out tentatively brushing his knuckles with my fingertips not knowing what to say. The silence lingers before I speak. "Is that what you need my powers for? Your father?" When he doesn't answer, I continue, "I can't bring your sister back, but I'll do whatever is in my power to help. I know what it's like to lose the people you care about." Ledger hand turns and his thumb brushes mine. We lay like that for quite some time, close but hardly touching.

"Have you ever worked on someone with the nullifying ability?" Ledger's question is so soft I hardly hear it.

"You mean someone that can nullify powers?" He stiffens almost imperceptibly at my question, but nods. "Not to my knowledge. I can't imagine my powers would work on someone with such an ability." I frown, and Ledger falls silent. When I look over at him, his brow is drawn, and his face is laced with an emotion I can't quite place. "Why do you ask?"

"Just curious."

"I wasn't able to save my father." I offer up a small piece of myself after he falls silent again. "Sandor confronted him at our home and when he spat at his feet the King speared him right through the chest with a sword. My mother woke me in a panic and carried me outside. My ability was starting to emerge, but I was so young and unpracticed." I reach for the power inside of me as a small comfort, and it warms in response.

"She begged for me to heal him, pleaded, and wailed as I tried desperately to conjure my power. I was so scared, so horrified, I couldn't even manage a small spark of energy. His warm blood soaked into the soles of my bare feet and then stayed crusted there for days after, until they allowed me to bathe."

The scene flashes in my mind, fresh and as terrifying as the day it happened. "Your blood, Layla, it is in your very blood." That sentence was the last thing my father had ever said to me. The words made as much sense to me now as they did the night he'd perished. I shake the echoing words from my head and continue, "His eyes had barely closed when the guards seized me, leaving my mother wailing in the streets holding his lifeless body."

I don't need to turn back to Ledger to feel his eyes on me. "I was wrong about you. You are so much stronger than you give yourself credit for." As he says the words his fingertips stroke mine. The small act somehow more intimate than I could have imagined.

He doesn't offer cheap words, instead a deep under-standing. I lay next to this man, my captor, feeling strangely safe and, for the first time in a long time, seen.

I rouse, being set in a soft bed, my bones aching from the hard ground. Warm arms release me, and I protest.

"Stay." The word is a foreign request on my tongue.

I swear I feel the ghost of a touch slide against my cheek.

And though my request goes unanswered his words drift into my ears, distant and hazy under the cloud of sleep taking over. "You're going to ruin me."

CHAPTER
THIRTEEN

It's quiet in the room the next morning, and I swallow my disappointment when I realize Ledger is gone. I go to sit up and realize a vine is twined around my wrist to the bed. I growl and yank at it, making it tighten.

"Really, Ledger?" There is a small nail sticking out of the wooden bed frame by my wrist, and I drag the vine over it.

I use the rusted edge to whittle away at the stem little by little until it snaps in half. Pulling my clothes on for the day, I strap the dagger Ledger had given me to my thigh. Mia had been nice enough to lend me a sheath for it.

I decide to go find Ledger and give him a piece of my mind. Grabbing the new cloak he found me, I throw open my door and tromp down the stairs.

I stop in the kitchens to grab a few apples and carrots to offer to Apollo.

The morning air is crisp as I step outside. A shiver works its way up my spine, and I savor the cool breeze enjoying the way it drifts over my skin.

Standing and relishing the feeling for another minute, I throw on the cloak. The rough wool scratches against my skin and warms me almost instantly.

The smell of hay hangs in the air as I enter. Apollo knickers as I approach; he looks saddled up and ready for the day. The stables are surprisingly clean and spacious. Saddles, bridles and grooming supplies line the walls.

"Hey, boy." I rub his nose and the white patch I like between his eyes. Holding out my offering to him, he sniffs curiously before accepting and nudging me with his head. I stroke his neck as he eats. "Do you want to know something? I used to dislike horses, but I fear you might have won me over." He nudges me again, and I smile, offering him another apple.

Apollo tenses mid-bite before pushing me roughly toward the open barn doors. I stumble back, almost falling. "Whoa, buddy, what's wrong?" I step closer to him, and he shakes his head, blowing out his nose harshly and trying to push me again.

I frown, confused until I sense another presence. My hackles rise as I turn around. My breath halts when I see Forde and a man I don't recognize standing beside him.

"Good morning, Layla," Forde greets, striding closer to me. My stomach somersaults uncomfortably, and I stagger back a step. His friend pushes one of the stable doors closed.

"Good morning, gentlemen. Forde, it's nice to see you again." I put on a pleasant look and stand a little straighter grabbing onto Apollo's reins.

"Oh, it's a pleasure to see you again, and alone! Where is Ledger? I thought for sure he would be with you?" The look in Forde's eyes can only be described as predatory.

"He ran out for some last-minute supplies; he should be back any minute." I lie as smoothly as I can.

Forde looks at his friend on the right, and he shakes his head no. "Anders here senses a lie. What reason do you have to lie, Layla?" They take a few more steps toward me. My hands fall away from Apollo, and he bristles next to me.

"You know what I learned last night?" Forde continues when I don't respond. He takes another step, holding out his hand to halt Anders. "After you revealed you were from Bellehaven, I did a little digging and learned that King Sandor has recently misplaced his healer." My heart pounds in my chest. "He's offering quite the reward for her return. Would you happen to know anything about that?"

His lip tips up as he waits for my response. "No, I can't say I do." My eyes flick to Anders and then to the open stable door.

"She's lying," Anders announces.

"I don't like liars, Layla." Forde's eyes narrow as he studies me. "You're a long way from where you should be. Come with us; we will take you back. I'll even consider giving you some of the reward."

My body tenses as he gets closer. "I won't go with you." I step back, and my heel hits the wall. I'd made a promise to Ledger, but more than that I didn't *want* to go back.

"I was hoping you'd say that. Do you know what I love most about the hunt?"

Apollo gives an agitated squeal from beside me. Forde is close enough now I can smell the scent of stale beer and the musk of his cologne.

"I like it when the animal doesn't make it easy for me." His hand raises, and I try not to flinch as his fingers brush my cheek. "I like the chase. But do you want to know what I love the most?" His breath fans over my face and his fingers graze over the pulse point fluttering wildly in my neck. My skin crawls, but I stand my ground. I hold his gaze as my hand inches toward the dagger strapped to my thigh.

Apollo's hoof slams into the barn door behind him, and I jump. I brush the hilt of my dagger, clasping my hand around the cold metal.

Moving as quickly as I can, I yank the blade up and attempt to find purchase in the soft skin of Forde's belly. I'm fast, but he is faster, his large hand closes around my wrist tightly.

He squeezes and twists my wrist in an unnatural position, making me gasp, and I drop the dagger. He catches it with his other hand in midair and slashes it against my cheek. I recoil against the sting.

"The fight—I like the fight." His hand seizes my face, his fingers digging into the skin of my jaw. He brings his mouth to my ear. "Fight me, Layla."

My knee lifts to connect with the sensitive flesh between his legs, but he catches my thigh. He yanks it roughly, and I lose my footing. My back slams into the ground kicking up a cloud of dust.

The air is forced from my lungs, and I gasp rolling over onto my knees. Before I can get my feet beneath me, his foot slams into my stomach. Pain explodes in my right side as my body is thrown back to the ground. I skid across the stable floor. My head swims from the lack of oxygen as I struggle to pull in even the smallest of breaths.

Apollo bucks unhappily as he pulls at his restraints. Forde stalks over to me, grabbing a handful of my hair and yanking on it painfully. "I wish we could stick around to see the look on Ledger's face." He looks back to Anders with a wicked grin and yanks me forward.

I scramble across the ground, scratching at his closed fist. The stinging from my scalp makes my eyes water.

He doesn't release my hair as he drags me to a horse that must be his. He pulls out some rope from the saddle bag and tosses it to Anders. "Tie her ankles." I struggle against his tightening grip.

Just as Anders grabs my ankle, I manage to elbow Forde in the ribs, and his grip falters. I fall onto my ass and kick out. My foot ricochets off Anders' face, and I scramble to my feet, running towards the open stable doors.

I don't get far before the cloak I'm wearing tightens around my neck, and I'm yanked back with full strength. My head pings off the earth so hard I see stars.

The stench of hay and manure choke me as I roll to my side. I push to my knees blindly, my eyes struggling to focus.

"I knew this was going to be fun." Forde's taunt cuts through my haze, and I force my legs to stand.

Apollo snorts angrily, and his hooves dance across the stable floors.

Anders rushes me, his stubby hands grasping onto the thin material of my tunic. The fabric rips as I push away from him, and the cold air assaults my bare skin. My undergarment is exposed along with my stomach.

He dives for me again, and I send my knuckles at his face. They make contact, and he grabs at his nose, crimson seeping through his fingers.

I turn, sprinting towards the exit. I feel the warmth of the sun, can taste my freedom as I reach the open doors.

Pain erupts beneath my skin; a weak scream tears from my throat before being stolen by utter agony. My body crumples to the ground, contorting and seizing. My ears ring.

Forde appears above me, smiling. His hand is raised, and his fingers dance as pain radiates through me.

The only thing I can think about is how many creatures had to go through this agony. How many creatures had this cruel ending, Forde's malevolent face being the last thing they ever saw.

Anders comes into view. His expression is that of pure wrath as scarlet stains his face and hands. Terror grips me as he clutches onto my legs, wrapping the rough rope around my ankles.

I writhe on the ground as Forde drags me by the rope back into the gods forsaken stable, a look of sick satisfaction breaking out on his face. I struggle to breathe, gasping for air, and try to find room in my lungs around the blinding pain.

A dull thud draws my attention as Anders drops limply to the ground. He fingers a dagger that is now embedded deep into his neck. His eyes go wide, ruby-red blood leaking out onto his pale skin. A strained choking noise escapes his mouth before his eyes go blank.

The pain in my body mercifully ceases, and my limbs twitch with the aftershocks. I lay listlessly on the ground, covered in a damp sweat.

Ledger steps into view, and a gray smoke pours from his hands. Vines hold Forde in place as his neck muscles bulge, fighting against Ledger's siphoning power as he pushes it down his throat. The air vibrates as I push myself up onto weak arms.

Forde sloppily throws daggers at Ledger, all of which he easily sidesteps. Fury laces his features, and though it's not directed at me, I can't stop the bolt of fear that tingles through me.

One of the daggers Forde throws glints in the sun a few feet away, stealing my attention. I realize it's mine, and I drag myself over to it, only able to breathe once the hilt is clasped in my trembling hand. I slice at the thick rope encasing my ankles until it drops away.

Forde's face turns a light shade of purple and spit drips down his chin as he struggles. Ledger descends on him, his vines snaking back into the ground. He slams his fist into Forde's face, knocking him back a few feet. He follows it with another blow to Forde's stomach that sends the air wheezing out of him.

Forde sways, a sickening crunch filling the air as Ledger's fist connects with his nose. He falls backward onto the ground, and Ledger wastes no time straddling him. He punches him again and again until Forde's face is a bloodied mess, the ground beneath him wet and tinged red.

The nauseating realization hits me that if he doesn't stop soon, he will no doubt kill him. "Ledger." My voice is weaker than I'd like. It takes him a moment, but his eyes eventually snap to me. They are crazed and distant, and I barely recognize him.

It looks like it takes him considerable effort to unclench his fists.

"The only reason you are not dead is out of respect for Stiny. Make no mistake, if you ever come near her again, I won't hesitate to make your death slow and painful. This is your one pass."

In one fluid motion, Ledger's dagger pierces through Forde's palm. The blade goes straight through, sinking deep into the earth. A strangled noise escapes him, and Ledger stands, going to me without looking back.

Forde lets out a garbled laugh. "You'll pay for that one, Ledger. I hope she is worth it." I frown at his words as Ledger approaches me, undoing his cloak and wrapping it around my exposed skin.

There is a slight tremor in his hands as his arm snakes around me, steadying me as he turns and leads us back to the inn.

He is patient, walking slowly, taking most of my weight. His power pulses off him in violent waves, making the hair on my arms stand on end.

I lean into him, soaking up his warmth, breathing him in, and letting his presence calm my rapid heart. "What the fuck were you *thinking*, Layla? You were supposed to stay in the room."

"Don't you think I know that, Ledger? Did you really have to bind me to the bed? I thought after last night we had formed some sort of trust between us."

"It's not about trust; it is about keeping you safe. I did it because you don't seem to have a semblance of regard for yourself, and when left to your own devices, you end up in situations like this."

His words shock me, and I struggle for a response. "I didn't know—wasn't aware of the danger." I stumble over my words. "King Sandor put out a reward for my return." Ledger curses under his breath.

Archie is quietly shutting the door to a room, disheveled and half-dressed when we pass him. He gives us a double take. "What in the hell happened? The sun has barely risen, and you two look like this?!"

"Forde happened. He was trying to take Layla back to Bellehaven to claim the reward King Sandor is offering for her return," Ledger says through clenched teeth. "Get the horses ready, we have to leave now."

"Jesus, I'm on it. Make sure she's okay." He nods towards me, and I look away, humiliated.

When we get to the room, Ledger sits me gently on the bed. I grip his cloak and my dagger like they are lifelines. I stare at my white knuckles, not ready to meet his eyes.

"Why were you in the stables?" He stomps to the bathroom.

"I was looking for you and wanted to see Apollo before we left. It was stupid."

"Yes, Layla, it was stupid." Ledger kneels in front of me and gently presses a wet rag to my cheek. I wince at the sting of alcohol and dare a glance at his face. He is eerily calm, his features stone cold. I can tell what he is feeling in the flaring of his nostrils as he stares at the cut on my cheek.

Our gazes collide, his green eyes holding mine hostage before he abruptly looks away, standing. The rag falls away limply in his hand.

His body is tense, his movements jerky as he throws a few things into his bag. "We need to leave. Can you ride?" He takes out a plain shirt and hands it to me.

"Yes." I take the offering, grimacing as I stand. My ribs scream in pain.

Ledger's eyes harden. "Put it on." His voice is quiet, re-strained. He turns his back to give me a moment of privacy. I pause before gingerly removing the cloak and torn tunic, trying not to jostle my ribs.

I slide the garment on, and Ledger doesn't wait for my response before turning around. His lips curl as he looks at my tattered top on the ground. "Lift up your shirt."

My mouth falls open slightly, wanting to deny his re-quest. I realize in my current state, riding Apollo will be ex-tremely uncomfortable.

My hands play with the hem of the shirt as I take in Led-ger's still form. He stares at me with a blank expression.

I raise the corner. The skin on my left ribs is no longer pale but an angry cherry red, blotches of purple spreading. Ledger glances down. I fear he will crack a tooth because of how hard he clenches his jaw. He stiffly walks to the bath-room, coming back with a roll of stretchy bandages.

"I'll need to wrap your ribs, or we won't make it very far." He approaches and I nod.

He bends down, unrolling the bandages. His fingertips dig lightly into my back. He huffs a breath that drifts over my skin. I bite my lip as my head drops back to count the nails on the patched ceiling.

His other hand shifts to my bare hip and my breath stalls in my lungs. His calluses scrape against my skin as he moves, and I fight to stay still. He's gentle as he maneuvers, so at war with his stiff posture and stoic face.

I flinch when he wraps the bandage firmly around the most sensitive part of my rib. He pauses, grinding his teeth together before continuing. My head spins as his fingertips skate over the flesh of my stomach.

He finally ties the bandage in place. He tugs the hem of my shirt softly, and the fabric falls, covering my torso. "We need to leave," is all he says before turning from me, grabbing his bag, and walking to the door.

CHAPTER
FOURTEEN

I LOOK DUMBLY AT HIS BACK, MY BRAIN AND BODY STILL reeling.

"Do you need me to carry you?" Ledger's back is still to me and my cheeks heat at his words.

God, I've never felt more pathetic than I do at this moment.

Indignation fills my veins at being assaulted and not being able to properly defend myself. I am sick of being a victim, sick of being weak and compliant. I never want to feel this way again. "I'd sooner throw myself down the stairs." I spit as I push past Ledger, ignoring the pounding of my head and the aching in my ribs. Weakness was something I was done feeling and refused to show.

I march right out of the inn and straight over to our horses. Cam is in his saddle on high alert as he scans the area.

Mia and Archie are whispering to each other and as I approach, they swiftly stop, looking at me cautiously.

Mia walks over as I grab the pommel of Apollo's saddle. The movement sends a sharp pain radiating through my chest.

"You okay?" Mia's voice is soft as she gently palms my shoulder. When I glance over at her, her brows are furrowed, and she looks genuinely concerned.

"I'm fine."

"I'm glad you fought back," she says, and I pause for a moment considering her words.

"Barely. He was seconds away from tossing me onto his horse and parading me back to Bellehaven. I want you to train me. I want to be able to really fight back." I have been so sheltered my entire life and have relied on Maddox for too much. I am sick of being a victim, sick of having not even a semblance of control over my life.

A small smile spreads across her face. "Gladly."

"Okay, we start when we arrive in Westray." I walk to Apollo. He nudges my middle gently. I wrap my arms around him and pat his neck as he nuzzles in further. "I'm okay, buddy; you did good back there."

Ledger studies our interaction.

When I'm ready, I grit my teeth, stepping into the stirrup and pulling myself into the saddle. The pain steals my breath, and it's an effort to keep my face blank.

I try to take some steadying breaths but with the tight bandages and my hurt rib, I barely manage a few unsatisfying gasps.

Archie appears, holding up a flask. "To help with the pain." He glances back. "Don't tell Ledger," He winks.

"Thanks, Archie." I grab the flask from him, unscrewing it and taking a sniff. It has a sharp, stringent odor that nearly makes me retch. Before I can talk myself out of it, I take a sip, sputtering. "That has to be the most disgusting thing I have ever tasted." I wipe my mouth with the back of my hand, grimacing.

"That's how you know it's the good stuff." He wiggles his eyebrows and walks away.

Ledger approaches, and I keep my eyes stubbornly ahead. Archie and he have a hushed conversation, and I nudge Apollo with my ankles.

To my surprise, he complies and begins trotting. I have to bite back my smile at the stunned look on Ledger's face as he jogs after us, grabbing Apollo's pommel and sweeping up behind me gracefully.

It takes him a moment to recover, but once he does, he reaches for the reins. "Brace yourself, blondie, this isn't going to be a pleasant day for you."

"No day that I'm stuck on this horse with you is a pleasant day, Ledger."

With that, he gives Apollo a soft kick and we set out for the day. The first hour of the ride is rough. Every jostle of my ribs sends shooting pains throughout my chest. I wince as I take small sips of the liquor, gritting through the pain.

My head spins as I shift, trying to find less painful positions.

Visions of the knife sinking into Anders' neck fill my thoughts, but I can't seem to find any remorse. I channel my indignation at the events into resolve. I should have shown up to more of Maddox's training sessions. I'm sure he will be thrilled when I tell him he was right.

I struggle to breathe sucking in pitiful gasps of air. My back aches from trying to keep still and straight. Ledger's hand eventually snakes around my injured rib, warm and steady.

"What are you doing?" I tense under his touch

"I don't enjoy seeing you in pain, and now that I've gained control of my emotions again—I'd like to attempt to ease it." I don't have a clue what he is referring to but realize when I lean into his touch that some part of me innately trusts him.

"You can do that?"

"I can attempt. It's difficult to do and if my concentration slips, I could siphon your power. If you can, hold completely still."

His power cools my heated skin as it seeps into me. It feels so different than I remember. It isn't unpleasant. I can feel the pull of him drawing from me, but it's not accompanied by pain. Instead, relief throbs through me, the twinges of pain fading until they are a faint pulse.

I take a deep breath as his power recedes back into him. His palm falls away.

My hand replaces his prodding the area gently. I turn my head to the side to peek up at him.

"Thank you." I know little about siphoning power but can tell by his change in posture that he'd taken my discomfort and made it his own. "You shouldn't have done that."

"You would have done it for me, or anyone here for that matter." He shifts in the saddle. "You can save my life twice and I can't take some of your pain?"

"Well, when you put it that way," I smile. "I guess now we're even."

CHAPTER
FIFTEEN

When we arrive at Westray, the sky is a dark gray. As we approach the castle, the guard yells something I can't quite make out.

"Welcome back, Your Highness; we have been awaiting your arrival." The guard nods to us as we pass him.

"Thank you, Orion," Ledger responds.

We cross over a large bridge. It is hard to see much, but I can make out beautiful white stones and see the moon reflecting off the calm water surrounding the castle. Westray already appears much grander than Bellehaven.

As we pass more guards they bow their heads in respect.

"We must get to my father; do you feel strong enough to see him tonight?"

My power rumbles from the depths of my belly, and I nod. "Yes, I do."

We ride a while longer before Ledger dismounts Apollo. He reaches up and places me on the ground next to him.

A short, stout, serious-looking man dressed in a royal red approaches us. "Your Highness, it's good to see you. I hope your travels were uneventful. I see you were successful." He nods in my direction. My stomach flips nervously.

"It's nice to see you, Humphrey. This is Layla; she has agreed to assist us. How is he?" Ledger asks.

"Layla." He says my name but hardly spares me a glance and doesn't wait for a reply. "I regret to inform you that I believe his condition has worsened since you've last seen him."

"Let us not waste any more time then." Ledger's hand comes to my back as he ushers me forward. My feet don't automatically work; my thoughts are racing as I stare blankly up at Ledger.

Mia steps up next to us and smiles encouragingly. "Come on."

Humphrey leads the way, and I reluctantly follow. Ledger keeps his eyes ahead as we walk. I'm momentarily stunned by the sheer eloquence of the castle. The ceilings are tall and grand, every stone even and square, as if the builders were determined for perfection.

Our footsteps echo and I imagine the castle during the day resounding with laughter and chatter. Despite its size and pristine appearance, it still manages to give off a welcoming, homey feel.

We stop in front of two grand doors with intimidating guards stationed outside of them. They nod at us and pull the gaudy gold handles.

The room is dimly lit and equipped with beautiful, lavish furnishings. I hardly notice as I zero in on the man lying on the lush bed in the middle of the room. No, not the man, *the King* of Westray.

I balk, flooded with my own naivety, drowning in the questions I should have asked. I clench my damp palms, letting my nails dig into the skin. My breaths come in short pants that send a mixture of dull and sharp aches throughout my chest.

While everyone else enters the room, I find myself shrinking back. Ledger's hand moves from my back to my clenched hand. He gently opens it, intertwining our fingers.

"Layla." My eyes snap to his, and I'm ambushed by the desperation that lines his features. "Please." It's a strangled plea I'm powerless not to answer.

I take another shaky breath, staring at our clasped hands before taking a step forward.

We get close enough that I can make out the hollow cheeks and pale, sallow complexion of Ledger's father. The resemblance to Ledger is almost startling, and I can imagine a time when he was handsome, full of life.

He lies motionless save for the shallow breaths that move his chest up and down. His sickly appearance is familiar to me, his once strong body frail from malnutrition and inactivity.

I reach for my power when it doesn't automatically rise to the surface. Everyone's eyes are on me, hopeful as they wait. The room feels stifling, my own body an inferno, pressure building in my chest.

I force myself closer to the sick man and raise a trembling hand to run over his forehead and down his face. I close my eyes to block out my erratic emotions. Ledger squeezes my shoulder softly, reassuringly.

I grasp at my power, willing it into my palms. When it doesn't answer me, my eyes snap open. I look vacantly at my quivering hands, not a glow to be seen. I try again to find any spark of power but only feel a cold sweat break out on the back of my neck.

I am that five-year-old girl again, blood covering my hands as I fruitlessly call upon my power.

The wails and pleas of my mother fill my ears. A vice grip squeezes my throat and chest until I feel like the one dying. I'm failing. Another life will be lost because of me, another tally mark added to my tainted soul.

"No, no, no, no, no." I don't realize it's me chanting this as I stare down at my 'bloody' hands. I'm losing my fight for breath, choking on my panic, the helplessness. My palms push at my ears trying to block out my mother's screams.

"Everyone out." The demand is hazy in the back of my mind.

"Layla, look at me." I'm frozen, I want to run, I want to scream, but my body doesn't answer me.

"Layla." Ledger's face comes into view, his warm hands encircling my face. "You need to breathe." He grabs my hand and places it on his chest. "Feel that? Feel the rhythm. In and out, okay?" I yank my hand away from his and grasp at the bandages on my ribs, needing them off.

Ledger notices and lifts my shirt, seizing the bandage and ripping it in half. It falls limply to the ground, and I gulp in air, letting the pain from my rib ground me.

"That's it." He brings my hand back to his chest, "In and out. You're going to be all right. Keep your eyes on me." I lock onto his forest-green eyes like they are my lifeline. My grip tightens on his chest, and his hand comes to wrap around mine.

It's a few painstaking minutes before my breathing slows to match Ledgers, and the dizziness vacates my head. I allow myself to rest my forehead on his for a moment.

"You're okay, you're okay," he chants, his thumb stroking my cheek. This moment, his actions, and the words he speaks feel so tender.

I pull away when I feel in control again, collecting myself.

"We don't have to do this tonight. I pushed it on you too soon. We can come back tomorrow."

I look at him and then back at his father. "I'd like to try again." I turn back to the bed, my stomach churning nervously. *You can do this.* "What is his name?"

"Callum," Ledger responds.

Taking a steadying breath, I close my eyes. My shoulders relax and clear my mind. The relief that courses through my veins as my power begins to vibrate through me is immeasurable.

Opening my eyes and tracking my still trembling hands, I hover them over Callum's body. A soft glowing mist begins to emit from them as I move, a buzz of power rippling through the room.

My mouth tugs down when I feel absolutely nothing from him; his body doesn't react to me. I try again, to no avail. This had never happened to me before. Bodies always bend to my will, react, and change.

Ledger's eyes are intently set on his father, hope lining his features.

"What exactly is his power?" I question as my power prods at the unconscious man.

Ledger's face falls, his skin instantly paling. "Is something wrong?"

"He's not responding to my powers."

"Well, try harder. I did not bring you here for you to fail." I can see as he slips his carefully crafted mask on. The one he uses when he's feeling any emotion he doesn't know how to handle.

My mouth snaps shut; now is not the time and place to argue. I open the lid on my powers and let it flow through me, my palms grow brighter. The hum of power in the room increases.

Nothing, I feel absolutely nothing from him, his body remains the same. His breathing is shallow, his skin still damp and sallow. I exhale, defeated, and cap my power, turning back to Ledger.

"Why are you stopping?" I can hear the desperation in his voice, can almost feel his internal panic.

"It's not working." I touch his arm gently and he averts his eyes. "Answer my question." I recall what he'd asked me in Grimwood, the odd timing, how specific it was. So, it's no surprise when he answers.

"He can nullify powers." There is a long silence in the room before Ledger continues, "I thought with him being unconscious, maybe you'd be able to get through." Anguish flashes across his beautiful features.

An ache forms in my chest for him. He already lost his sister and his mother, and by the looks of it, his father doesn't have much time.

His torment is almost tangible as he turns to his father, grasping at his bony hand.

My mind is languid, a feeling of helplessness washing over me as I watch the two of them.

"It's been a long couple of days. Orion will take you to your room. We will try again tomorrow." He doesn't look at me as he speaks.

Not knowing what else to do, I accept his dismissal, pushing open the heavy doors. Orion waits outside, the towering prince's guard. I wonder how I had never seen it before.

He must see the disappointment on my face because his own falls before he turns.

I follow him in silence until we get to a room with a smaller ornate door. He opens it and motions for me to go inside.

"Welcome to Westray Miss Sutton. Get some rest."

"Thank you, Orion." The door closes.

CHAPTER
SIXTEEN

I TOSS AND TURN, RESTLESS IN THE COMFORTS OF THE luxurious bed I lay in. I can't stop thinking of Westray's king and Ledger's devastating disappointment. I had utterly failed them, and that wasn't a feeling I was used to. It left me feeling raw and helpless, emotions that gnaw at my mental sanity.

I need to find the library and the serenity only books and research can bring. I creep from my bed, the marble floors chilling my bare feet.

The door swings open with a loud creak against the quiet of night. A guard stands at attention on the other side.

"Hello," I start. "Um, I was hoping you could escort me to the library?" He eyes me warily, taking in my night-gown and bare feet. "I wanted to do some research. I won't be long."

He nods in answer and starts walking down the hallway, his metal armor clinking. I scurry after him, barely closing the door. I follow him down the hallway until he turns and stops in front of two grand doors.

"Uh, through these doors?" I ask, and he responds by opening one. I pass him, walking through. "Thank you."

I lift my head as I walk into the room to marvel at all the books lining the walls. The library is grand and smells of the pages of old books and lilacs. I inhale deeply. The space is cozy and pristine, not a speck of dust to be found.

"Stunning," I whisper as I meander further into the space.

My feet move on their own accord, leading me further into the room. My fingers run over the edges of the spines and the preserved wood of the shelves. The library is dim, and a slight breeze rustles my hair.

I realize there are glass doors that open to the gardens outside. There is a sette and a few cozy chairs surrounded by flowers and plants.

It is so perfect I already mourn the moment I must leave. I could lose myself here for a very long time.

"There is no escaping you is there?" I jump at Ledger's voice, gripping my chest. I missed him sitting in the gardens. He lounges on a settee, a bottle dangling precariously from his fingers.

"That's rich coming from you." I stroll over to him snatching the liquor and taking a long swig, sputtering and coughing at the stringent taste. "You have horrible taste in alcohol," I choke, and his lip twitches as I hand the bottle back.

"Sleep eludes you?" he questions, looking up at the sky.

"It appears sleep eludes us both."

"Indeed." His face is blank, his shoulders slumped in defeat. His Adams apple bobs as he takes another long drag from the bottle.

It's then I realize he is bleeding; his face is swollen, and there is a line of dried blood from his temple to his jaw. His clothes are tattered and bloody. He holds what looks like a piece of crumpled paper in one fist.

"What the hell, Ledger? You're hurt!" My hands are already glowing as I hold them up. My power purrs at the thought of caressing his skin again.

He grabs my hands and pushes them away. "Leave me, Layla. I do not wish to be healed." He takes another swig of the amber liquid as my hands drop falling limply at my sides. My power flares angrily with the need to steal his pain.

"Are you going to tell me where these wounds came from? Or what that paper you are holding says? Was our journey here not exciting enough for you?"

He doesn't respond, instead cranes his head up to the stars. His tongue flicks out to lick some of the alcohol from his full lips, the movement catching my attention. He shoves the paper into his pocket.

"Fine. Keep your secrets." I snare the bottle from his hand before it can reach his lips and take another mouthful, wincing before forcing myself to swallow. "I thought maybe there'd be some books in here that could help with healing your father." I motion to the library, and Ledger's eyes drag over the full shelves. "Was he always sick?" I sink onto the settee next to him, careful not to brush his thigh with my own.

He picks some flowers next to the settee and begins weaving them together like I'd seen him do times before.

"He's been sick since I was a boy. Never this bad. He did what his body allowed but there were many limits. A lot of responsibilities fell on me." Ledger pauses from braiding the flowers together to take the bottle from me, but he doesn't drink. "With my mother gone, I raised my sister. I knew where I had to step up and what was expected of me. I owned what he couldn't. Took ownership of things I was far too young and underqualified to do. I overcompensated where I could to take the attention off of him." He sighs bringing the bottle to his lips.

It all makes sense now. Ledger is the epitome of a man who never had the chance to be a boy. A man who makes everyone's well-being his responsibility. A man who blames himself for the death of his sister, who will blame himself for the death of his father if I fail.

"I've been desperate to find a cure for him ever since my sister died. All consumed by it. I suppose if I can save him, it will somehow make up for me not being able to save her." His fingers tighten on the flowers as he stares at them.

"I'm sorry about your father. And I'm sorry you were forced to grow up too soon." I fidget under his gaze as it moves to me.

"You don't believe he is beyond saving?" He looks like he's holding his breath as he waits for my answer.

"No one is beyond saving, Ledger."

He pauses before nodding and tying the stems into a pretty loop. He hangs the finished product from his knee. His thumb and pointer finger glide over the petals before he glances back up at me. Taking the flower crown in his hands he holds it up.

"May I?" The question catches me off guard, but I extend my head forward anyway.

A grin tugs at my lips as he places it just above my ears. The sweet floral scent tickles my nostrils and when I look up, Ledger is staring at me intensely enough that I almost blush.

"Beautiful. You're so godsdamn beautiful." He shakes his head, the corner of his mouth tipping up.

"I never stood a chance."

The compliment is unexpected and makes my stomach flip. I snatch the bottle twirling it in my fingers while looking at the dark liquid. "How is strong is this stuff?"

Ledger lets out a laugh and I startle. His dimple pops as he throws his head back. The sound is pure, melodic and makes my stomach flip. It stops me in my tracks.

"I wish it was the alcohol." His laughter dies as his eyes rove over me, his neck flushed pink from the liquor. "Everything used to be gray before I met you, dull and uninteresting. Somehow, you've managed to bring color to it."

I'm rendered speechless as he slowly grasps the bottle intentionally brushing my fingers before bringing it to his mouth. He sways as he swallows and I reach out to steady him.

"We should get you back to your room, while you can still walk." I attempt to wipe the smile off my face. "Or before you tell me you love me."

Ledger huffs a laugh setting down the bottle and pushes up on wobbly legs. "I won't turn down the opportunity to get you alone in my room." He staggers forward and I toss my arm around his waist.

"Don't get any ideas prince, I'm too smart to be seduced by you." We leave the library and weave through the hallways.

"That's why I like you."

I roll my eyes. "You're a lot more fun when you're intoxicated."

"So I've been told." He lurches forward as we reach his room and we both almost topple to the ground. The guards standing at attention eye us, and I give them a timid smile.

Once inside, Ledger stumbles backward, shutting the heavy wood-carved door and steadying himself, and I cock my eyebrow. He gives me a knee weakening grin that has me fighting my own back.

I lead him to his bed and sit him down. "Medical supplies—where are they?" Dried blood is crusted on his skin, and I can't leave him like this.

"In the cabinet." He nods to the washroom and I jog over. Pulling out some alcohol and bandages from it, I then wet a cloth before making my way back over to him.

I bring it to his jaw and wipe away the crusted blood. Soaking a few cotton rounds in alcohol, I dab them against a shallow cut on his temple.

He winces slightly as his eyes roam my face. I grip his wrist, running another cotton round over the various cuts that litter his forearms. I admire the veins that run the length of them, the dusting of hair over his tanned skin.

He sits still, watching me in silence. I throw away the rounds and eye the cut on his neck that disappears into the collar of his shirt.

"May I?" I ask, eyeing the top button.

"You may." The sweet scent of alcohol washes over my face as he responds. Though I know the taste from the bottle, I wonder if it would be any sweeter off his lips.

My fingers brush his muscled chest, his abdomen flexing when they sweep over the sensitive skin there. On the last button of his shirt, my hands tremble. I carefully lift the torn side, folding it over his shoulder to get a look at the damage beneath. My knees nearly go weak as I fight to focus on the thin scratch marks on his upper body. His skin smells warm, inviting.

I scold myself. I'd worked on hundreds of shirtless men over the years and never remember being affected quite like this.

My breath hitches as I step between his legs to get a closer look. His thighs hug my hips. I skim the side of his neck with my fingertips, trying to determine how deep the wounds are. They go from his neck to the bottom of his chest but are mostly superficial.

Power trickles out of my fingertips against my will, and I snatch my hand back to avoid going against his wishes.

My cheeks redden as I push my abilities back down. "My power seems to have a mind of its own tonight. It doesn't enjoy the sight of you injured and likes being denied access even less." I wet a few more cotton rounds as I speak.

"Your power is fond of me?"

"I suppose you could say that." I glance up, seeing a ghost of a smile on his lips. I press a cotton pad to the scratch on his neck, and he grimaces. "Don't let it go to your head. I can assure you it is only because you are always bleeding around me."

"Mmmm," he hums back in answer, and it vibrates the air, drawing my attention to his lips, tipped up in amusement.

His power curls out of him in a swirl of smoke. It sweeps over my thighs from where he is gripping his mattress. It is cool and seductive and sends my mind reeling.

"What are you doing?"

I shiver as his powers ripple over me. Such an intense bliss fills my veins I fist my hands to keep myself from clutching onto him.

It hums over my skin much like his voice, in such tantalizing, powerful waves that my eyes drift shut. It's a welcome caress, a teasing taste of what he could offer.

"Do you like that?" The question is gravelly, seductive and it takes everything in me to respond.

"No." I refuse to give him the satisfaction.

"Do you want me to stop?" Power curls inside of me, dances over my body.

"No," I whisper, hardly registering my answer. I blink open my eyes to be met with Ledger's hooded gaze. My face is inches from his, and I'm leaning into him, chasing more of what he'd just inflicted upon me.

A fiery longing seeps into my veins as he inches impossibly closer, making my heart stutter. "My power is rather fond of you, too." His voice grates against my skin. He stops, staying perfectly still. I can feel his breath warm against my mouth and shudder closer.

My heart pounds in my ears as he waits for my next move. *I cannot do this with him*, can't let this go any further. I must heal his father and get back to Bellehaven. This would complicate things— but I am *so* tired of denying myself even the simplest of desires.

My tongue darts out, wetting my lips and his eyes dip, tracking the movement. I lean closer until our lips brush.

The small contact makes my head spin. An insatiable hunger I've never felt overtakes my body. Ravenous. This man makes me absolutely ravenous.

I wonder if this infatuation, this all-consuming desire, is what my mother had felt for my father. If that is why she had been so destroyed when she lost him.

The thought scares me more than I care to admit.

I let out a sharp breath before jerking away. I force myself to step back, even when my body and power want to rebel against the movement. His power recedes back into him. "I should go to bed." I avoid his eyes, my trembling hand fisting a bloodied cotton pad.

"What are you so scared of, blondie?" I can feel his eyes on me, blazing a path wherever they travel.

"I'm not scared." Another lie as I dare a look at him. His face doesn't show a hint of irritation or confusion. Like always he doesn't give away much, just an unwavering silent confidence.

"Is it *him*? Is that what is holding you back?" He frowns as he asks the question. I can't deny the feelings Ledger elicits from me, but they feel like a betrayal to Maddox.

I love Maddox. He's handsome, funny, and knows me better than I know myself. He'd fought for me so fiercely, and knowing him, he wouldn't stop until my return. The kiss we shared proved there could be more between us, that it could easily blossom into something incredible. But I didn't know if I could let myself go there.

The newfound desire for Ledger shocks me. It's getting harder to deny the connection we are forming. I'm fighting desperately to deny my feelings because there isn't a reality where I can stay in Westray. I have to go back to Bellehaven; emotionally investing myself in this beautiful man will do nothing but destroy me.

I have to keep him at a distance. He wasn't part of the deal. No matter how much I want him, I just can't see past the devastation my attachment to him would cause.

"Yes, it's him." I say what I believe will deter him and force my foot another step back.

Ledger shakes his head once, his lip barely tipping up. "I would be remiss if I didn't tell you that from the moment I laid eyes on you, I have been painfully uninterested in anything that does not involve you. I need your power, but I want much more than that."

My heart gallops in my chest and my palms sweat. I struggle for a response as my eyes flick to his door. "It's late." I round his bed, and he stands.

"Layla?" he calls as my fingers brush the cool metal of the doorhandle.

"Yes?" I breathe, pausing.

"Do you think you can forgive me for the unforgiveable things I've done.?"

"I already have."

CHAPTER
SEVENTEEN

MIA FINDS ME IN THE LIBRARY THE NEXT MORNING. I am skimming the three open books in front of me when she walks in.

"I thought you were hiding from me."

"Not hiding, just trying to figure out any solution to help Ledger's father. This morning, Humphrey told me his condition has started to worsen, and now it feels like I'm working against the clock."

"How long have you been here?" Her eyebrow quirks as she eyes my wild hair and the bags under my eyes.

"Since last night." I glance out the window, wincing against the brightness of the sun. I'd gone straight to the library after leaving Ledger's room. I knew I wouldn't be able to find sleep. I can hardly seem to remove Ledger and my impending future from my thoughts.

"Find anything useful?" She leans down fingering the open books strewn around the table.

"Not yet, but I'm sure it's here." I lick my finger turning the page.

"Why don't you take a break, train with me for an hour or two?" I continue reading, mouthing the words as she speaks. "Give your eyes a break." She shuts the book I'm scanning and holds it out of my reach. I open my mouth to object but when I see the determined look on her face, I snap my lips closed.

"Fine. You're probably right, I could use some fresh air," I admit, stretching my sore neck to the side.

"I brought you a croissant, fresh from the kitchens." She holds up her offering, and I snatch it from her, taking a bite.

"Thank you, I'll go change."

"Hold on." She stops me, gathering my wild, tangled locks into her hands. She tames my hair into a long braid that falls limply onto my lower back. "Much better." She smiles.

I change and then Mia and I walk to the training grounds.

I marvel at the incredible beauty of the castle, finally seeing it in the light. The stark white stone sparkles bright and seamlessly. The morning sun glitters through the dozens of windows lining the hallways. I can make out the cobalt blue shingles littering the many roofs that seemed to defy the wear and tear of the elements.

Everything appears so pristine, ageless as I drink it in. Mia opens the door to the training yard, and I step through. It's lush and green, the grass cropped short. There are well-used targets for archery on one side, and wooden dummies lined up along the other. An array of shiny silver weapons sits next to us.

Mia saunters over to the dirt running track that encircles the main training area. She bends down and begins to stretch her lean, muscled legs.

"Please tell me you're not going to make me run," I whine.

"We have to build your stamina and your speed, so yes, we run. Get to stretching," she demands. I curl my lip in displeasure but do as she says.

"We are going to start with two miles to warm up. Are you ready?" Mia shoots me a dazzling smile, and I grimace.

"Ready as I'll ever be." I try to muster some positivity, but it fades as I watch her take off. Her strides are long and fast, powerful and confident.

I spur my body into action, my ribs protesting at the jostling movements. I chase after Mia, determined to not to fall too far behind her.

The cool morning air whips at my skin, my braided hair lashing out behind me. After a few minutes, my lungs burn, and my muscles protest.

I watch Mia; her movements are lithe and nimble as opposed to mine, which are gawky and uncoordinated. She laps me continuously, but I force myself to keep pace and continue. I relish in the discomfort, the pounding of my heart. It feels equal parts good and miserable to push my body.

All the anger, frustration and fear of the past few days begins to melt away. The present moment comes into sharp focus.

The golden rays of the sun begin to warm my skin as it rises higher. I focus on the rhythmic hammering of my feet on the dirt. Sweat drips from my brow and runs down my face until I taste the salty perspiration.

Ledger enters the training grounds and my stomach flips when I see him. He glances my way before getting out various wooden swords and staffs, laying them feet apart around the yard.

"What is he doing?" I ask Mia as she slows to run with me.

"A few times a week, Ledger trains some children from the city. Some who are struggling with their powers, others who need a physical outlet."

"Oh, that's really... nice." My eyes widen a touch.

"Why do you sound so surprised? I know you haven't seen the best sides of him, but like I said before, where it matters, he's good. He struggled a lot with his powers as a child, especially because he has two. So, now he's made it one of his missions to make sure the kids of Westray don't struggle like he did," she says, annoyingly not out of breath.

I consider her words as I study Ledger. He meets my gaze, and I trip over myself, thankfully recovering before I can fall. Gods, the way he looks in this light, morning stubble and tousled hair, is a special kind of torture.

Children start to show up as I continue to run. They appear to be around five to fifteen years old.

I watch each of them greet Ledger with a high five or hug. He gets down on his knee when a particularly nervous-looking little girl walks in. He says a few things to her, and in seconds, she is smiling. After another moment, he even gets a laugh from her and ruffles her frizzy hair.

I can't seem to keep my eyes off him as he continues his lesson with the children. He's really good with them, patient and kind. When a little boy gets frustrated, he gets on his level. He takes the boy's arm and guides it with the wooden sword to demonstrate and then steps back and lets the little boy try.

I get glimpses of him as he moves from child to child, helping where they need. He gives them the right amount of space and instruction. I watch as their faces light up when they do something well and how he praises them.

I'm so focused on watching I hardly notice when Mia comes up beside me, eyeing me suspiciously. "Speed up, Layla, you're barely moving!"

"I'm going as fast as I can!" I yell back as my leg cramps. I collapse onto the grass, massaging the rebelling muscle. "I didn't realize how out of shape I am." I wheeze as Mia jogs back to me.

"That was barely over a mile, Layla." I give her a pathetic look, and she sighs, handing me my water bottle.

I notice a few of the older boys are practicing their magic as I drink. One of them throws fireballs while the other tries to put them out with his water ability.

He misses one, and I hear him hiss in pain as the fire singes the skin of his arm. I drop my water bottle and stride over to them before I can stop myself.

The one with the fire ability is profusely apologizing as the redheaded boy grasps his arm, howling in pain.

"Hi," I interrupt them, seeing Ledger coming out of the corner of my eye. "I'm Layla." They look at me confused. "I have healing powers," I offer, and they look at each other before gasping at my confession.

"I've never met anyone with healing powers!" the boy with fire abilities exclaims his brown eyes wide with shock.

"Well, now you have. Do you mind if I look at your arm?" I look at the boy. He has curly red hair and light blue eyes. I can make out blisters already forming on his arm and know he must be in a substantial amount of pain.

He seems hesitant as he glances at Ledger, who is now at my side. "Layla is an incredibly skilled healer; she saved me after I was attacked by some wild Kerolu in the woods." Ledger pulls down his shirt, exposing his scars.

The boys gape at Ledger's scars before the red-headed one winces, holding out his arm to me. "Will it hurt?" he asks when I raise my hands.

"No, it might itch or tickle even, but you shouldn't feel any pain," I explain, and he nods. I notice a smattering of freckles littering his face.

My power rumbles to the surface, flowing out of my palms and wrapping around the boy's arm. He gasps, bracing himself.

"Does it feel alright?" I ask and he pauses, relaxing and nodding his head. "What is your name?" I question while I continue.

"Holt."

"Holt. I like that name." I smile at him and withdraw my power.

"That is so totally awesome!" his friend exclaims when he sees the healed skin.

Holt looks astonished. "It doesn't hurt anymore." He touches it, smiling, revealing a gap between his two front teeth.

"It might be tender for a few days, but it shouldn't cause you any further pain," I explain. I feel eyes on me, and when I turn my head I see all the children gawking in my direction.

"Thanks, Layla." Holt turns to Ledger. "Can I see your scars again? I want to fight a Kerolu one day."

"No trust me, bud, you don't." Ledger mouths a thank you as I walk back to Mia who now stands with Cam.

"Hey, Cam!" I greet as I get closer. They both are holding staffs. "What are those for?" I ask.

Cam vanishes, and a brush of air on my neck is the only warning before he reappears behind me. "You've got to work on your reflexes, use more of your senses." He disappears, then reappears in one of the training arenas.

"This is really not my strong suit. Maddox used to make fun of my reflexes. He would always be right up on me before I realized he was even there."

"I'm a good teacher," Cam says confidently tossing me a staff.

The second I enter the training ring, Cam disappears. I look around looking for any hint of where he might reappear.

Before I can even blink, the staff slams into my back.

"Ow." When I turn around to face Cam, he is already gone.

This time, I move my feet and raise the staff, waiting for him to reappear. I catch his blurry figure in the corner of my eye but before I can react, he smacks me hard in the leg.

"I'm starting to not like this game." I shake out my leg, refocusing and swallowing the frustration that bubbles up inside of me.

"Try to close your eyes, it may help. Feel the air, how it changes, use your sense of smell, listen. Sometimes you see more when you can't see anything at all." Cam fades away, and I reluctantly close my eyes.

I hear his feet hit the ground softly to my left. My staff shoots out meeting air before his punches into my stomach, throwing me off balance and knocking me back. I struggle for a breath and when I do fill my lungs, I'm met with the stench of hay.

I'm transported back to the moment Forde's foot slams into my middle.

Eyes flying open, I drop to my knees to steady myself. I grip the staff tightly and then wipe damp palms onto my thigh.

Weak. That was all I would ever be. I shut my eyes against the images of Forde above me, the feeling of rough rope against my ankles.

I've been floundering since stepping foot out of Belle-haven. I've been beaten, bruised, thrown from one harrow-ing incident to the next. I'd failed Ledger's father and was currently failing myself.

"Sorry Layla, did I hit you too hard?!" Cam's eyes are wide, filled with concern. He leans towards me apprehen-sively from a few feet away, as if not wanting to get too close and upset me further.

"I can't do this." I throw the staff, and it falls to the ground sending up a cloud of dirt.

"Get up, Layla." Mia is next to me in the next second.

"I am good at one thing and that's healing. I'm just wasting everyone's time." My shoulders drop as I let out a frustrated sigh. I can feel Ledger watching from across the training grounds, awaiting my next move.

"You've forgotten your reason. You don't want to feel helpless anymore? Then fight. You don't want to be a victim anymore? Then fight. You have to feel weak to become strong." She grabs my staff off the ground and holds her hand out to me. "Now get up."

"All I've been doing is fighting Mia!"

"Well now you're going to do it with a purpose. On your feet. I'm not letting you give up that easily." I grind my teeth together letting Mia's words settle over me. Taking a deep breath, I slide my clammy hand into hers.

Once standing she brushes off my knees and places the staff back into my hands. I grip it hard enough that my fingers turn white and turn back to Cam. He looks nervously between Mia and me.

"I can sense your frustration, your anger. Use it. Channel it. Work with your emotions, not against them. Don't let them control you." Mia waits for my reluctant nod before stepping back.

Cam gives me a hesitant look.

"You're fine, Cam. I'm sorry I had a moment. Let's try again." I close the distance between us.

"Are—are you sure?"

"I'm sure." I'd asked for this; I just wasn't prepared for the feeling of vulnerability and helplessness to resurface. I'd made it to Westray, survived the Maladra and Kerolu. I'd escaped Forde, and if I encountered any of them again, I'd be prepared.

I close my eyes and bend my knees bracing myself. I hold out my staff ready for Cam's assault and let my emotions build my determination.

I can sense Cam's hesitation before he fades. My back spikes with awareness as he materializes. I hear his sharp intake of air as he waits for my reaction.

My body acts before my brain can command it and I swing around brandishing my staff like a sword.

It makes contact, bouncing off Cam's. A resounding noise echoes through the courtyard.

My eyes spring open to meet Cam's. He looks shocked, the whites of his eyes gleaming against the sun.

"Let's go again, and don't go easy on me." My eyes fall shut and I get in a defensive position once again.

A rush of air brushes my cheek as Cam departs. I move around the ring with my senses on high alert. Taking a deep inhale, I get a whiff of freshly laundered clothing. Cam.

I strike out, this time making contact with his body.

"Nice one, Layla." He grunts and I can't help but smother a grin.

We carry on like this until I am panting and sweat drips down my back. Cam gets in a few more- much lighter hits, but so do I, and each one makes me feel powerful and competent.

Cam fades only to emerge on my right. Our staffs knock together hard enough to make my teeth clatter. He's gone again and I sense him in front of me. We meet each other blow for blow until I make it past his defenses.

I don't know where my staff connects but by the pained wheeze that Cam releases, I know it can't be good. I open my eyes to him on the ground, gripping his groin.

"Oh shit, I'm sorry, Cam. Are you okay?!" Mia slaps a hand over her mouth to conceal her laugh.

"Good hit," he grits out, gasping for air.

The door of the training grounds knocks open as Archie arrives. "What's going on here? Fighting dirty, are you, Layla?" I hear the grin in Archie's voice as I drop to the ground next to Cam.

"Shut up, Archie. We were working on honing my senses. In my defense, it was his idea to have me close my eyes!"

I awkwardly touch Cam's shoulder as I try to comfort him. "Would you like me to try and use my power to take away the pain?"

"No, please no, I'm okay." Cam winces as he pushes himself up.

Mia snickers. "You alright, Cammy?"

"I'm fine. I think that's enough for one day."

"Are you sure? Let me just use my pow—" I try, and he cuts me off.

"I'm sure. I don't need your hands or power anywhere near my crotch."

"Okay, sorry again," I call back to Cam as Mia pulls me away.

"Don't worry, one time, I hit Ledger in the balls so hard he was limping for a week. An accident, of course," she whispers, and I snort.

"Thanks for not letting me give up." I rub at a bruising spot on my arm.

"I wouldn't dream of it. Remember this moment at our next training." She squeezes my arm and waves leaving through the door.

I linger in the courtyard after Mia's gone, watching as Ledger says goodbye to the children. He sneaks silvers into each of their bags as they depart. I marvel at his softness and the playful nature with which he addresses each of them. I find myself envious, wanting to experience that side of him for myself.

They all look at him like he's hung the moon, and I watch with rapt attention. For the first time, I get a glimpse of how much he loves his people and see the traits of a future king in him.

When they have all gone, he turns to me. I try to ignore the way my stomach flutters.

"I could use some help cleaning up if you feel so inclined."

"Put me to work."

He motions for me to go first, and I walk in front of him, suddenly self-conscious.

We bend down, picking up wooden swords and staffs off the grass. I'm hyper-aware of his presence, and as we work next to each other, I'm careful not to brush him.

"You're stronger than you give yourself credit for." He empties my hands and leans the equipment against the wall. "You have fight in you. You just need somewhere to direct it. Preferably not at me." Grinning he bends back down, loading up his arms.

"That may be true." I respond following his lead. "And you seem to really have a way with the kids," A soft smile graces my lips. "The ever-serious prince has a soft spot for children. Who would have guessed?"

"They've grown on me. We've been working together for a few years now. They have helped me as much, if not more than I have helped them."

"It's wonderful—what you do for them. I wish I would have had someone like you when I discovered my power." I finish stacking the wooden swords.

"That's why I started doing it. Children who are born with power need help channeling it. Honing their skills, releasing pent-up energy. It can be scary, explosive and overwhelming." Our fingers brush as we bend down to grab the same training weapon.

"How old were you when your powers came in?" I ask, snatching my hand back.

"I was five when my nature ability started to surface, nine when my siphoning powers took effect. The latter being harder to control. Every time I would touch someone, I would siphon their powers. I was scared to touch anyone for years."

"That's horrible." I pick up a staff and scrape at the chipping wood.

"I read every book I could find that had information on siphoning. My mother had passed by then and my father was sick, so Archie, Mia, and my sister would let me practice on them. I can imagine it wasn't very enjoyable, but they never complained." As he talks, I try to picture the little boy he was. "I was so fearful of my siphoning power that I didn't allow myself to kiss anyone until I was almost eighteen."

"That must have been very upsetting for all of the girls that met you before then." I laugh. He grins over at me, and I relish it when his dimple pops.

"Thank you for your help. If you ever want to join a session, I'm sure the kids would love to say they got to work with an all-elusive healer," he offers, and I nod. My heart squeezes as I picture what a life here could look like.

CHAPTER
EIGHTEEN

LEDGER PLACES HIS LARGE HAND ON MY SHOULDER. "You must stop, you've been at this for too long. I can feel your power waning."

My powers continue to delve into the King's body. I've been exploring every inch, every vein, every fucking nerve, and I can't get a single reaction from him.

It is like channeling my abilities into a black hole. The King's body is an impenetrable fortress, his nullifying power draining me. Still, I continue until my hands shake and my ears ring from exertion.

"Layla." Ledger's voice comes again, and I can't bring myself to look at him. The thought of burnout seems far more appealing to me than stopping and seeing the utter disappointment on his face.

"Just a few more seconds," I breathe. I push my power harder into the King's body, and my arms tremble. I grit my teeth against it. *I can do this. I won't fail. I cannot fail.*

My head begins to spin and my knees buckle. Ledger's arm wraps around me before everything goes, and I fall.

"What were you thinking?" Ledger is above me already, scolding me as I come to. "You'd rather force yourself into burnout than accept the fact this isn't working?" He looks angry as he helps me sit up. "I refuse to watch you do that again."

Ledger squats before me and his finger and thumb grip my chin. He turns my head roughly to the side. His other pointer finger brushes my ear and down my jaw. It comes away bloody.

"Gods." He stands, walking away briefly before turning back and yanking at the collar of his shirt. "I want to make myself clear. I won't watch you do that again. Not for me, not for my father." He bends down, picking me up and caging me into his strong arms.

"Put me down right now. I will not be paraded around the castle in your arms like a weak damsel." I buck.

He sighs, setting me down, but not before I feel his heart hammering wildly against his chest.

I sway as my feet connect with the ground, feeling my depletion. It takes immense strength and concentration to take a few wobbly steps forward. Ledger makes an exasperated noise before holding out his arm for me to grab. "You are the most stubborn woman I have ever met. Will you at least hold on to my arm to walk?"

My eyes flick to his outstretched arm. "No." I brush past him as I exit the King's quarters and feel his powers growl over the skin of my back.

"Any success, Your Highness?" Humphrey questions when he sees Ledger.

"Not yet, but we will keep trying." He grits out the words, and I avert my eyes.

"Of course." I hear the fret in Humphrey's voice. A reminder of his fading confidence in me. "Ms. Sutton, may I ask how long you've been the healer at Bellehaven? At what age did your abilities come through?" he asks as we pass, and even though the questions are rather direct, I answer anyway.

"Layla, call me Layla, please. I've been the healer in Bellehaven since I was a little girl. My abilities started to show when I was around four or five. I was quite young."

"Mmm." He makes a noise, and his lip curls up in the corner.

"I'm afraid I must get Layla back. Good night, Humphrey." Ledger slides his arm around my waist, taking some of my weight as we walk away.

"He doesn't seem to like me much," I comment as we walk.

"I wouldn't worry about it; Humphrey doesn't like anyone." Instead of going to my room Ledger pulls me across the hall to another door.

"Where are we going?"

"My room," he states, swinging open the door and pulling me inside.

"Okay." I stand awkwardly in the doorway. "And why am I in your room?"

"You extended too much power today. I want to make sure you are okay; you'll sleep here tonight." He removes his jacket and shoes.

"I don't believe I will sleep here. My room is just fine." I go to open the door, and his hand comes from behind, pushing it closed. "And I'm the stubborn one? Has anyone ever told you you're a little bossy? Controlling?" I mutter as I feel his chest against my back.

"I am a prince, after all," he drawls.

"What if I don't stay here tonight? Will you send me to the dungeons?" I eye his hand, which is still holding the door closed. As I turn around to face him, his other arm comes up, caging me in.

"You're too pretty for the dungeons, but I could tie you to the bed if that is what you'd rather?"

I swallow thickly as he grins down at me, that annoying dimple popping in the most alluring way. "He jokes. I was beginning to wonder if you had a sense of humor."

"Oh, I wasn't kidding, blondie. I can think of nothing I'd like more." His power snakes out in a cloudy haze, caressing my wrists and stroking up my arms. I shudder when it reaches my neck, tickling my skin before squeezing firmly, cutting off my air supply.

A bolt of desire strikes through me like lightning, sizzling my core. His head dips until our lips are a breath apart.

"You, writhing underneath me, begging for my touch," he purrs, and my head swims from lack of air and his closeness. Even if I could speak, my brain is empty of everything but him. "I would worship every inch of your body. Ruin you for any man that dares come after me." He makes it sound so appealing. I always swore I would never let myself be ruined by a man. What scares me the most is for him, I think I'd beg for it.

His grip on my throat loosens, and I take a pitiful breath.

"*Show me.*" The words almost leave my mouth in some kind of desperate plea. His power clings to my skin for a torturous moment before reeling back into him.

"I've never wanted anyone as much as I want you, Layla, and your complete disregard for your health and safety infuriates me," he growls. He tucks a stray piece of hair behind my ear and gives my mouth another leisurely look before backing away.

I realize, then, that I am clinging to the doorframe. I stay that way, stunned, as he removes his tunic, replacing it with a soft cotton shirt.

He walks another identical shirt over to me, holding it out for me to take. I hesitate, uncurling my fingers from where my nails dig into the wood.

"For you to sleep in. Unless you sleep unclothed, in which case, feel free."

I snatch the shirt from his hands and scurry into his washroom. Once the door is shut, I rest my back against it, taking a few grounding breaths. *Gods, I need to get a grip.*

I toss off my tight tunic and replace it with Ledger's oversized shirt. It hangs down to my knees. I keep my pants on, splashing some cold water onto my face.

Ledger opens the door, walks inside, and eyes the side of my face. Grabbing a cloth, he wets it and brings it to my ear, wiping away the crusted blood.

His touch is gentle, his presence familiar and comforting. He tosses the ruddy cloth onto the countertop.

"This seems a little scandalous. I wouldn't want anyone to get the wrong idea. I really should get back to my room," I try again.

"The only place you're going is my bed."

I follow him out of the bathroom, and he eyes the trousers I purposely left on. "They aren't coming off, Prince, so don't bother."

"As you wish." He lifts the covers of his bed and motions for me to get in. My eyes are bleary, my ears still dully ringing. I'm drained, completely depleted, and in desperate need of sleep.

I slip into the lush sheets, allowing the fight to leave my body when I feel how comfortable it is. Ledger doesn't get in on the other side but instead places a tray of food in front of me and drags a chair up to bed, sits, and pulls out a book.

"Where did this come from?" I question as my stomach growls.

"Humphrey sent some food after he saw us. Thought you could use it to help replenish your power."

"You aren't sleeping?" I ask. He must have been exhausted; it was well into the night by now.

"No. I told you; you extended a dangerous amount of power today, and I want to make sure you're okay."

"Ledger, I'm fine. You need sleep, too."

"And I'm fine here. Eat, Layla, and then rest." He looks pointedly at the tray of food and then opens his book when I take a bite.

"How do I know I won't wake up cuffed to the bed?" My stomach growls, demanding sustenance. I take a few bites of juicy guinea fowl and some kind of green vegetable.

"You'd have to ask nicely for that, and since manners aren't your strong suit, I believe you're safe for tonight." He watches me dribble honey over the melon on the tray and bring it to my mouth.

"You have a point." I grin.

After eating my fill, I push the tray to the other side of the bed. A yawn escapes me; I'm tired and satiated.

I can feel the food already replenishing some of my power reserves. My eyes grow heavy, and with no more energy left to fight, I sink into the soft pillows. They smell like the forest.

I stare at him as he reads, my eyes heavy. Ledger glances up from the page when he senses my gaze and raises an eyebrow.

"Night, blondie." Ledger rumbles as I succumb to sleep.

I dream of blood. Crimson thick on my hands, droplets littering my face, smearing across my chest, pooling onto my milk-white thighs. It soaks into my clothes, making them stick to me like a second skin. The scent of iron is so strong in the air I choke. It flows freely like a scarlet fountain vibrating and chanting to me with every heartbeat.

I startle awake late the next afternoon, my skin damp and my heart pounding. I push up, wincing at the bright sun, and notice I am alone.

My fingers caress the soft sheets. The bed is still perfectly made on the other side. I slip out of the down comforter and replace the covers.

I see a dried, pink lily sitting on his nightstand. It looks so much like the one I plucked after my encounter with the Maladra.

I should leave but glance around his room, appeasing my curiosity. I am in Ledger's room alone and my desire to explore the intricate parts of him that live here is undeniable. I amble over to his desk.

Atop it lies an intricate box and some letters in beautiful handwriting. I run my fingers over the velvet box and then brush the stack, each one signed, 'Love you dearly, your mother.' I catch a few words, 'Give it to someone deserving of your heart,' before it feels like too much of an invasion.

I meander to his closet. My nose brushes the collar of a wrinkle-free shirt, and I inhale deeply. The familiar smell of cedar and leather floods my senses. A smell that has become one of my favorites.

The thought of getting caught spurs me to leave, but I pause when I see Ledger's bloodied pants from a few nights prior when I had run into him in the library.

They sit rumpled in the corner of his closet and I can't help myself when I walk over to them and place my hand in the pocket.

My heart leaps when I feel the tattered paper still crinkled in his pocket. I debate leaving it, but my curiosity wins, and I pull it out. My hands quiver as I smooth the wrinkled parchment realizing it isn't just a random paper, but a torn page of a book.

I tense as I read, and what I see makes me wish I hadn't been so nosy. In the middle of the page written in bold lettering are the words. "Bring her back before we make you regret it."

I suck a sharp intake of air, fear flooding my veins. It is a stark reminder that my presence here is putting everyone in danger. The King of Bellehaven is a looming threat, and I know all too well he always delivers.

With Ledger's father's worsening condition and this new sobering warning, I know I have to find an answer fast. It's a crippling realization that no matter how much I may want to stay, I can't.

If anything happens to the people of Westray, specifically the four people I have grown markedly attached to, I will never forgive myself.

CHAPTER
NINETEEN

I RUB AT MY EYES, FORCING THEM TO FOCUS AS I FLIP another page. I've been reading for hours to no avail, and I can feel myself growing frustrated. The sun hangs low in the sky when Ledger walks in.

I chew absently on a piece of dried jerky, scanning the words in front of me as he approaches.

"I've been looking for you. Sorry I wasn't in my room when you woke. I had pressing matters I needed to attend to this morning," he says, peering down at me, or the open book, I can't tell.

I don't look up at him as he speaks, instead pulling out the crumpled paper from my pocket and tossing it at him. "Did those pressing matters have anything to do with this?"

He clenches his jaw and then his fist around the paper. "You let me worry about the King of Bellehaven." His voice is deathly low and serious.

"You want me to pretend every moment I spend here, and every day I fail to heal your father, I am not putting everyone at risk?!" I slam the book shut, standing up. "You do not know him like I do, Ledger—you don't know what he is capable of."

"And he doesn't know what I am capable of when the ones I care about are threatened." Ledger's power thunders through the room, shaking the walls and coating them in a foggy haze. Books topple off the shelves of the library. The chair and table creak as his vines snake up the legs.

I swallow, glancing down at them. "Bellehaven has one of the most powerful armies on the continent. I cannot allow anyone to be hurt because of me. I made a promise to you that I will help your father, and I will, but once that happens, I must go back." My voice is a pleading whisper, Ledger's face a mask of fury.

"You will not be forced into doing anything. He may have one of the most powerful armies, but they follow him out of fear, not loyalty. He has numbers but he doesn't have their respect or devotion. Westray's army is full of individuals with honor, strength and integrity. And I would have them fight for you, consequences be damned." His power wraps around my hips and tugs me to him, the air around me tinged with the faint smell of smoke.

I don't resist it, and once in front of him, I let my hand rest on his chest. "I can assure you, Ledger, I am not worth it."

"And I can assure you that you are. You are destined for more than what he allows of you. I can feel it, Layla, and if you don't desire that life anymore, then all you need to do is say it."

"You are asking me to leave Maddox, to forsake my mother. What kind of person would I be if I did that?" I aim the question at him and myself.

"If the King didn't have your mother, would you stay? Would you fight for a life here? With or without me?" He adds the last part.

"Ledger—" I start but he cuts me off.

"Please, Layla, give me something, anything. I feel like I am going crazy over here." He runs a hand through his hair.

"To dream of such things is a dangerous game, one I cannot afford to play." I bite my tongue from saying what I truly want.

He stares at me, the wrinkle in his brows and the frown on his mouth giving away his frustration. I know he wants me to fight for this life, for myself, for him.

I can tell he wants to argue, desires more of an answer from me, a real answer, but the truth is that I simply don't have one. He nods stiffly and my heart squeezes. His disappointment is palpable, and I force my eyes away. Archie,

Mia, and Cam walk in, breaking the tense moment. I lose a relieved breath taking a few steps back.

"Hope we aren't interrupting anything," Archie comments wiggling his eyebrows.

"Not at all," I respond, forcing a smile. "Did Ledger happen to mention he received a threatening note from the King of Bellehaven?" I ask, and Ledger shoots me a furious look.

"He did not." Mia looks at Ledger pointedly as she brushes past him, her scent of vanilla tickling my nose. "What did it say?"

"What do you think it said, Mia?" Archie grabs a book and plops down on the settee. "If I had to guess, it probably read something like, 'Give her back or else,'" he says, and Cam barks a laugh.

"Archie, this is serious," Mia scolds. "You, of all people, know what he is capable of."

"I do, and that is also why I am in no hurry to return Layla to him." He frowns. "Why does it matter what the note says? She can't go back until Callum is healed, and last time I checked he is still unwell." Archie turns his attention back to me. "You're too important, Layla, and we knew there would be consequences when we took you."

"Let the King of Bellehaven come; we will be ready for him," Cam chimes in.

"I would never ask anyone to fight for me like that and even a drop of blood shed over me is too much. What would

King Callum say?" Everyone is silent after I ask the question. "I'll take your silence as confirmation he would not agree with you." I sigh, losing my desire to argue.

"Now that you all are here, you can at least help. If we can find the answer to healing Ledger's father, then I can return to Bellehaven, and maybe we can avoid retribution." Even as I say the words, I know the King of Bellehaven won't let this go unpunished one way or another.

"Grab a book. If you see anything about nullifying powers or something useful that may help her breakthrough to my father, show me," Ledger addresses each of them.

"Get comfortable, we may be here a while," I add, grabbing a book and sitting next to Archie.

We all read for hours, stopping only when a housemaid comes to bring us food. My head lays on a pillow in Archie's lap. I pop grapes into my mouth as I scan the pages of the text I hold.

"Grape," Archie says, and I place a grape into his open, awaiting mouth. "You know, if you were wearing less clothing, this would be fulfilling one of my many fantasies."

Ledger growls from the chair across from us. "And if you don't start feeding yourself grapes, you'll find out what fantasies I have been having, Archie." The chair squeaks across the floor as he pushes up to stand. He throws his book onto the table and yanks another off the shelf.

Archie gives me a wide-eyed look, and I smother a smile.

"Grape," Cam calls and I toss him one, laughing as he catches it in his mouth.

"Not you too, Cam." Ledger scowls, making Archie snicker. "Are you even reading, Archie?"

"Of course, I'm reading, Ledge. I can't help it I get hungry."

I push myself up, scooting over to the other side of the settee, not wanting to further Ledger's irritation. "Guys, I think I found something," Mia calls from the table where she sits. We all jump up, crowding her. "It is in Urtash, the language of the old gods, so I can't make out much, but I keep seeing the word blood. Ledger, can you translate it?"

"Let me see." He grabs the text. We all hold our breath as he reads. My heart pounds as I wait. "It says if a healer's power was diminished or unreachable, a select few had the essence of healing within their blood. If they so desired, they could complete the sacred act of blood sharing to channel their healing ability."

My heart pounds. We all look at each other wondering the same thing. Could it work?

"We should go to your father. It's the first idea we have found in days, and I think it's worth trying," I suggest, letting hope swell within me.

"Okay," Ledger agrees, looking at everyone else, who nod back at him.

We leave the library together and make our way to the King of Westray's room. My stomach flips nervously the closer we get. Ledger orders the guards outside to stand down and they comply, opening the King's door. My palms sweat as we walk in.

Ledger's father looks worse than the last time I saw him. More frail, his skin yellow and sticky with perspiration. His breathing is loud and labored.

I reach for my dagger, dropping my hand and looking at Ledger when I realize I'm not wearing it.

Ledger grasps the hilt of his dagger. "Are you sure?" he questions.

"I'm sure." I nod at him. The metal rasps as he unsheathes it and hands it to me.

He lurches towards me as I grasp the razor-sharp edge in my closed palm and pull, slicing into my skin. Blood drips onto the floor as I approach the King.

"Layla." Ledger steps closer to me, and I hand him back his dagger.

Everyone watches as I step to the King's bedside, extending my fist. My blood leaves a trail as I bring the flow to his mouth.

My hands shake as the liquid trickles down, coating his tongue in a deep red. My head swims when he swallows. The tang of copper stings my nostrils.

I pull back my hand and Ledger is there, wrapping it in a cloth and holding it to his chest. We all stare at the motionless King, none of us breathing.

Minutes pass and nothing happens. My stomach drops, a sickening dread filling my chest. My heart aches for Ledger as he squeezes my hand gently. I swallow the knot in my throat, the bitter taste of defeat enough to make me gag.

I turn away, letting my head fall onto Ledger's chest. His hand rubs my back, and I cling to him. We stay like that for a long moment, the silence between us deafening.

"We will keep trying," he says, his voice thick with emotion. "You guys should get some rest."

I pull back as Mia steps up, enveloping him in her arms. "We are going to figure it out—we always do."

Archie claps him on the shoulder. "I can stay with you if you want?"

"I need to be alone with him, Arch," he responds, and I feel the failure all the way to my toes.

"There is still time," Cam whispers as he follows Mia and Archie out.

I stand awkwardly next to him, wanting to offer comfort but not sure how.

"Go. Rest, Layla," he demands, and I can feel his need to be alone with his dying father.

"I'm sorry," I whisper before walking out of the room.

CHAPTER
TWENTY

Once I am back in my room, I take a long bath, dumping various amounts of the fancy salts and oils that line the counters. I scrub the evidence of the day away ignoring the throbbing of my open cuts.

My hand leisurely drips blood into the clear water, rippling ruby at the surface before dispersing. I watch, mesmerized. My father's last words replay in my mind almost like a taunt. "Your blood, Layla, it is in your very blood."

What did it mean? And if it was true then why hadn't it worked?

When the water cools, I ease myself out of the stone tub. Wandering over to the vanity, I find some pristine white swatches of cloth I use to wrap the twin gashes tightly.

I find a lavender nightgown hanging in the closet and throw it on. Failure and defeat are eating me alive as I lay in bed. I fist my hands in the sheets, hissing at the sting, and wanting to check on Ledger.

He risked so much by bringing me here and it would all be for nothing if I was unsuccessful. Sighing, I get up and open the book I'd retrieved from the library. I translate the ancient language, word by word. It reads exactly as Ledger had said.

Maybe I wasn't one of the chosen few with power infused within my blood. My hand throbs as I look at the crimson soaking through the white cloth.

I jump as Ledger busts through my door. His eyes are wild, and his breathing labored. "You have to come—now."

I spring up and go to him, my stomach lurching into my throat. He grabs my hand and pulls me through the hallways. I jog to keep up with his long strides.

"What is it? Is your father okay?" My heart wallops against my chest. When he doesn't answer, I squeeze his hand anxiously. "Ledger," I say his name, but he doesn't stop or answer me until we are bounding through the open doors of his father's room.

Ledger is tense as we stand at the foot of the bed, the muscles in his body taut. "Look," he breathes, and I turn my attention to the King.

His sickly complexion is no longer a pale yellow but a rich golden that matches Ledgers. His sunken cheeks are full and have a dusty rose hue.

The hair atop his head isn't dull and dry, but a lush, shiny black. His once frail body, while still underweight, is now more of an athletic build.

He appears handsome and healthy and as if he is resting. His breathing is steady, and when I touch the pulse at his wrist, his heart is beating strong and sure.

I run the back of my hand over his forehead; his temperature is normal. "It worked," I murmur in disbelief. "It worked!" I say again louder, looking at Ledger.

His mouth is agape with astonishment. "He's— he's going to be alright?" His eyes roam his father's features.

"I can't be sure, but he looks like a different person," I say, awestruck as I study him again.

Ledger lets out a shaky breath. "Do you think he will wake?"

"I think it's possible," I respond as he touches his father's hand.

"Your Highness, is everything okay?" Humphrey cracks the door, his high voice carrying through the room. "I heard some commotion.

"I think we did it, Humphrey," he breathes as Humphrey enters, gasping as he beholds the King.

"It's a blessing from the gods," he whispers.

I stay for a few more hours, monitoring the King as Humphrey prepares for him to wake. His vitals improve and no matter how many times I check him, he still appears to be in good health.

Ledger stays by his side, his eyes rarely straying. He is quiet, barely even breathing as he waits for him to wake. I can taste his fear and see it in the lines of his forehead as each minute passes.

Finally, the King of Westray begins to stir, and then his eyes blink open. They are a devastating green, matching his sons. Ledger quakes letting out a noise of disbelief.

They embrace, murmuring to each other, and I back out of the room. The moment feels intimate, coated in many years of emotions I can't begin to fathom.

Humphrey notices and leads me out of the room. "May I escort you to your room, Miss Sutton?"

"Sure, thank you." I follow him through the halls.

"Now that His Grace is healed, will you be needing transportation back to Bellehaven?" he asks, catching me by surprise.

"Oh, um, I am unsure of my departure but thank you for your offer." I slow as we reach my door.

"You are a distraction for the prince. I see how he looks at you, his childlike infatuation. I fear you have forgotten yourself. Ledger is a prince, and you are just a healer. You do not mix into this world, and the sooner you go back to where you came from, the better." He sneers, and I rear back at his words.

My mouth opens and closes, trying to form a response.

"His Grace has not seen what I have seen, but I know he would mirror my words. Take this as a reminder because it seems like you have forgotten your place. Goodnight, Miss Sutton." He shuts the door, uninterested in what I have to say. I am left standing in shock.

As much as I hate to admit it, Humphrey was right. I had let myself get swept up in this world, in the allure of Ledger.

I lay down, attempting to sleep. It was well into the early morning now. I shut my eyes but with the adrenaline pounding through my veins and my impending return to Bellehaven that much closer, I find it almost impossible to rest.

I eat when a maid drops off food and then sit on the windowsill looking out into the dark.

A knock comes, startling me. I patter over to the door on bare feet and crack it. Ledger is standing there in a black button-down shirt. The first few buttons are undone, and his broad chest is peeking out. He has a shadow of stubble lining his square jaw. The sight of him makes my mouth go dry.

"Your Highness?" I question and get my desired reaction when I see his jaw tick.

"I hope I didn't wake you," he says.

"With the events of the day, I am finding it hard to sleep," I answer back.

"May I come in?"

I widen the door in response, stepping back. He enters, walking past me. The door clicks shut, and I stand awkwardly watching him.

"Do you mind?" He saunters over to the wine decanter and sets out two glasses.

"Be my guest." I watch as he pours two glasses of the burgundy liquid and walks one over to me. I can tell his palms are sweaty as I take the glass from him.

"Thank you." I take a long drag and let the rich, fruity liquid coat my mouth.

Ledger takes his own mouthful, and I watch his Adam's apple bob as he swallows. I fidget with the stem of my glass.

"How is your father?" I break the silence first.

"He is impossibly well." He clears his throat from a lump of emotion. "Thank you, Layla, truly. You are Westray's salvation, my salvation, and I am in awe of you."

"Well, you didn't bring me here to fail now, did you?" I throw his words back at him but with a teasing tone.

"I get it. I should not have said that. I can be a real ass at times."

"Your words, not mine." I grin while taking another sip.

"I was hoping to talk to you before morning. Honestly, I was afraid you'd already be halfway to Bellehaven by now."

"Considering I can't ride a horse, that would be highly unlikely." I smile into my wine glass.

"Have you thought of what your life could be here if you stayed?" The words tumble out of his mouth, and I realize he's nervous. "You could have your own healing wing. You'd be able to treat who you like when you like."

"My very own healing wing? Fancy." I entertain him. "And would your people have to pay to see me?"

"You could do it for no charge if that is what you wish."

"Where would I sleep?" I know I can't stay, but I need something to dream of when I inevitably must go back.

"In your room, of course." He looks around the room we stand in, and I like how he refers to it as mine.

I nod, taking a generous sip of the wine before placing the glass down to ponder his words. Having free will and being able to use my abilities to truly help people without stipulations has always been a dream of mine. For people to be able to get the care they need without having to choose between their health and putting food in their stomachs. It would be the life my father would have wanted for me.

"What will you do when the King of Bellehaven retaliates?"

"We will offer him riches, give him what he desires as long as it is not you. And if it is your mother you want, we can try to get her out. Bring her here." My heart flips at his offer, at the way he makes it all sound so deceivingly easy. I know the King of Bellehaven would not accept any amount of money. I couldn't think of a single thing that Ledger could offer him in exchange for me that he would accept.

As far as my mother goes, I would love to bring her to Westray, take her to the library, and show her the gardens. I just didn't believe she could travel so far in her condition.

"And if I wish to leave Westray?" I think I see a grimace pass over Ledger's face, but it is gone too rapidly to confirm.

"Then I will escort you back to Bellehaven myself."

"What do you want, Prince? Do you wish me to stay, or would it be a great relief to see me go?" I ask, already knowing the answer but wanting to hear him say it again.

"I will not tell you what to do, Layla. My opinion should hardly matter," he responds, and I try to hide the disappointment that passes across my face at his answer. "But it would be a great relief to think of something that isn't you. To be able to concentrate without my mind wandering to your beautiful face, your wild hair, your fucking frost-blue eyes," he continues and my heart gallops. "I've been able to think of little else. I fear, however, not even your absence will deter that."

I can hardly breathe at his confession. He always did have a way to stun me into silence. I find it hard to comprehend *I* have any effect at all on this beautiful man.

I will never admit it to myself but as much as I loathe this man at times, I desire him more. I want him beyond reason, a feeling I can't understand and stopped trying to rationalize long ago.

Maybe it is the wine or his confession, but I feel bold as I look up at him. Blood charges through my veins. "Then give me a reason to stay, Prince." I take a step closer to him, feeling the heat of his body through my thin nightgown.

His eyes darken as he studies me. "You should be cautious of what you ask. I am a starving man."

"I know exactly what I ask." I stare into his eyes as I say the words, hoping I sound more confident than I feel. I am *sick* of pretending, *sick* of denying myself of the things I so desperately desire.

It seems like that is all the confirmation he needs. He turns, placing his glass down before his attention drifts back to me, my body lighting up with anticipation.

His heated gaze meets mine before seductively, lazily sliding down my body. I flush in his wake; there isn't a single nerve ending that doesn't feel his eyes.

I could easily find myself addicted to the expression he currently wears as he devours me. I bask in his attention, crave it.

My heart jolts when his large hand comes to rest just below my breasts. He inches it down my body, the heat from his palm searing. His hand stops at my hip, and he possessively pulls me to him until my chest brushes his abdomen.

His free hand brushes the hair off my neck and then trails over my jaw to my chin where he gently grips it. He tilts my chin up, bringing our faces closer together, his thumb straying to my bottom lip and pulling it down ever so slightly.

His nearness makes my head spin, all my senses in overdrive.

His lips hover over mine, almost touching, "Stay," he whispers. I don't dare breathe when his full lips brush mine. "Put me out of my misery and let me taste you," he growls before covering my mouth with his.

His kiss is gentle, unhurried as he explores. When I feel the press of his warm tongue it brings me to my toes, chasing more. A hunger foreign to me overtakes my body.

His kiss claims me, strong and restrained. My hands tangle in the silky strands of his hair. His control is almost frustrating, while my brain screams only one thing over and over. *More.*

A dizzying current races through my veins at his touch, his very presence like a drug. His hands move around my body, starting at my hips, up my taut stomach, to my now-heavy breasts.

His touch is a light caress driving me out of my mind. All too soon his lips leave mine to trail down my neck, each damp kiss setting me aflame.

His mouth works its way back up, pausing at my ear. "I need to feel your skin, to taste it."

My hands move on their own accord, lifting above my head, giving him unspoken permission. Wanting whatever he is willing to give.

His fingers brush my thighs as he reaches for the bottom of my silky nightgown. The fabric draws over my skin as he drags it up, pebbling my flesh. He tosses it carelessly on the ground.

He growls, his eyes descending on me, clad in only a flimsy pair of underwear. He lifts my legs around his middle, taking a few steps and placing me softly onto the lush bed. My hair fans out around me, and I lay on display for him.

He marvels at me the way one would a painting like I'm a true work of art. His eyes burn a path over the plains of my body, snagging and clouding with lust. I try not to squirm, my body alight with such desire it seems an impossibility to stay still.

"I do not deserve to even be in your presence. You are the most beautiful thing I've ever seen," he breathes.

I bite my lip and let him drink me in until his eyes land on my face. I sit up and let my hands drift to the buttons on his shirt. My hands tremble as I undo them one by one, his exquisite, tanned skin revealing itself to me inch by tortuous inch.

When I get to the last button Ledger shrugs his shoulders, and the shirt falls to the floor. His hardened length strains against his trousers, and my fingers twitch with the need to touch it.

It hurts to look at him, from his beautiful, corded shoulders, to his lean, defined abdomen. Strength that shows in each strand of his taut muscles.

I run my fingers down his chest and over his stomach, his muscles tensing under my touch. I stop at the largest scar on his ribs and caress the raised skin, replacing my fingers with my mouth.

I hesitantly kiss his marred skin, eliciting a soft tormented groan that sends a thrill down my spine. I peer up at him from my lashes and his hands find mine. He kneels, placing my hands on the strong tendons lining the back of his neck.

His full lips once again find mine and we kiss with reckless abandon. My toes curl as our bodies meet, my nipples skating across his chest.

His hands explore the bare skin of my back and the soft lines of my hips. His touch is sure when he gets to my breasts, giving them a gentle but firm squeeze. I gasp as a jolt of pleasure shoots straight to my core.

His kiss grows more demanding, but he pulls back to speak his desire. "Stay." His voice is husky and full of tantalizing persuasion. The word echoes through my brain.

My thoughts are too fragmented to form a response as he continues to explore my body. I arch into him needing more.

He brings his sensual mouth to my dusty pink nipple and sucks, making my hips buck. My thighs are slick with evidence of my desire, how desperately I need more.

His magic descends over me peppering my skin until it settles over my neck, putting delicious pressure there.

"Say my name," he demands.

"Ledger," I breathe it, my fingers pulling his hair. He moans, and the sound makes the ache in my core almost unbearable.

He smiles as he sucks my other nipple into his talented mouth. He releases it with a pop, the cold air seeping into it, continuing my tortured pleasure.

He brings his knee to my soaked core, and I can't stop myself from writhing against it. Ledger looks down at me and his mouth curves up into the most beautiful smile I have ever seen, sexy and seductive. When his dimples pop, I feel like I might burst into flames.

"What is it that you want, blondie? Do you crave my fingers, or would you prefer my mouth?"

"Yes, anything, everything." My lust-coated brain can barely form words that make sense.

His hand slides down my body, stopping at my underwear. His knee moves away, and I whimper at the lost contact.

His fingers move to my entrance and my back arches as he enters one into my heat. Ledger makes a tortured noise. "Gods, you're so fucking wet."

My hips move at their own accord, chasing more. I nearly sob with relief when his thumb encircles my clit.

Ledger hums approvingly. "You like that?"

"Uh-huh," I mumble incoherently.

"You want more?"

"Yes." I don't even recognize my voice as I breathe the word.

He adds another finger, and I moan as he curls both of them inside of me. A delicious pressure builds in my core as jolts of pleasure ricochet through my body.

"Oh, gods," I moan as his power mists out of his palms, entangling with my own that now seeps from my body.

"Your body, this tight pussy is the closest thing to holy I've ever been. I'm not a religious man, but there is not a world where I would grow tired of worshiping you. Stay."

I feel his plea down to my very core, and I cry out as release whips through me. My fingernails scratch the length of his back, my own bowing off the bed.

I see stars, my eyes rolling into the back of my head. Ledger watches me as I come apart as if he is committing this moment to his memory, every moan, every fevered touch.

My power floods out of me in waves. My skin buzzes with it, and the room pulses.

It's Ledger's agonized sound that has my eyes opening. My power is wrapped around him. Ledger's head is tilted back, his brow furrowed as my power caresses him.

"Layla, I am desperately trying to make this night about you but if you don't rein in your power, I fear my control may snap." He shudders as my power continues its exploration.

I'm drunk with the knowledge that I have the ability to crack this man's unwavering control.

"Layla," Ledger growls, and I jump, grasping at my power. I close my eyes so I can better focus and clutch onto the tether, willing it back inside.

Once I'm sure I have control, I open my eyes. Ledger is catching his breath, his head bent, and his brow furrowed as his chest heaves.

After a long moment, he removes his fingers from inside of me.

My eyes drift to the length of him, straining against his pants. I reach, letting my fingers run over his hard rather impressive cock. He grabs my wrist pulling it away.

"Did I do something wrong?" My cheeks immediately heat.

His body is taut, still, as his grip remains. "You didn't do anything wrong, Layla. I'm trying not to fuck this up." He turns away grabbing his shirt off the ground, and my stomach drops, thinking he is going to put it on and leave.

Instead, he places my arms in each sleeve and begins buttoning it. His fingers find mine and he turns my injured palm over, revealing a now-thin scar.

"I get a bit of sick satisfaction when I assist you in doing that." He grins. He lifts me up, placing me in the bed and settling in next to me.

I turn so we are face-to-face, the moment more intimate than I am prepared for. My hands rest on his chest as he strokes lazily down my back. There are so many things I want to say, but I am tired and satiated and terrified of ruining the moment.

Instead, I study his beautiful face, enjoy his nearness, and breathe in his scent.

"Stay," he whispers one more time before sleep takes him. The darkness outside starts to bleed into a hazy gray, illuminating his sleeping form.

He looks so peaceful, so devastatingly handsome. He lays next to me, his arm now draped around my middle, like it's the most normal thing in the world.

I'm punched in the gut with an emotion I have trouble placing. It's something that feels so very foreign to me. A heart-squeezing yearning for this man, for a life that is not my own.

It steals the breath from my lungs and clogs my throat with panic. Things as beautiful as him weren't meant for people like me.

I needed space, needed his hands off me. Needed to inhale a breath that didn't carry his scent. I jerk away from him, but his hand tightens around me, robbing me of my fight.

I force myself to swallow the panic and blink my welling eyes. I relax into him, pretending for tonight, I am someone else. For tonight, I just want to be a girl being held by a boy. I allow my guilt and fear to fade and let myself imagine what it could be like for us in a different life.

If he was just a boy and I was just a girl.

CHAPTER
TWENTY-ONE

I STARTLE AWAKE TO A KNOCK AT MY DOOR. I NOTICE I'm alone, the side where Ledger lay last night, cold.

The knock comes again, and I spring out of bed fumbling over to the door. I open it to see a perky-looking Archie in his training gear.

"Rise and shine, beautiful! I heard the news; we did it!" Archie scoops me into a big hug, spinning me so my feet leave the floor. I laugh as he puts me back down. "I thought we could celebrate with a little training session."

His eyes drift, taking in my appearance, and I remember I am wearing only Ledger's shirt. Realization crosses both of our faces at the same time, and I attempt to push him out of the room just as he shuts the door behind him.

"Wasn't Ledger wearing that shirt yesterday?" Archie's voice follows me as I beeline to the closet. "I thought you'd been healing the King all this time. Wait, was this how Ledger thanked you?" I hear the amusement in his voice.

He stops outside of the closet as I throw on my training uniform, scrambling for an explanation. I stomp out of the closet, throwing the shirt at Archie's smug face as he leans against the wall. "You're mistaken. The shirt was hanging in my closet."

"You're a terrible liar." He looks pointedly at my discarded nightgown lying in a puddle by the bed. "Sexual frustration has been permeating from you two for days. This morning, however, you're looking refreshed and suspiciously relaxed." I throw my shoe at his head, and he, to my displeasure, dodges it.

"I'm glad he offered his services because if he didn't, I was about to. Just as a courtesy, of course." He smirks as I pick up the thrown shoe, yanking it on.

"Shut up, Archie. Are you here to train me, or are you just going to taunt me all day?"

"I honestly didn't know you had it in you. It's only been what, five hours since I last saw you and you've already healed the King and seduced the prince. I'm impressed." He beams at me as I push past him into the bathroom.

"Nothing happened," I call as I splash some cold water onto my heated face.

"Mia and I were taking bets on how long it would take you two to finally give in to each other. I didn't think you'd make it past Grimwood."

"It was a lapse in judgment; it won't happen again."

"Many girls have said that to me before, and it always happens again." He grins over at me, and I roll my eyes.

"Have you heard how the King is doing this morning?"

"When I saw him last, he was up, walking around, and looked healthier than I have seen him in years," he says, and relief courses through me.

"I should go check on him." I pull on my boots.

"He requested to be alone for the morning. I would check back this afternoon," he informs me. "I knew we could do it, Layla. In fact, I'd like to show you my own appreciation." He leans in, closing his eyes and pursing his lips, and I push his head away.

"Very funny. Can we go now?" He chuckles and motions me forward.

"Lead the way, my lady."

My BACK SLAMS INTO THE MAT, PUNCHING THE AIR from my lungs for what feels like the thousandth time.

Archie steps on my wrist, forcing my hand open for him to retrieve my dagger. I am eternally grateful my aching muscles from the days prior were healed last night because I can feel the new aches of today already setting in.

"You're sloppy and distracted, you should have seen me coming that time." Archie holds out his hand to help me up.

He's not wrong. Ledger is training with Cam in the square next to us. He isn't wearing a shirt, and the sounds coming out of his mouth are making my mind drift to the events of last night.

He seems lighter today, smiling and joking with Cam. It's so foreign to see, so charming I can't keep my greedy eyes from straying to him.

I grab Archie's hand and stand up brushing myself off.

"Go run a few laps. You can come back when your raging hormones have calmed." His eyebrows lift suggestively in Ledger's direction. I grit my teeth, willing the heat from my cheeks as we walk over to the track.

Mia is running and when she sees me, she runs to me, engulfing me in a hug. "I can't believe it worked! I never doubted you for a second!"

I hug her back.

"Thank you, Layla, really, Callum is like a father to me, and I don't know what I would have done if his condition didn't improve."

"You're the one that found the answer. All I did was provide my blood." I smile at her.

"I hope this doesn't mean you will be leaving soon?"

My heart drops with the knowledge I will have to go back. "I will stay another day or two, to ensure the King is recovering as he should."

"Let's make the best of it then." She grabs my hand, and we start to run. I focus on the contracting of my muscles and the burning in my lungs.

"How did Ledger's mother die?" I ask the question I'd been wondering, trying to keep up as she runs faster.

"Has no one told you?" I shake my head, and Mia considers me for a moment as if debating what to reveal before continuing.

"Ledger's mother was able to mimic powers or borrow them. She didn't use it often and thought of it as a violation. The night Lilly was born, she wasn't breathing. Her heartbeat continued to weaken until it stopped altogether." I stumble as my legs burn with effort, eager to hear more.

"One of her handmaidens had the power to create life. It was supposed to be used for crops and plants, never for a human. Ledger's mother was desperate, so she channeled power into Lilly." Mia's movements are lithe as she speaks.

"It worked, but she used a dangerous amount of power. Lilly's heartbeat returned as she took her first breath. His mother was thrilled, but that night, after extending so much forbidden power, when she fell asleep, she never woke again."

My heart sinks. "Gods above." My legs burn from the effort. No wonder Ledger wanted me to stay in his rooms the other night after I had burned through so much of my own power.

I run and run long after my conversation with Mia in hopes my head will blissfully empty. It doesn't. I can't get her words out of my head. Can't shake how much I ache for the boy Ledger once was.

When I make my way back over to Archie, he is talking to Cam and Ledger, who is mercifully now wearing a shirt. Ledger's eyes find their way to me and run the entire length of me, sending a thrill up my spine.

"Layla, are you ready now?" Archie asks.

"Ready as ever."

"Actually, would you mind if we tried something?" Ledger asks. "I'd like to test your powers."

I shrug, looking over at Archie. "Be my guest." Archie gestures to me and steps back.

"Actually, Archie, we'll need someone for her to practice on." Ledger looks at him expectantly.

"Meaning I have to be the test dummy? Why can't she practice on you?" he questions. Ledger gives him an expectant look. "This is because of the whole grape thing, isn't it?" Archie asks, and when Ledger doesn't respond, he concedes. "Fine, but my perfectly symmetrical face is off-limits."

I raise a curious eyebrow. "What are we doing? Did Archie get a nasty case of chlamydia?"

"That's an incredibly rude assumption, but since you're asking, I do have this mysterious bump on my—"

"Alright, Archie, not today." Ledger grins, and I avert my eyes so I don't get swept away by it.

"Explain to me how your power works," he asks.

"Not this again, Ledger." I turn from him, ready to walk away, when a root comes up to wrap around my ankle, stopping me.

"Sutton, this isn't that kind of lesson." He approaches me, his chest brushing against my arm. "But for the record, if you need more practice with that, I'm more than willing." His lips brush my ear making my knees weak.

"Now, let's try this again. How does your power work while it heals?" The roots release me and disappear back into the ground.

I sigh, thinking. "When my power enters someone, I feel their body respond to me. I picture bones fusing back together, skin mending itself, blood pumping at the right pace through veins, and their bodies complying. Other times, I think of things that make me happy. Things that make me feel good and let my power do the rest."

Ledger listens intently as I finish. "Have you ever thought bad thoughts? What would happen if you pictured a bone breaking or a throat closing?"

"I'm a healer, why would I ever do that?"

"To protect yourself. I want to see if you can harm the very same things you mend. If your power can work in the opposite manner."

"You've got to be kidding me. Why can't you volunteer Cam or Mia for this?" Archie protests. We both look at him until he huffs, conceding. "I'll do it for you, Layla, but go easy on me."

I send him a sweet smile.

"You're welcome, by the way," he says with a grimace.

Ledger steps up next to me so our arms are brushing. "Close your eyes and find your power." I do as he says and find it humming softly in my chest.

I startle as Ledger's hands come to rest on my hips. My pulse accelerates at the contact. The hold I have on my power trips as my attention shifts. My mind drifts to how deliciously his calluses scraped against my bare skin, the warmth as they caressed my curves, how his fingers felt inside of me.

"Is this alright? Do you have it?" he asks innocently.

I clear my throat, snapping myself out of the devious thoughts. My hands move to his, and I gently pry them off. "I am finding it hard to focus; maybe if I stand over here." I take two steps away from Ledger, noting the smirk he tries to hide.

I take a deep breath, scolding myself before reaching again for my power. The second I feel it, I nod my head, keeping my eyes closed. "I've got it."

"Okay, now send it out to Archie, let it do what it normally does." I take a steadying breath and do as he says.

The air shutters as my power skims curiously along Archie's body. When it doesn't find anything, it delves inside of him.

Archie inhales sharply as it skates over his organs and through his veins. "This feels kind of nice."

"Now focus on his heartbeat." Ledger's hand comes to my upper back. "Speed it up."

My power resists at first but follows my command.

"How do you feel, Arch?" Ledger calls to him.

"Like my heart is racing, breathless, lightheaded, my chest hurts a bit," he responds, and at that last part, I let off on the command.

"That was good. Now try slowing it down." I do as Ledger says, and Archie falters a step.

"And now?" Ledger asks.

"I feel tired, dizzy, and there is a sharp pain in my chest." Archie's eyebrows pull into a frown, and I release his heart from the command, bewildered.

"I think it's working. Now focus on his hands, move to a finger, and try to break it," Ledger commands and my eyes widen, thinking he must be joking. He just nods towards Archie.

I look to Archie to tell me to stop but he just makes a tortured noise. "Make it quick," he whines. "You owe me."

I take another deep breath and refocus on my power. I send it down his arm and to his fingertips. This takes more effort than I'd like to admit. I'm panting when I finally get to the finger of my choosing.

I focus on the bone in his pointer finger and imagine snapping it, breaking it clean in two. My power thrashes unhappily for a moment before Archie hisses a pained breath.

"Did it work?" My eyes snap open and Archie is grasping at his hand.

"What do you think, Layla? Now fucking heal me already," Archie barks, and I break out in a wide smile.

"I did it!" I smile incredulously at Ledger, and his eyes drift down, pausing. His own lips lift in a soft, proud grin I relish in.

"I don't know what kind of sick foreplay you two are into, but can you gape at each other later? This finger has been used to pleasure many women, and if it is affected at all after this, I will never speak to you again."

"Sorry, Archie, also that was more information than I needed." I walk to him and heal the very break that *I* made.

He tests it, wiggling it around a few times before he decides he's satisfied. "I've done my part. Never do something like that to me again, promise."

"I promise, Arch, and thank you for letting me practice. I really do owe you."

"I'll take my payment in beer, or if you're open to it—"

"She's not. You'll be happy with beer," Ledger interjects, and I smother a grin.

As I gather my things and prepare to walk back to my rooms, Ledger approaches me. "Coffee with a touch of honey."

I jump at Ledger's voice, my eyes springing open. "What?" I look down to see a mug of steaming coffee in his hands.

He offers it up to me. "Your coffee. I hope I didn't get it wrong. A touch of honey?" I look incredulously at him, taking the mug as our fingers brush.

The look on his face spurs me to take a sip of the piping liquid. I nearly moan at the rich, nutty flavor made perfectly to my liking.

"Thank you. I've found my will to live again after Archie beat it out of me."

"You did ask for his help training you."

"Don't remind me." I take another sip of the heavenly drink and try not to think of what conspired between Ledger and me before he left my room last night.

"You did good today," he praises.

"You may have created a monster. With enough practice, I may never allow a man to be within two feet of me ever again." I smile into my cup of coffee.

"Good. A man should not have access to you if that is not what you desire."

"I'm tempted to make my way back to Grimwood just to test my newly found skills on Forde himself," I joke, but Ledger's face becomes serious.

"You promise me you will not leave Westray alone. That no matter what you will not venture into those woods without protection." His face is serious as he speaks.

"Trust me, Ledger, I've seen what is out there. I am not eager to encounter those creatures any time soon, especially alone."

"Where is *my* coffee? For future reference I like mine black with sugar." I startle as Archie appears.

"I'm happy to share," I offer him my mug, and he accepts it with a slight bow, taking a few large gulps. "That's hot, you know?"

After another gulp, he takes a long inhale. "Thank you, Layla, you are a true angel."

"No problem." I turn the empty mug over in my hands, sighing.

We are all about to leave the training grounds when Humphrey makes his way over to us. I stiffen at his approach remembering the words he spoke to me.

"Your Highness, Archie," he greets them before eyeing me from head to toe. "Layla," he grumbles. "So sorry to interrupt but His Grace has requested Layla and Ledger's presence. Please clean up and meet him in the great hall." He looks pointedly at me as he says the last part.

I bristle, struggling to keep the emotion I'm feeling off my face. I glance over at Ledger and he responds for us. "I'll escort Miss Sutton when she is ready, thank you, Humphrey." Satisfied with his answer, Humphrey leaves us.

"I'm going to go test this new finger out. Good luck, you two!"

"Gross." I make a face at him.

"Shall we?" Ledger gestures for me to walk in front of him, so I do. He grabs the door, and we walk down the hallway together.

After Ledger walks me to my room I bathe, rinsing the sticky sweat from my skin, and hop out of the warm water. I brush my hair and rub some pink liquid onto my cheeks. My anxiety spikes as I stare at the fine clothes in the expansive closet. What does one wear to meet a king?

I rake through the dresses and decide on a simple blue silk dress that fits like it was made for me. I give myself a once over, running my hands through my hair before heading to the door. When I swing it open, Ledger is on the other side, knuckle in the air as if he was about to knock.

His gaze snags on me, his eyes doing a full sweep. "I like you in that dress."

"I hope it's appropriate to meet your father. I was going for something innocent and sweet."

"I'm pretty sure he will see through that the second you open your mouth."

"Hey!" I push his shoulder, and that damn dimple appears. My heart flutters at its appearance. As soon as it disappears, I already want to see it again. This new side I I'm seeing of Ledger is dangerous. The more he lets me in, the further I wanted to explore.

Now that the King is healed, I know I have to get back to Bellehaven, and I feel the ticking clock like my own impending doom. I don't want to leave, but I can't see any other option.

The walls I built around myself are crumbling at a rapid rate, and I can already feel the devastation setting in.

As we walk, my eyes filter around, drinking in the castle's artistry. It's a mix of elegance and charm. I could get used to so many windows and the beautiful greenery outside of them.

"I forgot to ask, are we mentioning the whole 'you kidnapped me' thing, or should I keep that to myself?"

Ledger stops dead in his tracks, making me stumble. His face loses a little color, which elicits a smile from me.

"Kidding."

"You think yourself very funny, don't you?" His body relaxes, and he continues walking.

"You don't?"

"Oh, I find you many things."

"Enlighten me." I smile, curious.

"Stubborn, frustrating, strong-willed," he begins.

"I'm flattered. I can't begin to conceive why you are not betrothed, you have such a way with words and women."

"You didn't let me finish." We stop outside of two double doors. "You're strikingly beautiful, kind, captivating, and by far the most intriguing woman I have ever met." He brushes some hair behind my shoulder, his hand lingering as if needing some excuse to touch me.

"Watch it, Prince, you say too many nice things about me, and I may never leave," I joke. Ledger falls silent as he looks at me, and I gesture to the doors. "Are we going to go in?"

He opens one side and my heart jolts. I hesitate in the doorway until Ledger's familiar hand finds my back. "I'll be with you the whole time."

"Reassuring," I mumble and feel his grin on the shell of my ear before I walk into the room.

I let my fingers drag against the spines of old books as we amble inside. I'm once again struck by how lovely the library is.

"This used to be my mother's favorite room, she would spend hours here. I used to join her reading, watering the plants— sometimes she'd even let me paint with her."

"It's perfect." My eyes roam the bewitching room again, and I have the sudden urge to feel the sun warm my skin. My eyes scour around, and it's only on my second sweep I notice the king sitting on the outside settee.

He is smiling at me, almost sadly, watching as I gawk. My cheeks heat, and I force myself over to him.

"My apologies, Your Grace, I don't think I will ever get used to a place that is quite so enchanting." I curtsey. "I'm Layla Sutton."

"Wonderful name. Please, sit. You reminded me of my Eloise the first time I showed it to her." He pauses as I hesitantly sit on the warmed cushion next to him. "I built it just for her, you know. I could hardly get her to leave for a second after she laid eyes on it. If there was ever a time I couldn't find her, this is where she would be. Now, when I need to feel her, I come here, her very presence is entwined in this room, these books, in this very settee." The King strokes the book in his hand gingerly, his face alight with a rueful smile.

"She sounds lovely," I respond.

"Lovely doesn't even begin to describe her." His eyes have a distant look as if he is now picturing her beauty. He shakes his head, clearing his eyes before continuing. "Now it is I who must apologize. I did not ask you here to bore you with woeful stories of the past."

"They do not bore me; I quite like to hear of her." I smile at the king. He looks so unlike the man I first saw, so full of life and almost impossibly younger. He is quite handsome, bearing a clear resemblance to Ledger. "You look well. How do you feel, if I may ask, Your Grace?"

"Call me Callum, please. I can't remember a time when I've felt this well, thanks to you. I awoke feeling like I had aged ten years backward. It is nothing short of incredible that power of yours."

"It was nothing really. I'm happy to have been able to help."

"I am curious how your powers were able to get through to me. I've never in all my life experienced a power effectively used on or against me."

"Uhm." I shift nervously and look to Ledger, who is sitting in the chair next to us.

"Father, Layla tried multiple times to reach you with her powers, but she was not successful. Instead of giving up,"—Ledger's eyes stray towards me, and my heart skips a beat—"we read in some old texts that sometimes a healer's blood could be infused with healing abilities." There is a long silence where I can't bring myself to look at the King. "So, Layla offered you her blood."

"Remarkable," Callum breathes. "You must not speak of this to anyone. I fear what one would do to get their hands on something as precious as your blood, especially Sandor. A man like him could find many uses for it, good and bad. It could bring him more wealth and power and upset the balance of the kingdoms." I balk at his words, fear snaking up my throat. I know how easily Sandor can infiltrate my mind and rifle through my memories, and I contemplate how I will hide such a revelation from him once I return. "How did you know it would be successful?" Callum asks.

I squirm uncomfortably before forcing myself to be still. "I didn't know if it would work at all, but we were out of options. My father never gave up on anyone. He always used to say, 'Everything has an answer, you just have to find it.'"

"Wonderful, I find those words to be very true." He pauses. "You're from Bellehaven?"

"I am."

"I know King Sandor. In the past, he has been hesitant to allow those with abilities to aid any of the neighboring kingdoms. He must have had a change of heart?" He looks at Ledger, and I fiddle nervously with my hands.

"I can be very convincing," Ledger says stiffly.

"Indeed, you've never been one to accept the answer no, even when you were just a boy. I suppose if anyone could have convinced him, then it would be you." He addresses Ledger and then turns back to me. "Thank you again, Layla, truly. The gift you have given me, to have more time with my loved ones, with this beautiful kingdom, is immeasurable."

"It is an honor, Your Grace," I respond as Ledger and I get up to leave.

We leave the King, and Ledger walks me back to my room. He produces a book when we get to my door. "I thought you might like something to read; this was one of my mother's favorites."

I accept the book from where it is outstretched in his hands and marvel at the golden sprayed edges. I falter at his thoughtfulness.

"I must get back to my father, we have much to catch up on. You'll be okay the rest of the day?"

I nod in response. "Yes, actually. I am meeting Mia. She wanted to show me more of Westray."

"Well, in that case, make a wish at the fountains." He produces a silver from his pocket and flicks it into the air.

I catch it in my open palm. "Will do, Prince."

CHAPTER
TWENTY-TWO

When I open my door, Orion is waiting for me. "Hello, Orion, nice to see you."

"Layla," he greets. "The prince requested I accompany you and Mia to the town square."

"Oh okay." We begin to walk.

"Are you settling into Westray?" I am secretly delighted in our conversation. Orion was a man of few words and the only person he seemed to speak to was Ledger.

"I am, it's beautiful here," I say as Mia joins us and we make our way through the castle.

The walk to town is stunning. We pass over the turquoise water surrounding the castle. There is a dirt path that crosses gentle grasslands and fertile fields.

We arrive at an enchanting little town. The buildings are built from a mixture of beautiful stones and cedar rooftops.

It's bustling with people, some merchants pushing carts and kids playing in the streets. I notice multiple blacksmiths pounding metals as we walk by, remembering Westray's main trade is weaponry.

"Ohhh, can we get a sweet first?" Mia asks as sweet smells drift into the air.

"I like the way you think." I smile and Mia clambers up to a cart. As we get closer my mouth waters at the sweet smell.

"Greta, you know I can never resist your utidilla cakes. Can we get two, please?" she asks.

"Mia, lovely to see you! Two utidilla cakes coming right up." Greta is a plump woman with a friendly face. She plates up two pieces of cake and puts a dollop of something I'm not familiar with on top.

"Thank you, Greta, it smells heavenly," I tell her as I grab the plate.

"Enjoy, dears." She smiles as Mia pays her. We find a place to sit by a babbling fountain in the town center.

Mia looks at me excitedly as I take my first bite. I moan as the delightful flavors hit my tongue. "That is incredible."

"Right?! It's my favorite."

I see two men across the way with a giant hunk of meat on a skewer. The older man turns it slowly, fire emanating from what I believe to be his son's hands, cooking a searing each side.

My brows furrow confused

"In Bellehaven, the powerful are required to live in a sanction away from town and their families." It was one of the reasons my father never declared his power. My mother didn't have an ability, and he never wanted to be without her. "Using your powers so brazenly is also not accepted. Abilities are to be used only for serving the King or Training."

"I'm not surprised," Mia chimes in taking another bite. "The people of Westray love it here and would protect it with their lives, those with abilities and those without.

"In Bellehaven, the gifted are not supposed to interact with the powerless. The King wants to keep bloodlines pure."

"He sounds selfish and despicable. I hear he has an agreement with Grimwood to allow creatures to get close to the town. Uses their presence to scare the people and discourage them from leaving."

I frown at her words, thinking back to all the injured soldiers I've healed and their gruesome wounds.

"I've also heard no one wants to cross him for fear he will alter or erase their memories. He isn't known to play fair, and it's said he can get into one's head with a simple blink." I'd experienced his powers as they slithered and raked over my mind. I'd learned tricks over the years to hide my most valuable secrets, but he was cunning and ruthless, and I dreaded his undivided attention.

Mia must register the expression I wear. "Enough about him. I know a place that has the most succulent seared duck woodlouse. Come with me!" She grabs my hand and tugs, and I stop her.

"Wait." I take out the coin Ledger has tossed to me and turn it around in my fingers.

I think of what I long for most, wish for something I'd never dare dream was within my reach, and cast the coin out. It sails through the air, spinning before landing with a splash in the fountain.

I laugh as a few children race to the water pushing each other to reach in and snatch it out.

They dash to Greta, handing her the coin and greedily digging into the hot utidilla cake she hands them. Mia chuckles next to me before tugging me off to the next cart.

"So, what is going on with you and Ledger? Care to enlighten me?" Mia asks as she takes a bite of tender meat. We are sitting on a bench tucked away from the crowds.

"Nothing." The answer is instant and makes Mia lift her eyebrow. "I mean—he's more than I could have ever imagined." My answer surprises me. "I'm scared, Mia. That I am going to hurt him. I have my mother and Maddox back... home." The word feels foreign on my tongue. "My feelings, what I want, what he wants, hardly matters when so much is at stake."

Mia gives my hand a squeeze. "For what it's worth, he's different since you've been around, happier than I've ever seen him. And from what I can tell, you're different too."

"Have your abilities ever reacted to someone?" I blurt, bouncing my knee.

"What do you mean?"

"Has your power ever intertwined with someone else's or awakened at the sight of them, responded to them?"

Mia frowns at my question. "Not that I am aware of, but I think I've heard of power having recognition. Our abilities were passed down to us from the gods and have served many before us. It is part of our soul, and it isn't out of the realm of possibility it can recognize another from a past life."

I nod, lost in thought, and am grateful Mia doesn't push further. I'm snapped out of my thoughts when a little boy approaches us. He stands in front of me, holding something small in his hands. "For you," he says, and I raise my hand to accept.

"Thank yo—" The word dies on my tongue as I hold up a small rose folded from what looks to be the page of a book.

"Where did you get this?" I demand, but the boy is already skipping away. My heart pounds as my eyes scour the town square. It couldn't have been a coincidence.

"Is everything okay?"

I'm standing now, my body tense, the rose clutched tightly in my palm. He wouldn't be foolish enough to be in Westray, where he could be recognized, would he? My stomach somersaults.

"Sorry to cut the night short but we must be heading back. There is a curfew in place due to increased activity in the woods." Orion approaches us and my brows furrow in response.

"What kind of increased activity?"

"There have been multiple sightings of Kerolu and Dire wolves near our borders. Highly unusual. I'm sure it's nothing to be worried about, but to be safe, the prince requested we escort you back."

Fear skitters up my spine, rooting in the pit of my stomach as unease fills my body. I can't seem to shake it as we make our way back to the castle.

I fidget with the paper flower, chewing the edge of my nail. I avoid Mia's gaze as it flits from the flower to my face curiously.

"Are you alright, Layla?" she finally asks as we walk back to the castle.

"Yes, I'm fine." The answer couldn't be further from the truth, but I don't know what else to say. "I'm rather tired, so I think I will call it a night."

"You're sure?"

"Yes, thank you for the lovely outing. I didn't realize how much I've hungered for a friend like you. Truly." I mean every word. It's difficult to imagine a world without her, and my chest aches at the thought.

Mia's arms wrap around me, and I return her embrace. "I feel much the same. Sleep well, Layla." With that, she leaves me.

Sleep doesn't come easy that night. I lay staring at the paper rose illuminated by the light of the moon. I toss and turn, my body restless, my mind alight with worry. I swear I hear a howl pierce the quiet of the night.

When I do find sleep, my dreams are plagued with visions of snapping teeth, razor-sharp claws, and agonized screams.

CHAPTER
TWENTY-THREE

THE CLANGING OF ALARM BELLS SOUNDS EARLY THE next morning. The floor vibrates with the pounding of feet. I scurry to the door, throwing it open, hearing commotion. Ledger rushes down the hallway, barking out orders, and I bound for him.

"What is going on?" I jog to keep up with his long strides.

"There has been a breach, and reports of Kerolu and Dire Wolves in the town center."

My stomach drops. I picture the townspeople, all the children. "I want to help."

"You should stay back until we get it under control. We will need you for the injured. I'll send for you when it is safe."

"I will come now. I will not sit idly by while your people are in danger."

Ledger clenches his jaw. His nostrils flare as he breathes a sigh of frustration. "I expected nothing less." He reaches into his coat and pulls out two impressive, sheathed daggers, shoving the hilts into my hands. "Protect yourself; remember your training."

The horses are saddled and waiting for us as we exit the castle. Mia, Archie, and Orion all rush to their horses along with many castle soldiers.

I jump on Apollo with Ledger, and we race to the town center. The world blurs by us in a whirlwind of colors. When we reach town, it is mayhem.

People are screaming and running, there are carts knocked down and blood in the street. There are Kerolu and Dire Wolves everywhere. The townspeople and soldiers fight them off the best they can.

When we jump off Apollo, Ledger pauses for a moment, turning to me. "I do not want to see any of your blood spilled today."

"Well, that makes two of us." I push past him and run; my attention is directed at a man struggling with a nasty-looking Kerolu.

I whip out my dagger and take a breath before loosing it. To my absolute surprise, it meets its mark, sinking deep into the creature's skull. The Kerolu drops with a thud, and I waste no time retrieving my dagger.

I open my mouth to ask the man if he is okay when his eyes widen, and he scrambles up, turning and running. I whip my head around to see a terrifying Dire Wolf charging towards me.

It is huge, its fur is mangey, and white foam drips from its jowls.

Panic laces through me as I throw my blood-slicked dagger at the running creature. It misses, whizzing past its head. I don't have time to reach for my powers; it's too close. My feet scrape against cobblestones as I try to scurry away from the pursuing beast, but there is nowhere to run. I brace myself for impact as the enormous wolf crashes into me.

I fly backward, hitting the building behind me. My head cracks off the wood, and the hit reverberates through my skull.

My vision blurs as I grapple to find my other dagger. The creature stalks towards me, a low growl vibrating the air and making my hair stand on end.

A large rock lays on the ground next to me and I close my palm over it. I clutch the smooth stone in my hand while inching myself to stand. The muscles in the beast's legs twitch as it prepares to lunge at me. I crouch, gritting my teeth and readying myself to fight. The beast lunges and before it makes contact, Cam materializes in front of me. His sword pierces through the wolf's skull.

Cam yanks his sword out of the creature's head, and my thrown dagger floats over to me, suspended in midair. "You can thank us later," Archie shouts from a few feet away, grinning.

"You okay?" Cam asks, and he waits for my nod before turning and getting lost in the chaos.

I swipe my dagger from the air and pull myself to my feet ignoring the pounding in my head. I take a steadying breath and try to calm my racing heart.

Ledger's fighting off two huge Kerolu to my left. He slashes and stabs, dodging their serrated claws. His movements are lithe and agile, practiced and nimble. It is impressive to behold.

My heart leaps when another Kerolu catches Ledger in its sights. It runs at him full speed. Ledger's back is turned to it, oblivious to the danger.

I jump into action, my feet pounding off the ground as I run. I fumble for my powers, knowing I won't be able to make it to him on time.

My power purrs to the surface and I send it out towards the sprinting creature. It glides along its body and sinks inside.

The Kerolu's organs are different from a human's, unfamiliar as I search for anything that will stop it. Terror floods my veins as it nears Ledger, its claws drawn.

A scream tears from my throat a second before I find its heart. I grip the organ and squeeze, commanding my power to stop it. The creature is mid-flight when its eyes roll back, and it drops to the ground, twitching. Its chest ceases to move as death claims it.

I stumble as I reel my power back in, feeling the depletion of the action. Ledger's eyes meet mine, his shock apparent as he realizes what I'd done. I attempt to wipe the terror from my face, giving him a slight nod. His focus returns to the Kerolu in front of him.

Moaning draws my attention. I turn to see a man on the streets, blood freely flowing out of his abdomen. I sheath my dagger and dart over to him. I grab his shoulders and drag him to a few feet from the mayhem.

White light seeps from my palms without me having to call for it. I rip the man's already tattered shirt, exposing his wound.

I find a deep gash, a part of his intestine showing. He seems in and out of consciousness as I speak to him, "It's okay, you're going to be okay."

The adrenaline in my veins makes it difficult to focus, but I take a deep breath and close my eyes as my hands drift over the wound. I'm relieved when there's no trace of venom; It must have been from one of the wolves.

I picture the wound closing, the skin knitting back together. I picture him healthy, returning to his family.

I open my eyes to a thin scar and pink, freshly healed skin. The man is unconscious as I slap his cheek. "Wake up, wake up, wake up."

Sounds of the ongoing fight assault my ears as the man's eyes flutter open.

"You're okay. You've got to move; go somewhere safe, please." Awareness registers on his face as he looks down at his abdomen. His mouth falls, clearly shocked, as I grip his arm, hauling him up.

"Go, now," I demand and turn my eyes, scanning the streets. There is a woman waving her arms. "Over here, help us!"

I can't help myself from seeking out Ledger again in the chaos. He is slicing and stabbing at a Kerolu, dodging its sharp claws, the other he had been fighting dead at his feet. I breathe a sigh of relief, turning back to the women.

I smell it before I feel it. A musky, rotten smell fills my nostrils a second before I am slammed to the ground.

My body is engulfed by rough fur and a muscular, incredibly strong body. I see a familiar-looking curved horn just as sharp teeth puncture my shoulder. A scream rips from my throat.

The Kerolu is incredibly heavy, so much so that I can't get my hands underneath me to grab my daggers. My head is turned to the side, my cheek smashed into the dirt beneath me.

The creature tears at the skin of my shoulder, its teeth leaving new puncture wounds in their wake. Pain lances through me. Blue blood pools on the ground beneath me, and I realize it's from the Kerolu. It is missing both arms.

I wriggle beneath the massive creature, trying to suck in air. Realizing I won't be able to roll the beast off me, I call on my powers.

I send the energy roiling through its body, clenching onto its lungs and throat. The creature struggles against me, short, ugly gasps leaving its mouth.

I squeeze harder, and my hair clings to my neck and shoulders. It feels like an eternity before the beast stills with a sick gurgling noise.

I flounder beneath the dead weight above me, a sense of hysteria overtaking me. The irony of seizing this Kerolu's life only to be suffocated beneath it. A laugh bubbles in my throat, one that very well would have escaped if I could suck in an efficient breath.

Seconds later, the weight is lifted off me. The Kerolu's body thuds on the ground next to me. I roll onto my back, gasping down air. I hear the sickening crunch of a sword and turn my head in time to see the metal yanked out of the beast's head.

"You okay, blondie?"

"Never better." I give myself a moment to recover before Ledger helps me to my feet. "Thank you."

I cradle my screaming shoulder. He looks ready to throw me on his horse and send me straight back to the castle.

"I'm fine," I assure him before he can say anything. He eyes the wound with wrathful intensity.

Someone is being carried into the alleyway and I know I need to help.

"Layla," he growls as I back away.

"Go kill the rest of these fucking things," I say to Ledger before sprinting over to the alley. It's clear this is where the injured are being taken.

"Over here, please, she's not doing well." A man waves me over. I see a woman on her stomach, claw marks slashed gruesomely down her back. She is writhing in pain, making garbled noises.

I already know venom is working its way into her system. I kneel next to her, my skin sparking with energy, ready to undo the damage done to her.

I raise my hands over her back, bracing myself for the pain that accompanies the poison. White light descends on her wounds. I grit my teeth as the black venom absorbs through my palms. I distract myself from the pain, picturing Ledger's face. The night where we spent together, his mouth on mine, that damn dimple.

My hands tremble as sweat drips down my back. The extracting of poison becomes an almost unbearable torture.

I let out a breath of relief as I sense the last bit leaving the woman's body. The wounds on her back mend rather hastily after that.

The man who called me over grabs my hands bringing them to his bowed head. "Oh, gods, thank you."

There is no time to answer him as I'm pulled roughly away and thrown in front of another. The man is propped up against the stone wall, his pant leg ripped, revealing a jagged bite.

The flesh from his ankle to his mid-calf is missing, stark white bone on display. His skin is pale, and his eyes are wild as they find mine.

"Am I going to be able to keep my leg?" he repeats the question again and again.

"Calm down, please. It's going to be okay; I'm going to help you." I reach for his face, stroking my hand over his forehead and down his cheek.

Once he has calmed, I focus on his leg, my hands already aglow. The man flinches back, his other leg kicking out at me, his fear apparent.

"Please hold him still." I aim this request at a woman standing close by. She comes and holds his leg down, murmuring comfort to him. I waste no time saturating his leg in glowing mist.

My eyes drift shut, imagining the muscle that is supposed to be there. I see the tendons and flesh molding back together. I picture the man able to walk again.

A few moments later, I inspect my work: the skin is red, raised in areas. He won't be without a scar, and it's not perfect, but the chunk of leg that was missing is now filled in and he will be able to use it.

If I had more time and if I didn't have to conserve what power I did have, I could have done better, but it would have to do.

I heal person after person. I'm coated in so much gore and blood I wonder if I will ever be truly clean again. The poison I remove leaves me feeling ill, the nausea in my gut so strong it's a miracle I haven't vomited.

I grit my teeth against the throbbing in my shoulder, fighting to ignore the acute pain. The man I'm currently working on has his eyes shut and eyebrows drawn in discomfort. My glowing hands move gently around the wolf bites until the frown on his brows ceases.

My head's spinning from exertion and blood loss, but I can't bring myself to stop.

"LAYLA!" Ledger's voice cuts through the mayhem making my stomach drop. I drag my body up and run, my feet reacting before my brain can command them.

Dead Kerolu and Dire wolves litter the streets. I limp around their lifeless bodies, trudging through puddles of blue and red blood. I don't see or hear any more fighting, an indication the battle is over.

"LAYLA!" His cry comes again. I frantically search the streets as I stumble down the cobblestones. My heart pounds in my ears as I round the corner, trying to push myself faster.

Ledger in the middle of the town square crouched in front of the very fountain I was laughing and eating at days earlier. He is huddled over a body, his scarlet hands splayed out on their chest.

My boots stick to the cobblestones as I stagger to them. Mia is crouched next to Ledger, her face looking grim.

My stomach drops when I see distinct red hair. It was the boy I'd healed in the training grounds. Ledger looks scared as he holds a cloth over Holt's wounds. I'd never seen that emotion on his face.

I drop to my knees next to him. They are enveloped in wet warmth as blood pools around his body, too much blood.

"Let me see." I touch Ledger's hands, and he pulls away the cloth.

There are open wounds in Holt's chest, and abdomen, and I can make out fresh bite marks on his neck. His breathing is coming out in gasps. His skin is clammy, a sheen of sweat on his forehead as I place the back of my hand on it.

He's cold. The sensation sends a shock of alarm up my arm. My power flickers in my palms as I hold them up. A steady stream of blood is flowing out of the open wounds, and I know they need to be closed, but I can detect Kerolu poison working its way into his veins.

"Am I going to die?" he rasps. His blue eyes find mine, and I can see the fear behind them.

"No. Holt, no, you aren't going to die." My voice quivers as I speak. "You must be brave, okay? I'm going to remove the poison, make it hurt less." He nods before I start the slow, arduous process. My dwindling power accumulates in my palms, and I grunt at the impact of the poison leaving his body.

His body convulses as the poison continues its assault on my system. I tense, and my hands aggressively tremble. My power and energy wanes dangerously low, but I refuse to stop.

"Stay with me, buddy." A whimper leaves my mouth as my power flickers. A warm stream of blood trickles out of my nose and over my lips.

A hand comes down on my shoulder, warm and familiar. The buzzing in my veins makes my skin vibrate, a scalding warmth blanketing me. A brief feeling close to ecstasy makes me sway as I look at Ledger.

My mouth drops open as I realize he is giving me his power. It works both ways, he can take and give. Something I wasn't even aware was possible.

"It hurts," Holt chokes as a tear falls down his freckled cheek. I focus back on him accepting the gift Ledger is giving. The second the first wound is free of toxin; I begin to heal it. His chest knits together in a jagged, sloppy scar.

"I know, I know. I'll take the pain away." My voice cracks.

Ledger lets out a relieved breath as the last of the chest wounds closes. I start closing the wounds on his abdomen.

I let out a shuddering breath, pushing my magic harder. I hear Holt's sluggish heartbeat, and panic creeps up my throat.

I beg my power to work faster, to close the wounds, to heal what had been so brutally broken.

"It doesn't hurt anymore," he gasps, and my heart drops.

"Holt, you've got to hang on. Please hang on." I beg him as his shallow breaths turn to gasps.

No, no, no, no, my brain chants as the glowing in my hands grow brighter.

A spark of hope fills my veins as his stomach wound mends. But then his gasps grow quiet. His chest stills.

I grapple for his heartbeat but can't seem to find one.

My brain goes blank as I look at his pale, freckled face. His eyes are open, his chest deathly still. My heart drops as I blink.

The trembling in my hands moves up my arms as I continue to pour my powers into him.

"He's fine, he's going to be fine." My vision blurs with unshed tears, the silence around me deafening.

Mia's face is grim as she falls back onto her heels.

"I'm going to fix it." My voice wavers as a tear skates down my cheek. My power falters again as I burn through the energy Ledger provided.

"Layla." His voice is a soft, gentle rasp in my ear. An unfiltered sob breaks from my throat.

"I can fix it." Tears flow freely down my cheeks.

My head swims as I sway to one side. I know if I don't cut my power off soon, I will burn out, but I can't bring myself to do it. I can't accept the reality this young boy died, and I couldn't save him.

"You have to stop." Ledger's hands come to mine doing what I can't. My power abruptly stops, and I sag back into him, another loud sob leaving my lips.

Blood, my blood. The thought flashes in my mind and, I reach for my dagger, ready to slice into my palm. Ledger stops me as if reading my mind. "He's gone, that won't help."

His strong arms envelop me as I stare at Holt's face, void of life. His fiery red hair flutters in the wind. Ledger pulls me away, lifting me up, and turns my face into his chest, where I soak his shirt with my tears.

"I'm sorry, Ledger, I'm so sorry."

He holds me up, my own legs too weak. Clouds gather, and the sky booms with thunder. Rain pelts my numb skin.

"You did everything you could." His lips brush my forehead. I fear if he lets me go my heart, along with the rest of my body, will crack in two.

I look up to see the devastation on Ledger's beautiful face as he stares at the lifeless boy. A boy he knew intimately, a boy he watched grow up.

My hands fist his shirt, grief and guilt hitting me like physical blows. His hand bands around my neck, his thumb stroking my pulse point.

Lightning cracks in the distance, filling the darkening sky with a flash of blinding brilliance.

My mind becomes hazy and unable to register much of anything besides Ledger, the smell of copper and pine.

I sit, unblinking, on Apollo, staring at my crimson-stained hands. No memory of how I got here, the only image in my mind of the boy, pale and lifeless. My ears still echo with the sounds of battle, screaming, metal on metal, and tortured moans.

The only thing grounding me, the only reminder I'm not still back there, is Ledger's arm around me, the steady stroke of his fingers.

CHAPTER
TWENTY-FOUR

WHEN MY AWARENESS SPARKS AGAIN, I'M IN WHAT I ASsume is Ledger's bathroom. I stare unblinking at my bloodied hands, noticing the violent trembling.

"Is she going to be...okay?"

"Just let me get her cleaned up." I recognize Ledger's voice.

Archie appears in my line of vision and his hands rest on my knees. "You did good today, Lay."

My eyes have trouble focusing on his face, and when I don't respond, he squeezes my knees and kisses my cheek before standing.

"Are you going to be alright? Gods, why was he out there? I just never thought—"

"Not right now." Ledger responds and Archie leaves.

I can make out the faint sound of running water but barely feel it as my hands are placed under the flow. The water turns ruddy as gore swirls down the drain.

Ledger scrubs my hands clean, his eyes searching my face in the mirror. He sits me down and brings a cloth to my shoulder. His voice is muted as he says something I don't comprehend.

He brings up a bottle of alcohol, and the chill of the liquid seeps into my damaged skin and down my arm. I don't even flinch. Ledger's eyes search my face, his own brows furrowing, reminding me I should be feeling something.

He continues working. I stare passively at the bite wounds as he dabs and places a clean bandage over them. He pauses, staring at my bandaged shoulder. His hand finds mine, squeezing gently and bringing it to his mouth, brushing my knuckles with his lips.

He leaves the room, and the sudden awareness I am alone makes my pulse accelerate. Horror and hysteria lap at my consciousness as the shock fades. My breath quickens, and my heart squeezes.

Ledger comes back in, carrying one of his clean shirts, and the look I'm wearing must give away my internal panic. He rushes over, kneeling in front of me, his hands coming up to frame my face. "Hey, it's okay, I'm right here, breathe." He strokes my cheek with his thumb, showing me more kindness than I deserve.

My eyes swell with tears, and I lean into him. "All I hear are his strangled breaths, Ledger. I can still see the light leave his eyes and his unblinking, lifeless stare. I let him die." I wail out the confession and my stomach bottoms out. "He was so young; he barely had a chance to live." The taste of salt on my lips permeates my tongue from the tears I hadn't known were falling.

"Look at me, Layla." It is an effort to look into Ledger's forest-green eyes.

"You did everything you could for him. Nothing that happened was your fault." His voice holds so much pain.

I know what today cost him, know how familiar he is with the soul-crushing feeling of loss. Whatever I'm feeling, he has to be feeling ten times over.

"You saved the lives of so many, and I can't begin to repay you for what you gave." His finger swipes a stray tear from my face. "Tell me how to help you."

We stare at each other, so desperately needing to feel something before the crushing weight of the day pulls us under.

My eyes slip to his lips, lingering as I take in their fullness. My gaze drags back up his face, only to drop again.

My trembling fingers rise to trace their soft fullness. A bolt of yearning thrums through my body. A look passes his features as he stills.

He allows my silent exploration as my fingers delve into the silky, sweaty strands of his hair. He smells of salt, iron and the forest. My eyes close as my forehead lowers to his. A quivering breath leaves my mouth.

We stay like this, my heart ratcheting in my chest, until I inch my lips inch towards his.

Ledger is unmoving before me, exhaling a warm, shaky breath that skates across my face. My own breath shudders out as my bottom lip grazes his.

The air around turns thick and charged. Desire stirs deep in my belly, and I grasp at it as our mouths collide. His body is rigid, his lips supple but unmoving. I nearly weep with defeat, despair filling the pockets of my mind.

Just as I am about to pull back, he reacts, his kiss soft, slow. He handles me like I am something fragile that might fall apart at any second, maybe I will.

I drink his kiss in, needing him more than I need the breath in my lungs. The kiss is languid, the taste of him enough to bring me out of my anguish.

"Layla." He pulls back gently, halting my advances, and a sob escapes my mouth. He pulls me to him, his arms snaking around me and pulling me into his solid chest. Another sob racks my body as my hands come around his waist.

We hold each other for a long time, taking solitude in one another. He pulls back, running his thumb over my damp cheeks. The realization that I can't save everyone, no matter how much I may want to, settles over me.

Holt's death would not be for nothing. I needed to remember his bravery, channel his fierce spirit. He was just a child, but fought valiantly for his city, for his people. He died an honorable death, and the Gods would bless him in the next life.

Ledger picks me up, carrying me over to his bed. He'd changed into a clean tunic and trousers. He sets me on the edge of the mattress, kneeling in front of me.

"Are you going to be alright?" He brushes some hair behind my ear. "I need to know that you are going to be okay."

I take his face in my hands, stroking the sides of his jaw. If today had taught me anything, it was that life was short, fleeting. I knew what the following day would bring, what my future held.

I've denied myself so many things in this life out of fear and duty. I've sacrificed my freedom willingly and would continue to do so, but tonight I want something for myself. I want him. I want to feel without the limitations I'd set for myself.

It's a selfish move, as I pull him towards me. For once I give myself fully over to my desires. Tonight, I would relinquish control, abandon my fears and lose myself in him.

I kiss him again, slowly, committing his lips to memory. Our mouths slide against each other until the ache in my throat is replaced by the ache for him, until my intent is unmistakable.

"Are you sure this is what you want? I am not an admirable man, Layla. It pained me to stop you once, I am almost powerless to do it again."

My throat burns. "I need you, Ledger."

His eyes pause on my face considering my words. "I don't want you to regret this in the morning."

"That isn't possible; I could never regret you." The words strip me bare.

Ledger swallows thickly. His eyes lower, raking down my body. I watch them darken, and it sends a zing of desire through me.

He grips his tunic, pulling it over his head and letting it fall to the ground. I run my fingers over his chest, his bared skin blazing into my palms.

"I've thought about this moment, about what you would look like naked, underneath me." He grabs the hem of my stiff shirt dragging it up my body and tugging it off. He sucks in a breath when he sees there is nothing underneath. "About what you would feel like." He drags his palm over my swollen breast, and I arch into it.

"About what you would taste like." He brings his mouth back down and my head empties of everything but the velvety sensation of his lips on mine. He seems to know how to kiss me just how I need him to, chasing away everything but the current moment. A hunger like I've never felt flares to life in my throbbing chest, and I moan.

"About what you would sound like," he whispers, smiling against my lips. He pulls back to admire my nakedness with hooded eyes. "Gods, you're beautiful."

He swallows hard, his breaths coming out in ragged pants. He sinks to his knees on the bed and his nose and mouth drag their way from my belly button to in between my breasts. My battle-stained skin prickles as his wet mouth finds my dusty-pink nipple, sucking it into his mouth.

I moan as blood courses through my veins like a raging river. He moves at a torturous pace, finding the ivory skin of my neck. His tongue darts out, licking the sensitive flesh. My head spins, and my sex throbs.

My emotions whirl and skid so intensely I can barely filter through them. His broad shoulders heave as my nails claw over his back. My fingers run over his biceps, brush his collar bones, and trail down his beautiful, spattered chest.

His hooded eyes drift shut as my hand moves down his taut stomach. His cock strains against his trousers, eliciting another thrum of want. My hand runs the length of it, and a breathy *"fuck"* leaves his mouth.

I unbutton his pants and pull, and he stands to step out of them, left in nothing but his briefs. He is so gorgeous it hurts to look at him.

He moves so he's above me, his rough, callused hands running up the sides of my waist. His touch is a welcome caress, an invisible warmth, and I crave it all the way down to my toes.

His wet mouth drags against the sensitive flesh of my neck, searing the skin. His eyes meet mine and I think of how it was easy it would be to get lost in the way he looks at me.

It's like he can see the rawness of my soul; perhaps it matches his own. He brings his lips to mine, offering me the reprieve we both so desperately seek.

Everything about him soothes my raging emotions. His nearness is so overpowering, my heartbeat chants his name.

I grip the snaps of my own britches and slither out of them. Ledger stills above me as his eyes rake over my exposed skin. I've been naked before but never this bare. There is nowhere to hide, he sees every bit of me, every ugly, unlovable part. I almost expect him to pull away, but his knuckles brush over the taut skin of my stomach. They trail back and forth over my hip bones.

His eyes find mine, and all I can see is adoration and desire, proof that he sees me, all of me, and wants me in spite of it all. His length brushes my belly as he bends down to feather his lips against mine. I lift to rub against it, yearning to feel more.

I squirm beneath him, dampness coating my thighs. His pointer finger slides down, and I jump as it traces my clit. My head spins with lust as I pant.

That same finger drags down over my opening. Our eyes lock as he slips it inside of me, my hips lifting to meet him, driving him deeper. I only exist where he touches me.

His jaw clenches. "Gods, Layla, I could live a thousand lifetimes, fight a hundred battles, and never be worthy of being in your presence."

I raggedly pant, my head spinning as his fingers curl inside of me. Pleasure builds deep in my stomach and as good as his fingers feel, I need more, crave it.

My fingers trail the length of his cock. "More, I need more."

His fingers slow before he pulls them from me, sticking them in his mouth to taste. My stomach flutters in anticipation. He inches closer and ever so carefully kisses me. The only thing I can hear is my pulse hammering in my ears as his kiss sings through my veins.

My desire overrides the feeling of vulnerability that threatens the moment. The walls I'd so carefully built between us crumble at a rapid rate, and I'm helpless to stop them. I want him to undo me.

Without breaking our kiss, I find Ledger's briefs and pull them down. My eyes lower in time to see his cock spring free.

I bite my lip and roam the length of him. He moves his hips, and the head of his cock presses up against my throbbing clit, making me gasp.

My hips lift, chasing the sensation and rubbing myself shamelessly against him. Such a potent need for him fills my veins. All I can think of is him. His smell, his hands, his mouth, his skin.

I grip him and move him further against my entrance. Our eyes meet, our ragged breaths melding together.

Our faces hover a breath apart as he eases himself inside of me. I make a breathless noise as I adjust to the size of him. He moves with vexing restraint. I push his hips with my hands, encouraging him deeper.

He groans, and his body tremors as the full length of him settles inside of me. I rock against the feeling of fullness, chasing friction.

"Fuck," Ledger breathes and moves his hands to my hips, holding them in place.

His pace is unhurried, and my nails dig into the skin of his back. Pleasure licks at my spine as he continues.

With each thrust, our powers lash out, caressing each other, intertwining. It's a heady sensation, addicting, and leaves me wanting more. My skin buzzes pleasantly, a faint glow filling the room.

Ledger kisses me with reverence, driving my need higher. His self-control unravels as he tries so desperately to keep himself in check.

I'm dizzy with need, every nerve in my body rushing to meet him. Every part of me vying for his attention.

My body is a raging inferno as heat builds. He grips my breast, his calluses dragging over my nipple. His teeth bite at my earlobe, and his power vibrates my skin.

I'd never experienced a pleasure so intense, so all-consuming. I knew after tonight, there was no going back. I was fully handing this man the power to utterly and completely destroy me, and I welcomed it.

His thumb finds my clit moving in small devastating circles. My hips jump as the fire deep inside my belly ignites. I'm utterly defenseless as pleasure courses through me. My back arches, and I cry out as my body quakes.

I tighten around him, and a strangled noise escapes his throat. "*Fuck,* Layla."

His hand moves to my hair, gripping it and pulling my head back, baring my neck to him. He buries his face there, running his tongue up the column of my throat.

His cock is throbbing inside of me, and I'm still clenching around him in the aftershock of my orgasm.

His thrusts become faster, more desperate. A moment later, a shudder racks his body, and a groan tears from his throat.

He collapses atop me, my head in the crook of his neck. We lay there a moment, him still warm inside of me.

"Now that I have found you, I am certain I will search for you in every life." I feel the words like an ache in my chest. He grabs my hand, the one I cut when I offered his father my blood.

He places a kiss on each fingertip before his thumb slides over the scar on my palm. He brings it to his mouth and places another full-mouthed kiss there, making my stomach flip.

I tug my fingers from his grasp and run them over the scars that trail his chest. Both scars tell our story, the story of us.

That moment, those memories weaving into a tangible bond. He picks me off the bed and walks us over to the bathroom, placing me on the counter to turn on the shower.

Warm steam fills the space and Ledger stands in between my thighs kissing me fervently. My legs wrap around him as he maneuvers us into the warmth.

Hot water flows down my back as he lowers us into the spray. He removes the bandage from my shoulder revealing freshly healed pink bite marks. He kisses the skin running the soap over my chest and down my abdomen.

He continues gliding it over the stained skin of my body with care. I lean into his touch, my knees going weak when he kneels in front of me running the bar of soap over my calves and up my thighs.

My toes curl as the soap coasts between my legs and a wicked smile crosses Ledger's face. His beautiful dimple makes an appearance stealing my breath.

"My turn, Prince." I stop his hand grabbing the soap as he stands. I run the earthy scented bar over his broad chest, skate it across his collar bones and down his strong arms, revealing his olive skin under the dirt and gore.

Ledger watches me intently, his smile gone, replaced with a look I can't quite place. His hand finds my neck and I lean into it as his thumb swipes over my jaw.

The moment goes from sexual and playful to intimate, and I'm not sure what to do with it. Exhaustion creeps back into my consciousness, and I sway on my feet.

The full weight of the day settles on my shoulders. Ledger must notice because he leans over, placing a soft kiss to my lips, before turning off the water.

We dry off, Ledger disappearing briefly, coming back dressed and with another shirt in his hand. He brings it over my head and helps my arms through the holes as it swallows me. The earthy scent of him fills my nostrils and I bring the collar to my nose and inhale. He watches the movement and his lip ticks up.

His fingers interlace with mine leading me to his bed. The lines between us blur as Ledger pulls me down next to him. My legs rub against the soft silk sheets before tangling with his. His arms band around me and I allow myself to take comfort in them, his nearness.

My body and mind are spent, fatigue sinking into my very bones. Sleep is no longer an option as I melt into Ledger, blackness claiming me almost instantly.

CHAPTER
TWENTY-FIVE

I STARTLE AWAKE WHAT FEELS LIKE ONLY SECONDS later in a cold sweat. My heart races and I struggle to catch my breath. Ledger is there, his voice a calm breeze cutting through my raging emotions.

"You were having a nightmare." His hand strokes over my back making my skin pebble. I fist the sheets to ground myself.

Flashes of Kerolu, blood, Holt's blank stare fill my mind. My mother's piercing screams, my father bleeding out in front of me. I squeeze my eyes shut and reach blindly for Ledger.

He finds my hand and guides it to his chest to feel his steady heartbeat and even breathing. "I know it is hard right now. My sister's death, knowing how brutal and terrifying her last moment must have been is a living nightmare. Having to relive it every night, a torment I wouldn't wish on my worst enemy." His brow furrows.

My heart squeezes for him. I am mourning a boy I barely knew, and it is unbearable. The guilt and pain of losing a sibling and not being able to stop it must have been shattering.

"The nightmares never stop completely, but for me, they became less frequent. I used to view them as my punishment, a constant reminder of my biggest failure. I'm supposed to be able to protect the ones I love, and if I can't do that then…" He trails off, and I lower my head so our foreheads brush. My hands find the back of his head, and I bury my fingers in his hair while trailing my lips over his cheek.

"Thank you," he whispers and brings his lips to my forehead. "All she wanted was to see my father live again. He meant a great deal to her. Now that he is healed, her death doesn't feel like it was for nothing. Your father would have been proud."

Our lips meet, and my power tingles the skin there as it rages inside of me. I kiss him fiercely as if I have the power to heal all the atrocities he's experienced.

His power rushes to meet mine, soothing me, consuming me until I can't decipher where I end, and he begins. I wonder for a moment if this is normal, if everyone's magic reacts so strongly to someone they care about.

"I want this life, Ledger," I whisper, and he stills. "I want you; I want Archie, Mia, and Cam. I want it all so much it terrifies me." I can't remember a time I let myself want something or someone, and I fear it will be ripped away from me and I'll never recover.

He draws a sharp breath. "Time has reserved a place for us, where the world doesn't seem so against the idea of us. I'm sure of it." My eyes well as we lay back down, and I press my back against the hard plains of his body. His arm slips around me, strong and reassuring.

The morning light rouses me from my deep slumber. I crack my eyes, turning to see Ledger slumbering next to me. His arm is banded tightly around me, and I want to nestle further into his warmth.

I stop myself from doing that, instead allowing myself another minute in his arms before untangling from him. I throw my discarded, dirty pants back on my bare legs, a reminder of how much of myself I gave last night. I feel vulnerable, laid out, and completely raw.

I don't regret a single moment, but waking up with him and having to face how deeply I feel for this man isn't something I am capable of doing at the moment.

I'd longed to feel this way, read about it in books, but that didn't prepare me for how all-consuming it truly is. Feeling anything besides guilt and sadness seems almost inappropriate after the way I'd failed yesterday. I wonder absently if Holt had ever been in love.

Thinking back to how young he'd been, he'd likely never had the opportunity, and the thought makes me hate myself more.

I look around the room, drinking in my surroundings. Before I force myself to leave, I want to commit it to memory. Every picture, every decoration, every fabric, each a small tell into who Ledger is, and I want to know everything.

He rolls over in the bed, spurring my feet to the door. I give his sleeping frame one last look before slipping out. The chill of the stone floors soaks into the soles of my feet as I pad to my room. I nearly make it to the door when I run into Archie.

My heart turns over as we stop a few feet from each other. He hesitates before closing the gap between us and enveloping me in his arms. My eyes well as I squeeze him back. "I'm sorry, Arch." It comes out as a whisper.

"Lay, don't be sorry. Promise me you won't blame yourself for what happened yesterday."

"What are they going to do with his body?"

"He will have an honorable burial. What family he does have will be taken care of. He was brave, overconfident, fierce, and so fucking stubborn," he says, and I swallow the raw noise that works its way up my throat.

"I don't understand; why were the wolves and the Kerolu in the city?" So many questions filter through my brain.

"The King is requesting all our presence in the throne room. Why don't we get you dressed and head there, I'm sure we will find some answers."

Archie sits on my bed, his elbows on his knees. He runs his fingers through his blonde hair, his usual lightness missing. I toss on random clothes, stealing nervous glances at him.

I go to grab my hairbrush when I see the small, white shell the Maladra gifted me sitting on the counter. The shell must have been placed here before my clothes were laundered.

I pick it up, studying the intricate details before sliding it into my pocket. The weight of it brings me comfort. I run the brush through my hair, plopping down next to Archie and tying on my boots. We sit in silence. His fingers thread through my own, and I let my head fall to his shoulder.

We soak in what comfort we can from each other. I am utterly drained, and the dark bags under Archie's eyes tell me he must be just as exhausted.

He rises, pulling me to the door with him. "You ready?"

CHAPTER
TWENTY-SIX

Mia gives me a sad smile as we enter and squeezes my hand as I pass her. I take a seat at the table next to Archie and brace myself for what is to come.

Orion appears, and my breath catches as Ledger follows him into the room. His eyes find me immediately, his body visibly relaxing.

He takes the seat next to me, and I get a whiff of his heady scent. It's an effort to keep my body rooted where it is. I am already yearning for his touch and the familiar warmth of him.

I grip the seat of the chair, letting my nails dig into the lush fabric. King Callum enters followed by Humphrey, and we all rise, bowing our heads.

"You may sit." He takes his own seat at the head of the table.

"I've called you all here to talk of the grievous acts that ensued yesterday. We lost fourteen honorable, innocent people. That number would have been much higher had it not been for all of your bravery."

"I want to personally thank you, Layla. It is my belief you not only fought yesterday but saved many lives. Westray is indebted to you." Everyone around the table nods, placing their hands on their chests and bowing their heads.

"Thank you, Your Grace." I fumble for my words, shocked by the show of respect. It wasn't until now I realized how protective I am of Westray, and how desperately I want to stay. I have truly come to care for everyone around this table.

Ledger's fingers brush the back of my hand. I meet his gaze, and the way he's looking at me makes my heart ache.

"I can't seem to make sense of why this may have occurred. We've had an agreement with Grimwood for many years, we are up to date on our payments to them. They should have been keeping all creatures away from our borders. I'm of the mind this was some kind of calculated attack, an act of retribution. Could it have anything to do with Layla being here?"

The color drains from my face, my heart ratcheting in my chest.

The room is silent for a moment too long before Ledger speaks. "It could have been an attack from Bellehaven. I took Layla without permission, and they sent a warning of retaliation if I did not return her."

"Ledger." Callum says his name and rubs at his eyes as he forms a response. "By bringing her here you have put all of Westray at risk. She must be returned." Callum looks at me and then at his son, his cheeks flushing in anger.

"I agree, Your Grace," Humphrey says from next to the King.

"I will not make that choice for her," Ledger declares, staring defiantly up at his father.

"You have taken her unlawfully. You know the punishment for such things. I'm afraid the blood of our people is on your hands." His disappointment is evident as he speaks to his son.

Ledger's chair scrapes roughly against the ground as he stands, and his fist slams into the table. "She saved your life and the lives of many people from Westray. Does that mean nothing?"

Callum bristles in his seat and my stomach churns. "Children died yesterday, Ledger, and that is just the beginning of what will happen if she stays." Callum gives me a remorseful look.

"I need air." Ledger storms out of the room. Anger radiates off him in furious waves. Orion prowls after him, his suit of armor clinking with each step.

"Excuse me, Your Grace." I stand bowing my head and following after them.

Ledger makes it across the castle bridge before dismissing Orion and charging into the woods. I stop next to his guard. He looks like he wants to disobey the order and bound after him.

"I'll talk to him," I say, and he looks at me wearily before nodding.

I wince as Ledger's fists slam into the tree, bark splintering the air around him. He hits it again and again until the tree turns red with his blood.

His broad shoulders heave in time with his labored breaths. I walk over to him silently, taking his bloodied hands into mine.

My power glides over his tattered skin, eager to mend the broken pieces of him back together. After the knuckles of his other hand are healed, I bring the fresh skin to my lips, placing a soft kiss there.

He doesn't pull away. Instead, his fingers tighten around my own while the other hand snakes around my back, pulling me closer to him.

His chin rests on the top of my head as he leans into me.

"This is all because of my presence here, Ledger. I must go back," I whisper.

He sighs, closing his eyes; he looks so very tired. "You don't know that, Layla. We don't know that it was an attack from Bellehaven."

"If it wasn't, then it's only a matter of time. I know King Sandor, and he won't stop until he gets me back. He is never going to let me go." Emotion clogs my throat at the thought of leaving Westray.

"I want to give you something." Ledger pulls out a delicate silver chain. Hanging from it is a stunning emerald that matches the color of his eyes. It's surrounded by small sparkling diamonds. "My father gifted this to my mother after I was born. I never saw her without it."

"It's beautiful." It sparkles in the sun as I study it. "I could never accept that, Ledger."

"I couldn't imagine anyone else wearing it until I met you. I want you to have it." He goes to clasp it around my neck, his fingers gentle as they whisper over my skin.

I watch, barely breathing. The cool metal brushes my neck and I shiver. Just as he finishes clasping it, I feel a rush of air, and then Maddox appears behind him, holding a large dagger against Ledger's exposed throat.

"Maddox," I gasp at his sudden appearance. My first instinct is to go to him, but the dagger at Ledger's neck freezes me in place.

"Don't move or I will slit your throat." Maddox presses the blade into the thin skin at the base of Ledger's neck drawing a few drops of blood. "I'm here to take her back to Bellehaven."

"I was wondering when you were going to show up." Ledger throws his head back, slamming into Maddox's nose and ducking out of his hold. I yelp, jumping towards Maddox when Ledger draws his own dagger, holding it up and standing in front of me. "Stay behind me, Layla." He crouches in a defensive position ready to fight. "It is her decision if she stays or goes. You do not get to make that choice for her."

"She doesn't belong here. She belongs back in Bellehaven. With me." Maddox's chestnut eyes meet mine, blood trickling out of his nose.

I don't know what to say, what to do. Maddox lunges for Ledger; his fist makes contact under his left eye.

Ledger's head snaps back from the blow. He recovers quickly, landing his own punch to Maddox's stomach. I hear the air wheeze out of him. Maddox's dagger whips up, cutting Ledger's shoulder.

The power inside of me, however, depleted from yesterday, rumbles unhappily to the surface.

"Stop!" I yell as they continue. Ledger manages to slice his dagger across Maddox's chest. They punch and slice at each other, ignoring my pleas.

With each blow and drop of blood, my power roars to life. "STOP!" I shriek, holding up my glowing hands.

I immobilize both of their arms, forcing their hands open and their weapons to drop. Maddox's eyes widen and he looks at me like I have two heads.

I force them to their knees and they both seethe as they catch their breath. They don't fight my power; instead, let it command their bodies.

"I will not stand here and watch you two kill each other."
I look at both of them.

Guards wearing the signature silver of Bellehaven start to descend from the woods. My brows furrow as I look at Maddox.

"Stand down," he orders them. "You have to come with me, Lay. It's your mother. My father has had her in the dungeons for days. She isn't doing well." My heart falters, and I lose control of my power. It recedes sluggishly back into me.

"What?" My voice is breathy as I sink to my knees in front of Maddox.

"I'm sorry, Lay. I tried to get her out of the castle, but she wouldn't leave. She will barely eat; she just lays there chanting your name repeatedly."

"My name?" My stomach flips as he nods. I look over at Ledger, who is wearing a pained expression. Like he already knows what I am going to say.

"Layla don't do this," Ledger begs.

"What choice do I have, Ledger? He has my mother." I stand to face him.

"I'll go with you; we'll figure it out." He steps toward me, and the guards draw their weapons. I can feel the faint hum of their powers as they prepare. Maddox's face twists in confusion.

I huff out a humorless laugh. "Sandor could take you as a prisoner, or worse, kill you for what you have done."

"I will send—"

"Stop, Ledger." I silence him with my raised hand. "I must go to her. I have to get back to Bellehaven. I won't give King Sandor a reason to hurt her or the opportunity to shed more innocent blood over me. Please, just let me go," I plead with him, my voice cracking in time with something in my chest.

The tortured look on his face is almost enough to break me. I've let myself indulge in the dream that I could live this life and be someone else for too long.

The reality is that I am tethered to Bellehaven, destined to live my days serving and obeying. The incapacitating ache that blooms in my chest makes me long for a time when I was blissfully ignorant and unfeeling.

"Get me out of here," I whisper to Maddox, my voice cracking. The world blurs, and for a moment, I'm torn between two lives: the freedom I've tasted in Westray and the duty that's always defined me in Bellehaven. The man who has always been my safety and the man who turned my life upside down.

My mother's face flashes in my mind. Holt's unblinking stare, and I know I have no choice.

"No, no, no." Ledger's anguished voice cuts through my haze. A vine, an extension of his desperation, wraps around my ankle almost painfully as we turn. Maddox hacks at it, and it falls away limply, like my dreams of a different life.

I force myself to look forward, each step away from Ledger feeling like a betrayal—of him, of myself, of the person I'd started to become. But I keep moving because that is what I've always done, what I'll always do for the people I love.

The guards descend as Ledger attempts to pursue us. He draws his sword, unleashing himself on the guards around him.

"Layla!" Each scream of my name makes something in my chest throb. My nails scratch at the skin there, needing relief from the pain. My power pulses unhappily under my skin and my legs strain against my command to keep walking away.

Ledger spins, his power lashing out, his sword singing through the air and into flesh. His movements are strong and skilled, but his face is desperate as his eyes flicker to me.

He slashes down guard after guard until I can no longer bear to watch. Maddox pulls me through the woods at a pace so brisk I struggle to keep up.

"Almost there, Lay." He throws me on his horse, and I give Ledger one last look before I force my eyes forward. No part of me *wants* to leave this place, to leave him.

The horse races through the woods, the trees blurring around us. Maddox holds me tightly to him. "I got you," he murmurs into my ear.

I swallow the sob that works its way up my throat and cling to Maddox's arm. The further I get from Westray, from Ledger, the harder it is for me to breathe. We ride higher and higher until we get to a tall peak.

Maddox takes me with him when he dismounts and sets me on a tree stump. He kneels and I wrap my arms around his neck, clinging to him as tears cascade down my cheeks.

His arm comes around my waist while his fingers stroke my hair. "I've missed you, Lay." I clutch him tighter, breathing in his recognizable scent. *Gods, I'd missed him so much.*

"You're alright," he murmurs. "It's okay, you're safe now." I release him and blink my eyes against the sudden onslaught of emotion. I wasn't alright, was far from it.

"He can't hurt you anymore. I'm sorry I couldn't get you out sooner." A sob ratchets my body and Maddox frowns as his thumb brushes away a stray tear.

His warm hand wraps around mine. I didn't realize I'd been scratching at my chest. His eyes linger on the necklace lying just below my collar bones. His brows draw together as his eyes flicker from my face to the beautiful piece.

His confusion is evident causing my heart to race. I keep my lips sealed, terrified of what might come out. I'd fallen for the prince of Westray. My captor. The last man that I should have let myself care for.

The ground rumbles as horses gallop straight for us. Maddox stands, his hand going to the pommel of his sword. I let out the breath that I had been holding and push up on weak knees.

Tamish appears from the tree line, followed by a few guards and Forde. I frown, fear snaking through my veins.

"Why is Tamish here? And why is he with Forde?" I wipe my damp cheeks with the back of my hand.

"My father ordered him to go with us to bring you back. He didn't trust I could do the job." His jaw feathers and his eyes narrow as they near, slowing their horses.

Tamish jumps from his horse and strides towards us. His sword is out, and the tip is covered in scarlet blood. "You made the right choice, darling." He directs the comment at me, but I hardly register it.

"Why is he here?" I glare over at Forde, and he gives me a cocky smirk.

"When I saw Tamish and Maddox come through Belle-haven looking for a healer girl, I knew I had to help them. They agreed to offer me the reward if I could flush you out of Westray. I hope Ledger and his crew received my gift." I bristle at his words.

"You unleashed the Dire wolves and Kerolu onto the in-nocent people of Westray?" I grit my teeth.

"You are lucky that is all I did, especially after his behav-ior in Grimwood. Ledger took something that wasn't his. He must learn those things have consequences."

"Fuck you," I seethe, lunging for him. Maddox holds me back.

"Do calm down, Layla. Honestly, what did you expect? If you ask me, we went easy on them." Tamish wipes his bloodied blade onto his pants, and my power sizzles.

"Why is your sword bloody?" My stomach churns uneasily.

"The prince was more zealous than we anticipated." He sneers.

"What did you do?" I ask, hysteria building inside of me.

"The King asked I deliver a message." Tamish sneered. "He doesn't like his things borrowed, especially not by Westray. The balance of power between kingdoms has always been precarious, and your little adventure could tip us into open conflict. Sandor is...displeased about the lengths he's had to go to retrieve you. I simply made that clear to the prince."

"Take me back," I demand, turning towards Maddox.

"You're not going anywhere, girl." Tamish steps in between us. My power pulses beneath my skin.

"For the love of the gods, I didn't kill the boy. We don't want a war with Westray yet; he will recover." I picture Ledger hurt, and it makes me want to slit Tamish's throat.

"I need to go back." I sidestep Tamish and plead to Maddox. I can almost taste his confusion, see the questions bubbling inside of him.

"You do not belong there. Do not further humiliate yourself. Get on the horse and let this fade into a distant memory," Tamish says, gesturing to his horse. "We can do this the easy way or the hard way, and trust me, girl, you won't like the hard way."

I release the hold on my power and propel it towards him. He staggers back a step as it slams into him. I squeeze at his windpipe, and he gasps, grabbing at his throat.

Tamish struggles against my hold, and I fight to keep him still. His knee hits the ground, and my power flickers. My abilities are still deeply drained from what I'd expended the day prior.

A sick smirk slides over Tamish's thin lips as he lifts his own hand. Blinding pain explodes in my body, and I collapse and lose all control.

My limbs twitch, and I scream silently as his rank power filters through my body. Agony. It is so acute I retch, bile dripping over my cheek and mixing into the dirt.

"STOP! Tamish, please." I hear Maddox begging and feel his hands somewhere on my body. I can see Tamish's hand hovering out in front of him, pumping me full of his torment. I get a glance of Forde's giddy face

I latch onto my own power, gathering the pitiful remains of it, and manage to shove what I can out towards him with the intent to fragment the bones of his fingers.

Before it can reach Tamish's outstretched hand, a guard steps out from behind him, stopping my attack and ricocheting it right back to me.

My piercing scream echoes in the distance as the bones in my hand shatter. I grasp my arm to my chest, tears streaming down my face. Maddox is yelling, his panicked face blurring above me. I moan as Tamish sends one more pulse of wretched pain through me.

"Put her on the horse," he demands, and Maddox arms wrap around me.

"You're okay—you're going to be okay," he whispers, breathing his apologies into my ear.

My body spasms with the aftershock of Tamish's assault as he places me in the saddle. Hand throbbing, I fight for consciousness. My mind screams, begging my body to move, to fight, but it doesn't obey.

My legs and arms remain limp, and my power is an unhappy flicker in my core. I want to war, to cry, to burn down this unfair world.

Instead, I sit on the horse as it carries me away from Westray. Away from the people I have come to love and cherish and the man I've allowed myself to care for so deeply. The fight in me wavers, unclear and displaced.

I feel like a prisoner once again. I can't fathom how I am supposed to return to Bellehaven after my world's been turned upside down. I am brimming with emotions and life I've never dared let myself feel before, and I know I'll never be the same again.

CHAPTER
TWENTY-SEVEN

Ledger

Watching her leave with him sends me into a desperate sort of hysteria. I refuse to accept the reality that she is going back. The second she uttered the words, she wanted this life, me, I knew I'd be too selfish to let her go.

The guards descend on me, hurtling their powers and swords in my direction. My body moves without command, without regard for myself. Its only desire to get to her.

I slash and parry, dodge and drain my way through the men. The last time I felt so out of control was when I found my sister and unleashed myself upon the Kerolu.

My feet move one in front of the other in her direction. Her hand is in his, her eyes are on me, devastation lining her features.

The anguish in my chest is acute, my determination thick in the air. I don't care how many men I have to kill, don't even register the blood spraying through air, coating my skin. All I can think about is her.

Her blonde hair flashes through the greens and browns of the forest like a beacon.

My powers rage inside of me, boiling and lashing out the further she gets away. There are two guards on the ground struggling against my vines as they wrap around their throats, depriving them of oxygen.

I drain the abilities of another two guards, the veins in their necks protruding as they strain against me. Their power wells inside of me, overflowing and fortifying as it surges through my blood until they drop to the ground unseeing.

The men keep coming, glancing nervously at the others as they swing their swords in my direction. Power curls out of me in thick tendrils of smoke, invading, seizing, feasting upon their abilities.

She reaches his horse, and he throws her atop it. She is no longer looking at me. Her body is rigid as he mounts behind her.

I let out a guttural, agonized roar as my sword carves through flesh and bone. She doesn't even pay me another glance as the horse gallops away.

I'm so lost to my rage, to disbelief that she would leave— just like that, I hardly register it when a sword plunges into my side. My magic snaps back into me with such force that I stagger back.

I look up to see Tamish, the Kings hand. He wears a sick smile of satisfaction as he twists the sword and then yanks it out sending me to my knees.

My breath shutters out and I struggle for air on my next inhale.

"A gift from King Sandor. You shouldn't take what doesn't belong to you." He spits the words as I grab for my side. Blood soaks through my shirt warming my palms.

He gives me a mocking look before raising his hand. I know what's coming yet do nothing to stop it.

My body convulses, my limbs lock up. The blood from my wound pools beneath me. I welcome the debilitating pain, the breath-taking agony.

Westray's soldiers pour into the woods armed and lethal. The air vibrates with their raw power. Bellehaven's men hesitate.

"Fall back." Tamish's voice cuts through the chaos. "RETREAT!" His hand drops, releasing me from his hold. Soldiers run, swords clash, the air becomes thick as abilities are unleashed.

I take in a gasping breath, searching the woods for her. No flicker of blonde hair, no shimmer of pale skin. My vision blurs.

Pain laces through me as I push to my stomach. Coming up on my elbows, I drag myself over the leaves and dirt. I can taste the damp earth, the tang of iron. I crawl after her as cold seeps into my bones.

"Ledger!" Archie is next to me, his eyes wide. He searches my body, his face palling as his gaze catches on my crimson-soaked shirt.

Mia is there now too. She's cursing; her hands press into my side to stop the bleeding. The wound is throbbing, my head is spinning.

Both of them are shouting at me but I can't make out their words. The world starts to dim, the familiar dull and gloom of my existence settles back over me. She was the color and she chose to leave.

I'm being transferred onto a stretcher, a bitter tasting tonic sliding over my tongue.

"Where is Layla, Ledger?" Darkness flickers at the edge of my vision.

She's gone. She made her choice, and it wasn't me. It was never going to be me.

"She left."

THANK YOU FOR READING! Did you enjoy? I'd be honored if you would leave a review. Nothing helps an author more and encourages readers to take a chance on a book. Book two, *UNLEASHED* COMING SOON!

ACKNOWLEDGMENTS

This book would not have been possible without the feedback and help of so many. Thank YOU to start, for taking a chance on my book and reading it. Thank you to all my beta readers, Monica, Tessy, Izzy, Kate, Allie and Mikayla, each suggestion made this book better and helped me learn. Thank you to my editors, Vallie, Oskar, and Kaitlynn.

Thank you to my husband who never stopped encouraging me, you're everything I've ever dreamed of and more. Thank you to my friends and family, who have always cheered for me so loudly, I could hear nothing else. And lastly thank you to my son Summit, who watched me write this book during many bedtimes. May you grow up to love reading, lose yourself in mythical worlds and complex fictional characters. May you learn about the human experience and develop empathy for those around you. May you grow up to be a good, kind man.

Thank you, *thank you.*

ABOUT THE AUTHOR

STACI JOST GREW UP IMMERSED IN ADVENTURES ABOUT wizards, dragons, vampires, and far-off kingdoms—and her fascination with the fantastical never left her. Now a passionate wordsmith and creative spirit at heart, she draws on her gifted imagination to weave hard-hitting romantic fantasy novels, capturing her readers with heart-pounding stories about larger-than-life characters with a satisfying dash of spice.

When not dreaming about her next story idea, you can find Staci hiking or skiing, doing hot yoga, or tucked away in the corner of a cozy coffee shop with a good book. She currently resides in Crested Butte, CO, with her husband, their wonderful son, French bulldogs, and a black lab.